She wet her lips in unconscious invitation

"I really should go." Matt took a deep breath and stood up. Much more of this and he would forget his good intentions all over again.

"Do you have to?" Liz's voice was regretful and her eyes glowed with unspoken meaning. "It is difficult, knowing how good it is between us when we... And, well, it's going to be a whole month. My mind is producing all kinds of trite excuses," she confessed a touch hysterically. "This thing is bigger than both of us. I can't fight myself. We're only human."

She was trembling. Matt knew all he had to do was take a step forward and she would be in his arms. For a full minute they stood looking at each other. Then he took that step....

Margaret Chittenden has always loved Edinburgh. She spent a few summers there as a child and remembers being fascinated by the castle that stands high on a rock above the city. As an adult she's fascinated by the possibility she may have lived there long ago in another century.

This author of numerous romances and mysteries has also written a mainstream novel, *Forever Love*, about a heroine who unravels a murder mystery—from her own previous life! Margaret lives near the Pacific Ocean, where she and her husband have transformed a weathered old cottage into a dream home—by hand.

THIS TIME FOREVER

MARGARET CHITTENDEN

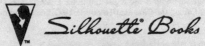
Silhouette Books

Published by Silhouette Books

America's Publisher of Contemporary Romance

This book has to be for my dear friend
Donna Carolyn Anders

 SILHOUETTE BOOKS

ISBN 0-373-51188-4

THIS TIME FOREVER

Visit Silhouette at www.eHarlequin.com

Printed in U.S.A.

CHAPTER ONE

IT WAS HAPPENING AGAIN.

Gazing out of the airplane window, Liz Brooks could feel the familiar frightening sensation pressing all around her, as though someone was wrapping her body in a muslin cocoon. Her limbs were becoming strangely numb, her eyelids heavy.

Fight it, she instructed herself. *Don't give in to it. Wiggle your toes, your fingers, open your eyes wide, think about something else. Concentrate.*

Stop the airplane, I want to get off.

She had felt fine when she came aboard in Seattle for her flight to San Francisco, looking forward to the travel agents' convention, delighted to find there weren't too many passengers on board so she could have both window and aisle seats to herself.

And now this.

Don't think about it.

As soon as the plane leveled out, she opened her briefcase, pulled down the table in front of her and started going over her presentation.

For an hour and a half she kept at it, fighting the lethargy that kept threatening to overwhelm her, ignoring the pilot's invitations to look out the windows to left or right as the plane passed over various landmarks, avoiding the interested glances of the man across the aisle whenever she lifted her head, stopping only to accept coffee and snacks from the pretty brunette flight attendant.

She didn't pack her papers away until she suspected the plane would soon be descending, making its approach to San Francisco Airport. Then she sat very straight, concentrating all her will on staying alert.

Keep your mind occupied. Don't let up yet.

The plane was flying through a cloud bank that looked heavy with rain. Liz hadn't thought to pack a raincoat. The first three weeks of July had been hot and dry in Seattle; she was out of the habit of carrying rain gear. She looked down at the crisp linen of her blue summer suit and worried that it would wrinkle irrevocably if this cloud dropped its contents over the city.

Straining to see through the fogged-over window, she was suddenly reminded of a time when she was a child and she'd awakened to frost patterning her bedroom window with a crystal leaf pattern. It had seemed to her then that if she could somehow thaw a small portion of the pattern, she would be able to look out on a changed world.

No. Don't think about changed worlds. Think about ordinary things, the muffled drone of the engines, the cool air from the vent blowing on the top of your head.

A peculiar silence was settling over her, a stillness so complete that she could barely hear her own pulse fluttering in her ears.

Terrified, she struggled to open her eyes wide but she couldn't—the intensity of her narrowed gaze had become fixed and sightless and there was a buzzing sound all around. She was floating now, drifting through air that was heavy with mist, free of the airplane, free of her body, free of all that was familiar and safe.

THE EXTRAORDINARILY handsome man was there again, looking down at her, smiling, his golden hair shining in the sun. Such bold blue eyes he had, and such a brilliant smile. His name was Robert, she knew. Robert Charles McAndrew. And her own name was Jeannie Findlay. She was wearing a high-necked, bottle-green dress with a row of buttons marching up the front of the bodice and a full skirt that was draped back to hang in folds at the rear, its hem brushing the tops of her black boots. A perky felt hat trimmed with feathers was cocked at a rakish angle over her forehead. Her hair was a dark auburn, curled frothily in front and rolled up at the back and sides. Her face was heart shaped, her cheeks naturally flushed with pink, her eyes bright brown, alert and intelligent, set off by a thicket of dark auburn lashes and smooth bird's-wing eyebrows. She was sitting on a bench in a parklike area and she could see Edinburgh Castle looming high above her on its rugged rock.

A CHIMING SOUND INTRUDED. Then the flight attendant's voice saying, "Please fasten your seat belts."

Liz's eyelashes fluttered; she could feel them fluttering. For a second she could see her own hands clasped in the lap of her blue linen skirt. She tried to separate them, but they seemed locked in place and now her vision was clouding again and pictures were shimmering in front of her, drawing her into them.

ROBERT WAS NO LONGER with her. She was wearing the same dress and hat but she was in a different part of Edinburgh. The Cowgate? She was climbing a flight of stone steps, climbing slowly because of the old trouble with her hip. And she was frightened.

When she reached the top, a man was standing in a doorway looking at her belligerently. Angus Macdonald his name was. He was a customer—no, the husband of a customer. A short man, he was wearing a long striped apron and a small round cap, also striped. He was angry for some reason.

His fist connected with her stomach even as she saw the sudden glitter in his eyes, and then as she staggered backward, winded, her mouth forming an astonished O, he took another step forward and shoved her with all his might.

Behind her was the staircase she'd climbed, steep and narrow. She made a grab for the rail and missed. And then she was staggering, stumbling, falling downward, her legs and arms twisting under her as she fell and fell and fell....

THE PLANE was on the ground. Liz blinked, feeling disoriented, then turned her head to see a group of passengers frozen in the act of removing jackets and tote bags and briefcases from the overhead bins. They were all staring at her as though she'd suddenly grown two heads. The pretty brunette flight attendant was pushing through them. She looked scared to death.

"Are you okay?" she asked Liz, leaning over the empty seat beside her.

"I'm...well, yes, sure, I'm fine. Why shouldn't I be?"

"You cried out," she explained, sitting down beside Liz. The other passengers had turned away now, all of them looking mildly embarrassed as they resumed their preparations for disembarking.

Liz swallowed and turned her own head away. She could see her reflection clearly in the window. She looked pale, she thought. And rather severe. When she was working, she usually tied her long, curly and often unmanageable copper-colored hair in a French braid. She hadn't realized before that the style made her cheekbones stand out so that they looked almost Slavic. Her eyes appeared huge, luminously blue.

"What did I say?" she asked, glancing back at the flight attendant.

The woman shook her head. "You didn't say anything. You *screamed*—several times—as if you were in pain. Gave us all a start. Were you dreaming?"

"Dreaming. Yes—I mean—well, I guess so. I must have been. God, I'm sorry, I can't imagine…"

The woman patted her knee. "It's okay," she said kindly. "Just so you're all right."

"I feel fine," Liz said, but she didn't. She wasn't sure she'd ever feel fine again.

"THE THING IS," she said to Erica Walter hours later, "what if I have one of these…episodes…when I'm driving?"

Erica was a psychologist, an old friend from University of Washington days, a tall, vibrant blonde with a willowy figure and a sharply intelligent face. Liz had come to her clinic without even calling ahead, as soon as she'd finished giving her lecture. She had no idea how the hell she'd gotten through the day.

"I have no memory of the landing in San Francisco Airport," Liz said urgently. "I just vaguely remember the sound of the seat-belt light coming on. This is the third time I've flipped out. The first time I was in my apartment in Seattle, looking down at the rhododendron bushes in the front yard. The last time I was jogging around Green Lake, for God's sake. When I came to I was sitting on a bench, gazing into space like a zombie. What's the thing in psychiatry—a fugue state—some kind of psychological amnesia?"

"After a fugue, the patient can't usually remember what he or she did during it," Erica said carefully.

The patient.

"How've you been feeling lately, by the way?" Erica asked. "Any problems at all, anything on your mind?"

"Nothing."

"How's your love life?"

Liz laughed shortly. "Less than zero," she said, then hesitated. "I did get a marriage proposal—from Allen Harper. You met him last time you were in Seattle."

"The CPA who bored me to tears with his description of some lumber company's chapter eleven proceedings?"

"That's the one."

Erica grinned. "I take it you turned him down?"

Liz sighed. "I did. Though I must admit I was tempted to accept—for all of five minutes."

Erica raised her eyebrows. "Why?"

"I'm tired of the dating game. Most of the men I meet are only interested in short-term flings. I've been wondering lately if it wouldn't be a good idea to settle for loyalty, kindness, companionship."

"Liz dear, you're twenty-seven—not sixty-seven." Erica reached over to tap her knee lightly. "Forget Allen, he's not for you. Wait until you find someone who makes your heart go pit-a-pat."

"The kind of men who make my heart go pit-a-pat don't want to get married. They want to go wham bam thank you, ma'am."

"There's somebody out there for you." Erica was silent for a minute, then she said, "Did the flight attendant mention any kind of strange behavior—while you were...out of it?"

"No. She said she'd noticed I hadn't put my tray back up, and mentioned it to me. I was looking out the window and didn't answer her, so she figured I'd dozed off. And then soon after the plane landed, I suddenly started screaming.''

"Not surprising," Erica said. "You were falling down a flight of stairs. Enough to make anyone scream."

"But that wasn't me, that was Jeannie." Liz hesitated. "It felt like me, though, just like the other times. I was right inside her skin, unaware of any other life, unaware of…myself.''

She shook her head. "It seemed so real each time, Erica. After the first time, for several days, I kept thinking I wasn't dressed properly because I couldn't feel Jeannie's dress and petticoats swishing against my legs. I'd look in a mirror and be surprised to see blue eyes instead of brown, my carroty curls instead of Jeannie's auburn hair. I still don't feel as if I'm quite…here." She looked around Erica's office, which was furnished in starkly contemporary fashion. Liz's taste ran more to country style with lots of antiques, but even though she didn't particularly like contemporary furnishings, until now she'd never felt *alien* among them.

Erica was frowning. "You mentioned Jeannie's dress—did you get any idea of period?"

"Gosh, I didn't even think of that. Yes, judging by Jeannie's clothes—there was a suggestion of a bustle, and Robert was wearing a morning coat, I think. I'd say late nineteenth century maybe. With the state centennial last year, Seattle newspapers were full of historical pictures."

"Do you have any idea what might have triggered your experiences?"

Liz nodded. "My mother's company, British Travel Services, recently signed up the Prince Hotel chain. As the sales rep I'll be leaving in a couple of weeks to visit all the hotels the chain owns in Scotland. I've had to do a lot of reading up on the country—maps, brochures, that sort of thing. The first time I flipped out was right after I started planning the trip.''

''Before that there was nothing at all, nothing... unusual?''

Liz hesitated. ''When I was a kid,'' she confessed reluctantly. ''In school. I kept drawing this castle. It was some kind of compulsion. Every time the teacher said draw something, I drew a castle. I had no idea what it was until I brought some of the drawings home and my mom told me it was Edinburgh Castle.''

''The same castle Jeannie saw.''

''Yes. And there's more.'' She took a deep breath. ''Mom used to take me on the ferry to Victoria on Vancouver Island. I used to freak out over anything Scottish— dolls dressed in tartan, tea caddies with pictures of Scottish thistles on them, cairngorm brooches.''

''Your mother's English. Had she ever visited Scotland, told you about it?''

Liz shrugged. ''Not that I remember.'' Leaning back on the white leather chaise longue Erica had urged her into when she arrived, she looked up at her friend and grinned wryly. ''So what do you think, Doc, do you want to analyze my childhood traumas?''

Erica looked at her steadily. ''I don't think we're dealing with a childhood trauma here, Liz.''

''I thought everything went back to childhood.''

''It often does, but in your case, I believe it might go back even earlier.''

Liz sat up and stared at her. ''What are you saying?''

Erica took a deep breath. ''I'm talking about spontaneous regression. I've heard of it, read a lot about it. This is the first time I've known anyone personally who has experienced it.''

"Spontaneous regression?" Liz echoed. "What the hell is spontaneous regression?"

"An involuntary return to a former lifetime."

"You mean reincarnation?" Liz swallowed hard. "You have to be kidding."

"I'm not, though."

Liz laughed nervously. "Sorry, I'm not a believer. None of this new-age stuff sits well with me. I don't even eat health food. I'm an old-fashioned girl." She looked directly at Erica. "You were an agnostic in school."

Erica nodded solemnly. "I'm not nearly as adamant as I used to be, Liz. I guess in those days being an agnostic fitted my scientific bent. And my education and training in psychology were strictly scientific. Not once during my studies was the word reincarnation, or even the concept, mentioned. I've always dealt only in things that I could observe and record."

She smiled wryly. "Subconscious factors, yes, those I've always believed in. Most people's problems stem directly from events they've buried. It's my function to help my patients bring the buried problems to the conscious level where they can be dealt with—nothing even vaguely supernatural about that. All the same, after reading about spontaneous regression and reincarnation I've come to believe it's possible there might be something to it. And your experiences sound similar to case histories I've read."

She frowned. "Hypnosis might help. I started using it on my patients a while ago. It's very effective. Hypnosis goes directly to the subconscious while at the same time lessening the patient's inhibitions, the guards we put up on our own minds."

Liz shook her head. "This is too much, Erica. I can't believe we're sitting here calmly discussing reincarnation.

My reincarnation.'' She smiled wryly. "Not that I'm feeling too calm.''

"You don't want to believe in reincarnation?"

"No way.'' She laughed shortly. "I'll grant you that *something* sure as hell happened to me. But it must have been a hallucination each time—some kind of waking dream. Or ghosts walking around in my head. But not reincarnation. I'd sooner believe I'm crazy.''

Erica grinned, then raised her eyebrows. "You mentioned that Jeannie limped?"

"Yes. Some kind of hip problem.''

"Right or left leg?''

Liz didn't have to stop to think. "Left.''

Erica pursed her mouth. "I seem to remember you had to give up volleyball in school. Some trouble in your left leg, wasn't it?''

Liz stared at her. "You want me to believe I carried the injury through? Come on, Erica.''

"I've read of people who have terrible migraines in this life discovering under hypnosis that in a former incarnation they were shot in the head, or even guillotined.''

Liz shuddered. "I'm beginning to be thankful Jeannie only fell down the stairs.'' She leaned forward. "Whatever's going on, I'm not driving a car until it stops. I can just see me flipping out to visit Jeannie when I'm tootling along I-5 in rush hour. Instant wipeout.'' She sighed. "Sorry, Erica, I'm not about to accept your reincarnation theory, but if you want to try hypnosis on me, I guess I'd be willing to let you. Not that I think it'll work.''

"On the contrary,'' Erica said. "You're an intelligent woman, Liz. Intelligent people are usually easier to hypnotize. But I'm not going to do it.''

"Thanks a lot, friend.''

Erica leaned forward. "You need an accredited hypnotist, yes, which I am, and one trained in psychotherapy. But you also need someone who can regress you under hypnosis to this past life or whatever it is. All kinds of situations are liable to come up during past-life regression. Whatever you say, Liz, I'm convinced that's what we're dealing with here. And I'm not equipped to handle anything like it.''

Turning away, she picked up a pad of prescription blanks and began writing. ''I'm giving you the name and address of a hypnotist who coincidentally happens to live and work in Seattle. He's a very intelligent man. A qualified psychotherapist. You can trust him completely. He used to be a medical doctor.'' She grinned. ''He's also single—divorced, and much more interesting than your friend Allen. Worth meeting for his own sake.''

''I get enough matchmaking from my mother,'' Liz said shortly. ''Besides which, I don't get mixed up with divorced men. It usually takes two to ruin a marriage.''

Erica shook her head. ''Matt's divorce wasn't his fault. His wife left him when he gave up his practice. She said any doctor who'd walk out on a thriving practice had to be nuts.''

''She could be right. Why *did* he give it up? How many MDs give up their practices? Did he give it up voluntarily?''

''Absolutely. He wanted to go beyond conventional medicine.'' She hesitated. ''He's now the head of the Psychic Research Institute in Seattle.''

''Psychic Research? You want me to let myself be used as some kind of guinea pig?''

Erica shook her head. ''I think you need to find out what's going on inside your brain.''

''You do think I'm crazy.''

''As a matter of fact, I think you're saner than most.

You've had some weird experiences that you don't understand and you are striving to understand them. Crazy people don't always do that.'' She stood. "Let's go get some dinner, okay? I'm starved. How about seafood? There's a place near here that serves the best prawns you ever tasted.''

To Liz's surprise, Erica gave her an undeniably wistful smile. Wistfulness was not a part of her friend's makeup. "I envy you, Liz,'' she said softly. "I've been regressed myself, but all I came up with were very dim impressions. You've had this window into a vividly real other life granted to you.''

Because she was suddenly afraid, Liz answered flippantly. "Maybe Jeannie was killed when she fell down the stairs. Maybe that's why I keep repeating the same scene. There's nothing to come after.''

"Did it seem to you that she might have been killed?'' Erica asked.

Again Liz didn't hesitate. "No.'' A finger of apprehension touched her spine, sending a chill through her body. "I can't tell you how I know that. I just do.''

Erica nodded. "Go see Matt,'' she urged. "I think he could help you embark on an immensely rewarding journey, a journey few people take, a journey into your own past. You should be very excited.''

"I can hardly wait,'' Liz said flatly. But she took the slip of paper Erica held out and read the name Erica had written in her neat, somewhat Gothic handwriting. Dr. Matthew Lockwood. "I'll think about it,'' she said, not intending to at all.

ON SATURDAY EVENING she was sitting in her Seattle apartment watching television, some mindless game show that she didn't have the energy to get up and switch off.

She'd mislaid her remote control somewhere among the sofa cushions. Without any warning at all, instead of looking at the crazy antics of the participants, she was somewhere inside her own head, watching herself—no, not herself, Jeannie Findlay—folding a piece of wide ribbon in a very decorative way. She was pleased with the result, pleased, too, that her hands were cool and dry so that the light colored ribbon remained clean and fresh. Jeannie was sitting on a rickety chair in a bare-looking room. There was a small coal fire burning fitfully in a black grate.

Clanging bells startled Liz back to her own living room and the flashing images on her TV set.

The next day she dredged up enough courage to call the Psychic Research Institute. Not at all sure it was the right thing to do, she made an appointment with Dr. Matthew Lockwood for the following Friday. In the meantime nothing weird happened at all. She flew to Texas and back, gave a seminar in Tacoma, dated a couple of times—and tried not to think about Jeannie Findlay and Robert Charles McAndrew.

Dr. Lockwood's office was much cozier than Erica's, she thought as she entered it nervously on Friday. It was furnished like a living room with a comfortable-looking recliner, and a pair of sofas bracketing an empty fireplace. On the hearth stood a primitive carving of a Canada goose that she'd have given anything to possess. There were glass-topped tables scattered about, some good botanical prints on the walls, a couple of interesting sculptures, plants, magazines and lots of books. The room had a totally relaxing, unthreatening, *normal* ambience, which was probably the whole idea. Most likely anyone coming here for the first time would be as petrified as she was.

That was a good word—petrified—she decided. She was standing almost at attention, her hands clenched so tightly in her jeans pockets that she wasn't sure she'd ever be able to take them out. Her heart was beating a rapid tattoo against her ribs. If Dr. Lockwood was one minute late she was going to run like a rabbit. What on earth had made her think she wanted to be hypnotized?

He didn't keep her waiting. He came in right on time holding a sheaf of papers, which he set down on his desk as he looked at her. She hadn't quite known what to expect of a director of a psychic research institute, had imagined a gray-haired ascetic type with a goatee, shoulder-length hair and the gaunt face and penetrating eyes of a prophet. But the reality was a tall, slender, good-looking man in his mid-thirties. His hair was brown, on the shaggy side but not overly long. His face was lean, scholarly, his gray eyes kind rather than penetrating. They appraised her in a way that was more friendly than clinical. She liked his eyebrows, she decided. They slanted upward in the center when he raised them, giving his face a puckish look.

He could have been a university professor, or an author ready to pose for a book jacket photograph. All that was missing was the pipe. He wore a fairly ancient tan corduroy jacket, cream-colored chinos, a faintly striped shirt and a tie that looked as if he'd loosened it with an impatient finger. "Miss Elizabeth Brooks?" he said.

It was the strangest thing. As soon as he spoke, Liz's pulse, which had been hammering away in her ears, slowed to a normal rate, her clenched hands relaxed and she was able to draw them out of her pockets. Right away she knew she was going to like him, knew she could trust him absolutely. Her relief was almost palpable.

She said something. Afterward she couldn't remember what, whether or not he answered her. It didn't seem to matter.

There was something about his comfortably rumpled appearance that appealed to her enormously, though he was certainly nothing like the happy-go-lucky jock type she was usually attracted to. All the same, he obviously took good care of himself—there was more than a hint of muscle under the soft corduroy jacket. And he had a definite presence—an aura of competence and self-confidence. He had a solid handshake, too, firm without being aggressive—her fingers retained the warmth of it long after he let her hand go.

Gesturing to the recliner, he sat down on a swivel chair behind his desk, raked one hand through his unruly hair and gave her another long, straight, friendly appraisal, after which his eyebrows slanted up again. "Dr. Walter called me about you," he said.

Liz grinned wryly. "I suppose she thought I'd chicken out."

"Did you want to?"

"Yes."

He laughed. If she'd had a shred of nervousness left it would have been dispelled instantly by the warmth he generated when he laughed. He must have had a terrific bedside manner when he was a doctor. "I won't ask you to do anything you don't want to," he promised.

She leaned forward. "Did Erica tell you what happened to me?"

"She said you had apparently experienced spontaneous past-life regression on three occasions. I understand you're afraid to drive in case of a recurrence."

"I've been riding around in buses and taxis."

"We can take care of that fear with a posthypnotic suggestion if you like. I can suggest that you will not regress unless you're in the presence of a qualified hypnotist."

She frowned. "That seems too much like relinquishing

responsibility, giving myself over to someone else. Is there another way?''

"How about if we plant the suggestion that you'll only regress if you really want to?''

"That would be a relief." She forced a grin. "How about a posthypnotic suggestion to make it all go away?''

"Is that what you want?''

She shook her head. "I'd spend the rest of my life wondering what it was all about. But I have to tell you, it's Erica's idea that I've got myself involved in some past-life drama, not mine.''

"What do you think happened?''

She sighed. "I don't know. It's as if there are two worlds—completely separate—and somehow I've found a way to slip from one to the other. I suppose it could be a hallucination." She looked at him very directly. "I don't do drugs. But people can hallucinate without them, huh?''

He nodded, then frowned. "I asked Erica not to tell me any details of your…incidents, Miss Brooks. I prefer not to be influenced by preknowledge. Which is why I'm going to ask you not to describe your experiences to me. I'd rather have you relive them under hypnosis so that I can go through them with you." He raised his eyebrows. "How do you feel about that?''

She was suddenly nervous again. "Terrified," she admitted.

"You're very honest about your feelings," he said approvingly. "Are you too scared to try?''

For one second she hesitated, and their eyes met and held. There was a peculiar little silence. Then he smiled. Such a smile he had—at once intimate, sympathetic, whimsical, sexy. His gray eyes seemed to fill with light.

Liz took a shaky breath and clenched her fists on the arms of the recliner. "I'm here. I came to find out what's happening to me. Erica says I can trust you. So what do we do?''

He grinned. ''You look pretty tense to me,'' he said. ''Let's not rush into anything.'' He pulled a pad toward him and picked up a pen. ''Suppose we complete a short history first so I can get to know you.''

He asked a lot of personal questions, none of which she minded answering, none of which any doctor she'd ever seen hadn't asked her. No doctor had ever been quite so patient, however. Matt Lockwood seemed to have all the time in the world.

She lied only once—when he asked if she'd had any prior psychic experiences. For one thing, she wasn't sure drawing a castle qualified as psychic. For another, she didn't want to seem too weird. Psychic was awfully close to psycho.

When he finally set the pad aside, he raised an eyebrow. ''I imagine you have a few questions yourself?''

She nodded. ''A thousand or so.''

''Fire away.''

She looked at him curiously. ''Erica said you were a medical doctor and gave up your practice. Did you get bored with it, or what?''

''Not at all. I enjoyed being a doctor. And I was a good one. I started out in family practice. I had studied hypnosis in medical school—the American Medical Association gave it official sanction thirty years ago—but I didn't use it at first, not until one of my patients was having a difficult pregnancy. The results delighted us both—she sailed through the rest of her time and the birth was virtually pain free. Afterward, when she had difficulty losing the weight she'd gained, I used hypnosis again. Word got around and people who wanted to lose weight, or to give up smoking or drinking or drugs, began coming to me.

Pretty soon I was using hypnosis all the time, with excellent results.''

"Erica uses hypnosis," Liz murmured.

He nodded. "It works. People tend to forget Freud stated that hypnosis was the most efficient key to helping people." He grinned. "I'm not sure Freud would approve of regressing people to former lives, however. In the beginning, the farthest I ever deliberately regressed people was to the womb. The results of that were startling enough."

"So what made you think of going farther back?"

He hesitated. "I didn't think of it. A man who came to me for help with a diet confessed he had a crippling fear of heights. Under hypnosis I suggested he go back to the origin of his problem. He suddenly started talking about a former life in which he had spent some time mountaineering in eighteenth-century Switzerland. Apparently he fell into a crevasse and was killed. Sitting in my office, totally relaxed, he vividly relived the entire experience. The whole thing shook me even more than it did him, but most astonishing was that from then on he had no more fear of heights." He laughed shortly. "He still ate too much, but he was able to climb up a ladder and repair the roof of his house."

He shook his head. "Some of my colleagues suggested the man was fantasizing—those who didn't think I'd taken complete leave of my senses, that is. I pointed out that whether the experience was real or imaginary, at least it had worked for my patient, and that was the main thing. Several months later, when another patient regressed automatically and very convincingly, I started attending seminars and workshops in past-life regression—reading, questioning, gradually developing techniques for assisting my patients to relive former lives. In every case, chronic symptoms disappeared and did not return. I became so involved in past-life regressions that I began neglecting other aspects of my practice. It seemed a natural progression to open this institute. We have several highly trained personnel, Miss Brooks, all involved in various aspects of research and healing."

"Do you suppose you could call me Liz?" she asked hesitantly. "Miss Brooks makes me feel uncomfortably like a schoolmarm."

He grinned. "Liz it is. I don't want you to feel in the least uncomfortable. And my name is Matt."

What a relief that he was so friendly, so normal. "You talked about symptoms," she said hesitantly. "I don't really have any, you know. I mean, I don't have phobias. I'm not *sick* in any way."

As soon as she said this, she remembered the leg problem that had bothered her in college. But that was a coincidence. It had to be. And a year of chiropractic had taken care of it.

"You do believe absolutely in reincarnation?" she asked.

He nodded without hesitation. "I do. There is an inherent reasonableness in the idea of reincarnation. My belief stems from that and not just from my patients' experiences. Also, I had some personal interest even before all of this—the institute, my change of job—came about." There was an intensity in his gray eyes that impressed her. There was no doubting his sincerity. She liked this man, she thought, even if she couldn't accept what he was saying for herself. She liked this man a lot.

"I believe each of our lives is a period of learning," he continued matter-of-factly. "I believe we learn from our mistakes and our successes, from our pain and our joy."

Before Liz could digest all of this, he said, "I know

reincarnation seems an incredible theory when you first run into it, Liz, but if you think about the incredible things we take for granted in life, it's a little easier to accept. A tadpole hatches out of an egg, then it becomes a frog. A caterpillar turns into a butterfly. A seed turns into a flower, or a cabbage. Really *think* about the male sperm penetrating the female ovum—the fetus developing *inside* the mother, becoming a baby that forces its way into the outside world, grows into a child and then into an adult and gradually gets older and dies. Incredible, all of it. Impossible, if you stop to think about it. But we know this is what happens.''

''I've read a little about reincarnation,'' Liz admitted. ''Nowadays it's impossible not to. And I have to admit, it *sounds* logical. I mean, I can see where it explains so much about why some people seem to have such terrible things happen in their lives, while others seem to get through without any problems at all. But I have to tell you, I haven't made any leap into faith. I'm extremely skeptical.''

''And do you still have nine hundred and ninety-nine questions?''

She laughed. ''I guess not. Not now anyway. Maybe one more, if I can phrase it without telling you everything that happened to me.''

''Go ahead.''

''Well, when I was experiencing these…episodes, or whatever you call them, I was another woman, or at least it seemed as if I was another woman. But she didn't look anything like me. She was shorter, even skinnier, if you can believe that, brown eyed, auburn haired. If I were to believe in reincarnation, which we've already established I don't, then I'd have to believe she *was* me. It doesn't quite jell, does it?''

"It does if you realize that reincarnation deals with the soul and not the body. The body is only the outer covering." He laughed. "You're tensing up again. Look at it this way. What are you wearing?"

The question mystified her, but she'd come this far.... "Jeans, sneakers, a yellow cotton blouse. I thought casual clothing might help me relax," she added defensively.

"Good thinking. What did you wear yesterday?"

"I had a business meeting yesterday." She thought for a moment. "I wore a tan rayon Liz Claiborne suit, a cream-colored blouse, high heels. And my hair was tied back in a French braid."

He glanced at her mane of curly hair and smiled briefly. "In spite of those changes, would you say you're the same person today?"

"Well, of course...oh, I see. You mean that if I did have another life, I'd be the same person today that I was in that other life, but I have another body so I look different."

"Exactly. In each incarnation we have a different physical body and appearance, a different name, different parents and environment, but these changes do not in the slightest imperil our individuality."

She sighed. "My mind's boggling, doc. Maybe it would be better if we just got started."

"By all means." He indicated a tape recorder on his desk. "I'll be recording everything you say."

"Okay."

"I want to assure you that nothing you say will go beyond these four walls without your permission."

She hadn't even thought of the possibility. She trusted him, not just because of Erica's recommendation, but because he was so straightforward, so friendly, so normal.

"What do I have to do?" she asked.

"Relax. Put your chair back—just lean back and it will

go with you. That's good. Now if you look up at the ceiling here, you'll see a small dark circle painted on it.''

"Got it," Liz said.

"I want you to keep your gaze on that spot for a while and listen to the sound of my voice. In a minute or two you'll notice that your eyes want to close. That's perfectly natural. Just let them do so whenever you are ready."

Was she really going to do this? Of course she was. And she wasn't afraid anymore. Matt Lockwood made the whole thing seem so...reasonable.

He had a nice voice, she decided. It wasn't all vibrant and meaningful as she'd expected it to be, the way Hollywood portrayed a hypnotist's voice. It was just calm and friendly and matter-of-fact. Soothing.

"Let the muscles at the back of your neck relax," he suggested. "Imagine they are really limp, like rags. Then let that feeling travel down through your body. You can close your eyes anytime you want to."

She did want to. The little circle had become very faint. The familiar lethargy was stealing over her, but she had no desire to fight it this time. She just let it come, warming her, relaxing her. She really did like listening to his voice. He was telling her that in future she would only experience regression if she wanted to, that it wouldn't happen to her against her will. She needn't be afraid to drive or to carry on her day-to-day work schedule.

For now, she should imagine that she was floating slowly, chair and all, very comfortably, through a wide, light-filled tunnel. She would see various passages opening and when she came to one that looked familiar, one she wanted to explore, she could move forward along it. Anytime she was ready. Anyplace she wanted to go. Any particular passage that seemed the right one. Anytime she was ready. She could hear the clock ticking, birds chirping in

the trees outside. There must be a window open. To the
left of her chair a shadow was forming, the shadow of a
large craggy rock...

CHAPTER TWO

"Where are you, do you know?" Matt asked.

"I'm in Edinburgh, of course," Liz said. "Where else would I be?" She hesitated. "No, wait a minute, this is different. We're leaving Edinburgh, going out to the country beyond Leith, Robert says. We're going on a picnic. Imagine that. Jeannie Findlay's going on a picnic."

Oh, it was such a lovely sunny day, with little puffy white clouds dancing across the sky in the breeze. The same breeze was blowing the ribbons on Jeannie's sailor hat out behind her. There was only a hint of autumn in the air. The carriage bowled along merrily, its varnished surfaces shining in the sun. She and Robert sat up front, with him holding the reins. The horses needed no guiding. They, too, seemed happy to be outdoors on such a day, and their heads arched high as they trotted along.

Jeannie looked behind her and caught her breath at the view of the city they'd left behind—the beautiful stone-built town of Edinburgh with the great castle on one side and the Calton Hill on the other, Salisbury Crags towering beyond. Even the cap of blue smoke hovering over the city looked pretty in the sunlight.

She faced forward again. Robert was smiling. He'd taken off his hat and he appeared as carefree as a lad. "There's cold grouse and bannocks and fruit and a fine bottle of wine in the basket there," he said.

"A meal fit for Queen Victoria," Jeannie said happily.

She was going to enjoy this day, she decided. She wasn't going to worry about the work she'd left at home in her flat, about the money she'd be short after missing yet another day, money she sorely needed.

"CAN YOU HEAR ME, Liz?" a voice asked.

"Yes," Liz said, though it seemed an effort to speak.

"Are you still in the carriage?"

"No. It's all gone. I don't know where it's gone." There was only darkness in front of her now. And a great sadness.

"I'm going to wake you up, okay? When I count to three, you'll come back to the present, feeling rested and relaxed."

"HOW DO YOU FEEL?" Dr. Lockwood asked as Liz blinked.

The room was shadowy. It had rained earlier and the sky was still cloudy. What light there was barely filtered through the trees outside. Douglas firs. A few oaks. A row of alders. The institute was in a heavily wooded area outside Seattle. It was all very quiet and restful, but she wished she could see the expression on Matt's face, get some idea of his reaction.

"I'm okay," Liz said softly. "I feel good, I guess. You told me I'd feel good, didn't you, just before you started counting so I'd wake up."

"Just stay still for a few minutes. Let yourself get used to being here."

"I didn't want to let go of it," she said regretfully. "It was such a good feeling. I was so...happy."

After a moment's reflection, she added, "It was interesting to me that I appeared to be right there in Scotland, riding around in a carriage, yet I could hear you asking questions and I could hear my own voice answering. But at the same time, I was Jeannie. And then for just a minute or two I was all the way into it and I didn't remember you or me. I wish it had gone on longer."

He was fiddling around with the tape recorder, rewinding the tape, she supposed. After a minute or two he got up, walked over to the window and stood there with his hands in the pockets of his chinos, gazing at the trees outside. He didn't say anything; probably he was giving her time to come all the way back.

"What did you think?" she asked nervously when his silence became somewhat oppressive.

He turned at once. "Forgive me," he said, his voice brisk. "I was so...involved in listening to you, I became disoriented myself. It happens that way sometimes."

He seemed to be studying her face. She wished she could see his more clearly. "Don't worry about the brevity of it," he said. "It wasn't a deep trance. It takes practice sometimes."

"I thought it was noteworthy that I mentioned Queen Victoria. I told Erica I thought the...episodes took place in the late nineteenth century, so that holds together, doesn't it? At least my crazy imagination creates authentic fantasies."

He didn't answer.

"It was different this time," she added. "The scene, I mean."

He sat down at his desk. His face was still in shadow. "Tell me about the other times."

"The first time I was standing in my apartment looking down at the yard, then all of a sudden I was sitting on a bench looking at Edinburgh Castle and the man I somehow knew was called Robert was there. Then I sort of segued into climbing to an upper story in an old building, and a man named Angus Macdonald pushed me—Jeannie—downstairs. The second time I was jogging around Green Lake—same scenario. The third and last time I was on an airplane flying to San Francisco. When I fell—when Jeannie fell down the stairs—I screamed and scared the dickens out of the other passengers. That's when I went to see Erica. I had one other episode, a quickie—is there such a thing as a miniregression? I was at home watching television and I saw Jeannie in my mind, folding ribbon. She was in her own flat, I knew that, and I called it a flat, not an apartment. There was a coal fire in the room. The whole scene couldn't have lasted more than a few seconds. Robert wasn't there.''

"Do you know Robert's full name?''

"Robert Charles McAndrew,'' she said without hesitation.

Apparently he wrote the name down on the pad in front of him. "Did you get any idea of relationship?''

She shook her head. She wished he'd switch a light on so she could see him better. There was a stiffness in his voice that hadn't been there before. She felt…awkward, though she hadn't felt any constraint earlier. "I think I liked him a lot—Jeannie, I mean, liked him a lot. I think maybe she was falling in love with him. I don't blame her, he's gorgeous. Robert Redford in *The Great Gatsby*, elegant but on the roguish side.''

She thought he might have smiled, but he didn't say anything.

"Can I sit up?'' she asked.

"Certainly.''

"I guess that was pretty boring for you, huh? No battles or royal palaces. No Cleopatra sailing down the Nile.''

Matt was making notes again and ignored her attempt at levity.

"I'm really curious now," she said. "I'd like to know how Jeannie and Robert got together in the first place. I mean, she seemed to be poor—she was worried about missing a day's work. Robert was very well dressed and the carriage apparently belonged to him, so he would seem to be fairly wealthy."

She paused. "What do you think?" she asked again. "Am I the reincarnation of Jeannie Findlay?" She had meant to ask the question in a deliberately dramatic manner, making a joke of it, but it had come out sounding anxious instead.

Matt didn't answer right away, but when he did his voice was matter-of-fact. "I'd like to wait a while before giving an opinion," he said.

It was silly to feel so disappointed. What had she expected, that he'd get all fired up with excitement over her amazing experience? He must listen to this kind of stuff all the time.

She didn't try to hide her disappointment. "I hoped you'd be able to tell me right away what was going on and why."

He shook his head. "I lay no claims to psychic ability." He hesitated. "We do have a psychic on staff. Dr. Ledbetter. He conducts channeling sessions, group and private. You can certainly consult him, if you wish."

"I've read about channeling. Spirit guides, that sort of stuff."

"A little more scientific than that."

She'd offended him, that's why he was acting so stiff. She had to stop sounding as if she was scoffing. "I'll stick with you, if that's okay," she said solemnly.

"Fine." He glanced at her, then away. "If you don't mind, I'd like to play the tape of today's session and listen to it alone and then see you again in a few days."

She shook her head. "I won't be here. I'm leaving town on Monday. I'm going to Scotland for a month."

"To Edinburgh?" He sat forward abruptly. She'd obviously startled him.

"It's a case of the egg coming after the chicken," Liz explained. "I started planning the trip to Scotland several weeks ago." She explained about her mother's business. "It was after we started talking about Scotland that I began having these...episodes. So I guess that's what triggered them."

She shrugged. "I'm not just going to Edinburgh. I'll be visiting all the Prince Hotels."

He had finally switched on a lamp, but she still couldn't read his expression. His face was smooth, professionally neutral, the way her gynecologist's was when he asked her intimate questions. His eyes were as gray and clear as the sky on a winter morning. "Is there a Prince Hotel in Edinburgh?" he asked.

She nodded. "The Prince William." She laughed nervously. "Maybe I should skip that one, skip Edinburgh altogether."

He frowned. "It might be a wise idea at that. I'm not sure you should expose yourself to—"

She held up a hand, palm out. "Whoa," she said. "I was joking. Wild horses wouldn't keep me from going to Edinburgh." She hesitated. "I've got to admit to being scared, though. I mean, this is a business trip. I definitely don't want to freak out my clients. You don't think I'll suddenly...regress as soon as I get there?"

"You'll only regress when and where and if you want to," he said emphatically.

"Was there anything different about my...regression?" she asked as she stood. She wished she could think of something else to call it. Giving it the same name he did made it seem she was accepting it, and she wasn't. No way. "I mean, compared to your other...clients...patients?"

"There's no set form for these things," he said slowly. "Some people receive only small impressions. Others say it's like viewing a movie. Still others participate fully, to the extent that they appear to be living the other life and forget the present one. I think you had a glimpse of that. Next time perhaps you'll experience more of it. Some people get very emotional. Many, like you, describe what is happening very calmly. Occasionally someone will speak in a foreign language. You acquired a faint Scottish accent as you went along."

He seemed tired, she thought. And his former friendliness had disappeared altogether along with his smile and the puckish tilt of his eyebrows. Did these sessions drain the hypnotist, the way séances were supposed to drain the person conducting one?

"I still don't believe it," she said, wanting to be frank.

He smiled tiredly. "That's your privilege, of course." He looked away. "I do want to assure you that your experiences are not at all extraordinary," he added.

She felt vaguely relieved. If you were going to be weird, it was nice to know you weren't abnormally weird.

"Shall I call for an appointment when I return?" she asked.

He nodded immediately and stood up. "Definitely. Yes. Please do. I wish you weren't...I wish I had seen you sooner, I might have been able to prepare you. I'm not sure—"

He broke off, worrying his hair with one hand. Then he looked at her for a long moment, his lips parting as if he were going to say something more, but instead he shook his head and compressed his mouth. "A month then," he finally murmured. "Yes, that's probably a good—"

Moving around the desk, he opened the door for her, as though all of a sudden he was in a hurry for her to leave. "Have a good trip," he said politely. He didn't offer to shake her hand again, which she'd been rather looking forward to.

Had she offended him in some way, she wondered again as she walked toward the bus stop. He wasn't nearly as friendly after the regression as he had been when they started out. Pity—she'd liked him. Face it, she'd felt enormously attracted to him. But right now, she wasn't sure if she wanted to come back to see him or not.

MATT LOCKWOOD slumped back into his chair the moment Liz left the room, feeling as though all the strength had drained out of his legs. Placing his elbows on his desk, he pushed his fingers into his hair and rested his head on his hands, his eyes tightly closed, silently trying to will the tension out of his body. He had no idea how he had managed to function during the last half hour. The minute Liz had said, "I'm in Edinburgh, of course," his brain had frozen in place.

Taking a deep breath, he sat up straight and stared at the recliner Liz had occupied, wishing he could will her back into it, question her, hypnotize her again.

He had always known she would come. Always.

Pressing the intercom button in front of him, he said, "Get me Dr. Demetrius, will you, Sally?" He hoped his voice didn't sound as ragged as he felt.

When the phone buzzed, he took another calming breath and picked up the receiver. "Ione, could you please come to my office? I know it's close to quitting time but I need to see you."

"Ten…fifteen minutes?" Ione asked. "I'm just reading a transcription of a tape."

"Right now," Matt said tersely, hanging on to his last ounce of control so he wouldn't yell at her.

"On my way, boss," Ione said, sounding mildly offended.

A couple of minutes later she entered his office, a short, unashamedly overweight woman with frizzy gray curls, bifocal spectacles and a luminous smile. She was wearing a brown polyester pantsuit that was at least ten years out-of-date. She was Matt's colleague, his closest friend, his mentor, his confidante, his surrogate mother.

"You'd better have good cause to use that tone of voice with me, young man," she said with mock severity. Then her smile faded. "What's wrong, Matt? Are you sick? This damn flu that's going around…"

He shook his head and waved her to a seat on the other side of his desk. "Do you remember when you regressed me the first time?" he asked urgently.

She nodded. "Four years ago. When we first started talking about opening this place. You'd had a couple of spontaneous regressions already."

"Do you remember who I said I was in my last life?"

"All the people I see and you expect me to remember something from four years ago? You want me to get your folder from my office?"

"No. I want you to dig into that fantastic memory of yours and give me the answer now."

She sighed exaggeratedly, closed her eyes for a minute, then opened them and smiled in triumph. "Robert Charles McAndrew."

"And the woman's name? The woman Robert Charles McAndrew was in love with?"

She raised her slightly bushy gray eyebrows. "Give me a break, Matt. No. Wait. It was Scottish, too. Jennie?"

"Jeannie. Jeannie Findlay."

"As I recall," Ione said slowly, "there were meetings of those two people in other lives, previous lives. Different names, of course, different countries, but you seemed convinced they were the same people."

Matt nodded. "There was a time in Persia in the seventeenth century. She was wealthy, I was not."

"Ah, yes, I remember you talking about mosaic tiles on the outer walls of her father's house."

"There was also Denmark. I was a fisherman. She was a weaver."

Matt stood and paced back and forth a couple of times behind his desk. He was starting to feel it now, letting himself feel the excitement.

"I've just met a young woman named Liz Brooks," he said. "She's a travel agent. No, not exactly an agent— she's a sales representative for a travel marketing company."

He bent over the desk to refer to his notes. "British Travel Services in Seattle. She's leaving for Scotland on a business trip on Monday. Ever since she started planning the trip she's been having what she describes as episodes."

He straightened, shaking his head. "She just walked in that door and I regressed her, all unknowing. This is what she came up with."

Reaching over, he activated the tape recorder, then leaned his hands on his desk, staring intently at Ione while the tape played and Liz talked of Jeannie Findlay and Robert Charles McAndrew going on a picnic.

"Dear God in heaven," Ione said faintly when it was done.

He sat down. "You're our resident expert on couples

who've reincarnated together," he said. "Tell me what to do."

"What *did* you do?"

He pushed a hand through his hair. "Behaved like a village idiot with my mouth hanging open. What *could* I do? She has no background in reincarnation theory, except for a little pop reading. Thinks the whole thing sounds logical, but she's not making any leap into faith."

He sighed. "I'm quoting her exactly. She's totally skeptical. She assured me in several different ways that she's not buying my theories. So what could I say to her? 'Excuse me, miss, I know we haven't met before, but I'm the long lost lover you've been searching for.' We're strangers to each other, Ione. There was no way I could even give her a hint of what I was feeling. I had to take refuge behind some stiff professional facade. She probably thinks I'm an unfeeling stick. Maybe she'll decide never to come back. Maybe I'll never see her again." He felt a wave of despair at the thought.

"You have her address, don't you?" Ione pointed out calmly.

Matt laughed. Ione was always able to bring him down to earth. "She came here at the recommendation of her friend Erica Walter in San Francisco," he told her. "Erica's a psychologist. I met her at a hypnosis seminar last year. She figured Liz might have experienced spontaneous past-life regression. She was right. Boy, was she right."

"So, is she pretty, this Liz Brooks?" Ione asked.

"Vividly so. Extraordinarily colorful—blue eyes, milky skin, hair like a forest fire, wonderfully defined cheekbones. She could be a fashion model. Tall, slender, sits and stands very straight. Very nervous at first, but trying not to show it."

"People are always nervous the first time."

"She came to me for help, Ione. Out of all the people she might have gone to, she came to me. She's lived in Seattle all her life, just as I have. And she's twenty-seven, just as Jeannie was."

"And you are thirty-five." Ione gave him the benefit of her gentle smile. "Haven't you been connected with re-incarnation theory long enough to know there's no such thing as coincidence? That's the great beauty of it. Was it coincidence you both came back in the same time frame? Was it coincidence that you both were born in the same town? Don't I see it over and over with the couples I work with? When there's a strong bond in one life, sooner or later people come together in another one."

She frowned. "As I remember it, even under hypnosis you couldn't recall how your time together in Scotland had ended. If it wasn't resolved, then all the more reason for you to meet again this time around."

She studied his face for a minute, then reached across the desk to place her hands on his clenched fists. "Relax, Matt dear, you won't get anywhere by jumping on your horse and riding off in all directions. Let me think now."

She took off her bifocals, polished them slowly with a tissue from a box on Matt's desk, then settled them back on her snub nose. "This is all very interesting, you know," she said. "We may have a first. It's usually so simple. People without any conscious memories of past lives to-gether meet in this life and feel immediate attraction, or repulsion, depending on their karmic history. Somehow there's a subconscious recognition of each other. They say, 'I feel I've known you before.' Or even the old line, 'Haven't we met somewhere?' If what we have is a man and a woman, and the attraction develops into love, we don't necessarily have a happy ending. When they come to me, it's usually because they are having difficulties. By regressing them to their previous lives together, I can often find the roots of their problems. However..."

She paused, leaning forward. "In your case, and that of Miss...Brooks?...you each had knowledge of at least one other life together *before* you met each other. Tell me now, were you attracted to her right away?"

He smiled wryly. "I told you what she looks like."

"You've regressed gorgeous young ladies before. Did you *feel* anything?"

He decided to be cautious. "I thought she was very attractive, but as this was a professional interview I should ignore that fact."

"You're so disciplined, Dr. Lockwood." Her voice was loaded with sarcasm.

He let out his breath on a long sigh. "Okay, Ione, yes, I was immediately attracted to her. Strongly attracted. How could I not be? She lit up this room like a flame. When I came in and saw her my first thought was that I should lock the door so she couldn't get away."

"And she?"

"Was friendly, but nervous. And also attracted. There was a moment, early on..." He sighed. "After the regression I was in total shock. I've no idea what she felt then."

"So. Did she make another appointment?"

"She said she'd call. But I'm worried about this Scottish trip. She's liable to regress. I gave her a posthypnotic suggestion that she wouldn't unless she wanted to, but I think she may decide to."

"So perhaps she'll learn more about her life as Jeannie, more about Robert Charles McAndrew, and come back and fall into your arms."

"You're not being a whole hell of a lot of help, Ione."

She made an exasperated sound. "My dearest Matt, what do you expect? The ethics of this situation are perfectly clear. You must wait until she returns, and regress her again, if that's what she wishes. You must set aside your personal feelings and pretend she is unknown to you. If you cannot do that, you must refer her to a disinterested party. Me, for example. You must on no account reveal any specific knowledge of your own that would shock or upset her. Actually I'm not at all sure you shouldn't refer her to me at once.''

He shook his head. "I don't want to do that.''

"Can you maintain a proper professional distance?''

"I think so, yes.''

She studied his face for a minute, then she stood and headed toward the door. "I wish you luck, my friend. You may have a long and difficult road ahead of you.''

CHAPTER THREE

A MONTH LATER, Liz was seated at a small table in the dining room of the Prince William Hotel in Edinburgh. She was sharing breakfast with the hotel manager, Ian Cameron, a nice middle-aged Scotsman who was smartly dressed in a meticulously tailored charcoal-gray suit. Liz was wearing one of the three dress-for-success outfits she'd packed before leaving Seattle, a navy blue blazer, beige skirt and a crisp white blouse with a floppy paisley bow at the collar. Her hair was bound severely in its French braid, tied at her nape with a narrow navy blue ribbon.

Beyond the tall mullioned windows the morning mist shrouded the ancient city of Edinburgh—nothing unusual there. Yet Liz's hands felt clammy against the warm tea-cup and there was a tightness in her chest that was interfering with her digestion of the oatmeal porridge Ian had insisted she sample. Yesterday's experiences had unnerved her more than she cared to admit, even to herself. And in a little while she was going to have to force herself to go back into the streets of Edinburgh. Her pride—and yes, her curiosity—wouldn't let her do anything else.

There was only a sprinkling of guests in the dining room, a subdued handful of English, German and Scandinavian tourists who seemed cowed by the Prince William's newly restored baronial splendor.

"I wish you hadna left Edinburgh till last," Ian Cameron grumbled, raising slightly grizzled eyebrows.

"It seemed logical to begin with the Prince Andrew in the Orkneys and work my way south," she said apologetically. She could hardly tell him she'd wanted to approach Edinburgh obliquely because she had been terrified of what might be waiting for her. Actually she had almost decided to avoid Edinburgh after all, but then she had decided she'd never been a coward and she wasn't going to start now. If Fate had surprises in store for her in the old city, she might as well face up to them and get it over with.

"But you allowed only two days for Auld Reekie. How can you get to know a city in two days? Did you at least go on a tour of the castle yesterday?"

"Of course." And had been scared half out of her wits by the eerie familiarity of it all—St. Margaret's Chapel, the historical apartments, the curving ramparts of Half-Moon Battery, the steep cobbled passageways.

Déjà vu.

More than déjà vu.

Strangely, as she had walked the Royal Mile that stretched from the castle to Holyrood Palace, much had seemed familiar, yet much had seemed changed—especially in the Lawnmarket, an area of antique stores and tartan souvenir shops. But how could it seem changed if she had never seen any of it before? Several times she'd experienced the terrifying feeling that if she just slid her eyes slightly sideways, she would see something other— something that wasn't really there.

"Ah well, what's done canna be undone." Cameron smiled ruefully. "You'll forgive me for waxing poetic, Miss Brooks. It's not often I'm blessed with the company of a bonny young lass to light up the dark corners of this old place. I wish you could prolong your stay."

Liz spread butter on a scone. "I think I've got everything I came for," she assured him. "I'm all clear on the workings of the Prince William and its sister hotels. I have all the brochures I need and lots of maps and photographs. I'll be giving seminars throughout the United States this fall and winter, promoting the Prince chain to tour wholesalers and travel agents who set up FITs—foreign independent travel. I'll use slides, videos and other promotional material to show the accommodations available, recreational opportunities, scenery and so on. I think you'll see a marked increase in tourist interest."

He nodded. "And in Yankee dollars, I hope. We had quite a few Americans during the Edinburgh festival, but the earlier part of summer was dismal. It takes time for people to learn there's new management. You wouldna believe the condition this place was in—the plumbing alone...and Americans do like their plumbing." He grinned. "I'm glad the powers-that-be were clever enough to hire you. I suppose with a name like British Travel Services, your firm specializes in British hotels? You have other clients in Scotland?"

She shook her head. She was feeling less nervous now. It felt good to talk about her work. Normal. The longer she talked the longer she could delay doing what she had made up her mind she was going to do. "This is the first time we've ventured into the Scottish market," she told Ian Cameron. "We had talked about it, but the Prince chain contacted us before we got around to doing anything. My mother owns the company and she was English originally, you see. Her parents owned hotels in Middlesex and Buckinghamshire. We started out with areas Mom knew well."

"Your mother was a war bride?"

"No. My dad was over here during the war, but Mom's ten years younger. He met her on a return trip in 1958." No need to mention they'd divorced twenty years later.

"Which makes you less than thirty. Och, I've forgotten what it's like to be that age—with no responsibilities, no worries."

If you only knew, Ian Cameron, she thought, but contented herself with smiling vaguely.

"I've had a terrific month," she said after a moment's silence. "Scotland is so beautiful. I'll have no difficulty convincing people of that. The scenery is stunning, and the people generous and courteous and very friendly."

"Aye. We're not as reserved as most people think." He leaned forward, those grizzled eyebrows of his shooting upward again. "I'd be happy to show you some of the environs of Edinburgh," he offered. "There's no reason I can't take the day off and drive you out into the Lothian countryside—to Linlithgow perhaps, where Mary Queen of Scots was born. The Stuart Kings…"

"I have several appointments today," Liz said hastily. It was a lie, but she could hardly tell this nice, normal, ordinary man that she was halfway expecting to spend some time in another century, living somebody else's life.

A couple of hours later, she was sitting on a bench in Princes Street Gardens, looking upward to where Edinburgh Castle ought to be, dismayed by the persistence of the mist. Thick, gray-white, impenetrable, it filled the ravine and totally blocked the castle from view.

As far as Liz could tell, this should be the right perspective from which to view Edinburgh castle as Jeannie had when she first showed up in Liz's mind. But how could she expect anything to happen if she couldn't even see the damn castle? She wouldn't have time to come by here in the morning, her train for London would leave too early.

"I want it to happen," she murmured. "I'm going to sit right here if it takes all day."

Fifteen minutes later, her patience was rewarded by a tinge of brightness in the sky, backed by a high and craggy shadow. She remembered reading in one of the brochures she'd acquired that violent eruptions of lava eons ago had created the rugged castle rock as well as the mile-long slope on which Old Edinburgh had been built.

Behind her was New Edinburgh, a mere two hundred years old and one of the first examples of large-scale town planning in Britain. In marked contrast to the huddled mass of buildings known as Old Town, New Town's severe and elegant Georgian buildings had been erected in a gridiron pattern with squares at each end. It was a city of wide streets, chain stores, shopping arcades, coffee bars and boutiques and fast-food outlets. She'd experienced a little déjà vu there, too, yesterday, but with nothing like the strength of her feelings for Old Town.

She could clearly hear the bustle of Princes Street behind her—the car horns, an occasional squeal of tires, someone shouting a greeting, the drawn-out hiss of air brakes and the rumble of the maroon-and-white city buses. All the same, the gardens had a secluded air, in spite of the railroad that cut through them and the heavy traffic on The Mound that joined the old town to the new. Squirrels scrambled up and down the trees, scolding passersby, hunting among fallen leaves for acorns.

Above her the mist was thinning now, eddying in the light breeze that had come up, offering teasing glimpses of gray buildings. A phantom city, a legendary city, a Camelot, turreted and spired, was forming slowly, magically, out of the mist.

And then without any warning at all, the mist vanished as though it had never been. Her drawings had been totally accurate, Liz realized with a sinking feeling in the pit of her stomach. Yet somehow the buildings of old Edinburgh, etched against the clear blue sky, seemed darker, sootier than when she'd looked at them yesterday. Chimneys were sending up thick columns of smoke. That's why they used to call Edinburgh Auld Reekie, Liz remembered. The smoke was from coal fires. Surely they didn't still burn coal for heat? Hadn't she read in Fodor's guide that Edinburgh was a smokeless zone now? She hadn't noticed any air pollution yesterday.

Still gazing upward, she became aware that the sounds behind her had changed. Now she was hearing the clippety-clop of horses' hooves and the rattle of large wheels. A parade of some kind? Why was it impossible for her to turn around?

There was a rushing sound in her ears, and a movement of air so strong that it seemed to be trying to lift her off the bench. The sounds behind her had become strangely muffled, she realized, and her pulse was beating loudly in her ears. She held her breath, straining upward, waiting, watching, listening…

JEANNIE FINDLAY had felt slightly dizzy when she first sat down on the empty bench. "That's what comes of walking all the way to New Town from the Lawnmarket without a bite of breakfast," her friend Mhairi would tell her, no doubt. Well, she'd left home early, with a delivery to take to a customer in George Street. She had brought her drawing book along, thinking it was time she spared an hour or so for herself—but she hadn't thought to bring a bit of oatbread, too.

She was feeling better now. Opening her book, her fingers clumsy in their worn gloves, she studied the castle again, determined to capture it properly for once. She had tried so many times, simply because she loved looking at it and wanted a picture of it to hang on her wall. Unfortunately her efforts invariably frustrated her.

Biting the tip of her tongue, she began drawing, commencing with the dominant structural lines, contours and masses, with many a stop to measure with her thumb on her pencil. Shading carefully, she added the more important details, then the minor ones, then stopped to look at what she had wrought.

She had to laugh. Her picture looked like a child's toy fortress drawn by a four-year-old. If she didn't laugh she would cry over her lack of talent. How could it be that she could draw a complicated hat for a customer with no difficulty at all, yet the castle would not come out right?

Her fingers were cold; perhaps that was... Och, no, she thought. She could at least be honest with herself. She'd had no better luck in midsummer.

A pair of children were having a grand time playing with a ball nearby. As Jeannie closed her book over her pencil and brushed a few dry leaves from her skirt, she watched them, envying them their freedom. They were handsome boys, perhaps eleven years old, apple cheeked and healthy looking, dressed in trews and warm jackets tailored of the finest cloth, a disquieting contrast to some of the ill-nourished, bandy-legged bairns who lived in her tenement.

She felt a spurt of resentment that was all too familiar, though it was not directed at the innocent children, but rather at the system that divided the human race into rich and poor.

Sighing, she stood, wiggled a little to adjust her stays and turned away just as one of the boys missed the ball and it bounced past her. Without stopping to remember she was a woman grown, Jeannie lunged to catch the ball, unfortunately not seeing the pair of long legs in striped trousers that had appeared from nowhere to trip her up. Off balance, carried on by her own momentum, she fell over the bench she'd just left, striking her head smartly against a tree just behind it, knocking her hat off and the breath from her body.

As stars danced a Highland fling in front of her eyes, she knelt on the bench, blinking hard in an attempt to clear her vision.

"I was trying to catch the ball myself," a man's voice said somewhere in the shower of stars surrounding her. "I was taking a constitutional—didn't see you until it was too late. Your green frock, the trees... I simply didn't notice. I do apologize."

It was hard to hear through the din inside her head. Pain was shrieking from ear to ear, stabbing her eyes. But there was no mistaking the man's accent. A Sassenach, without a doubt.

"Please say something," the voice begged. "Are you going to swoon? Dash it, I've no sal volatile with me. You came quite a cropper. Did you break any bones, do you think?"

Her vision was beginning to clear, but she was still too stunned to answer. But then she became aware that the man was running his hands familiarly over her arms and shoulders and down over her body, and she dredged up an indignant breath. "Take your hands off me at once," she ordered sharply.

"I'm simply making sure you're in one piece," the man murmured. He sounded offended, but he removed his hands from her person.

Very carefully Jeannie turned around and lowered herself into a sitting position on the bench. The boys had evidently run off. Afraid of getting into trouble, no doubt. Gingerly touching her scalp, she winced as her fingers encountered a bump the size and texture of a hard-boiled egg. "I'm put in mind of Walter Scott's Minstrelsy of the Scottish Border," she murmured through the pain. "'He belted on his gude braid sword and to the field he ran; but he forgot the helmet good that should have kept his brain.'"

"A witty woman as well as a pretty one," the man said in an admiring voice. "Here, let me see how bad it is." Holding her head firmly against his middle with one hand, he moved his fingers through her hair, snagging them on her hairpins.

"Be careful," Jeannie warned.

"The skin isn't broken, there's no blood," he said, then whistled under his breath, tightening his hold on her head. "By Jove, you've got a very large lump here."

"I can tell that," Jeannie said, exasperated. "Now if you'll just let go of my head, I could perhaps refrain from suffocating."

He released her once again. "I say, I'm truly sorry. I didn't realize I was causing you further discomfort."

Jeannie flexed her neck from side to side, then took a breath and risked straightening her throbbing head.

The man was still hovering over her. He was a young man, she decided. It was difficult to be sure when her eyes were watering with pain and he kept wavering in front of her. "Hold still now," she told him, and quite suddenly she saw him with startling clarity.

The most beautiful man in the world.

Long after, she would remember that first thought and the queer heaviness that came to her limbs.

He was not so young after all. Past thirty anyway. Seven or eight years older than she was, well built, clean shaven, his thick fair hair cut short, shining like afternoon sunshine on a field of barley. He had the bluest eyes she'd ever seen—bold blue eyes with little lines at the outside corners—eyes made for laughing.

"I believe I should take you to the infirmary," he said briskly.

"I'll no be beholden to a Sassenach," she said, pulling herself to her feet. "If you'll just find my hat for me and my drawing book, I'll be—" She broke off as the ground shifted under her boots.

The beautiful man took hold of her arm and she didn't have the strength to resist him. Gently but forcibly he sat her down again. "I think perhaps you shouldn't try to move for a few more minutes," he advised. Then he disappeared. No, he'd just gone behind the bench to retrieve her hat. Sitting down beside her he carefully brushed dust from it with the palm of his hand and gave it to her. As she took it from him, his fingers touched hers and she suddenly seemed to have lost the ability to breathe. She certainly didn't have enough strength to put the hat back on. Lifting her face, she gazed up at him with the hat held limply in her lap. There was a silence that seemed to last for a long, long time. She felt as though something inside her had opened, letting in a warmth like summer sunshine. She could even *smell* the sunshine, and a warm earthiness coming up out of the ground.

He cleared his throat. "An exceptionally dashing hat," he said.

"Hat? Oh, my hat. Thank you. I made it myself. Well, I shaped it and sewed all the trimming on," she added, ever a stickler for the truth when it wasn't necessary to lie. "I bought the body of it from the wholesaler of course, as I usually do."

"You're a milliner?"

"Aye." No need to tell him of her other occupation. He would think less of her, and she didn't want a Sassenach looking down on her, especially such a handsome Sassenach.

"My congratulations." She wasn't sure if he was teasing her. It might just be the way his smile formed, crooking up one corner of his mouth.

"Your drawing book, ma'am," he said and she took the book from him. It was open to the sketch she'd made. "Not quite so fine as your hatmaking," he commented.

"I canna seem to get it right, no matter how I try," Jeannie said mournfully. "I can only draw hats. Mind you, the great fashion designer, Mr. Worth, couldna draw, either. He used to have lithographs made of heads and arms and then he sketched in his dresses." What a chatterbox she'd turned into suddenly.

"Not enough shading in the middle here, perhaps," he said, leaning over her book to pencil in a few lines. His breath was sweet on her face and she didn't pull back. "This part needs work," he murmured. "It's the perspective that's not quite…" With a few whisks of her India rubber and a dozen strokes of her pencil he transformed her drawing into an almost-exact replica of the castle.

"You're an artist!" Jeannie exclaimed.

He laughed, deep, rich throaty laughter that made her feel warm inside again. "A flattering response, but untrue, I'm afraid," he said. "I'm the new president of the Royal Edinburgh Bank."

"A banker!" Jeannie shut her mouth firmly and resolved not to open it again. With shaking fingers she set her hat on her head and pushed home the hatpins, hoping she wouldn't stab them through the lump that was still throbbing up there.

She stole a glance at her companion. His own hat must have been knocked off in the collision, too. He was brushing it off now—a black top hat of the best quality. He was dressed in a fine suit of clothes—gray striped trousers and a morning coat over a white shirt with a stiff collar and loosely bowed tie. Obviously he was not only a Sassenach, but one of the gentry.

He had evidently caught her peeking at him. He smiled again. It was easy for him to smile it seemed. Jeannie thought of herself as good-natured, but sometimes it was hard to smile the way life was.

"Does your head feel better?" he asked gently.

"Aye," she lied. "I'll put a wet flannel on it later."

He looked at her very directly. His face was solemn, but that corner of his mouth was crooked again. "Do you know what today's date is?" he asked.

It seemed an odd sort of question, but she answered anyway. "It's the sixth of September, 1888."

"And do you remember your name?"

"Do you think I'm daft?"

"My dear young woman, I'm simply trying to determine if the blow to your head has had an injurious effect."

"Oh."

"Your name?"

"Jeannie Findlay."

"Jeannie. Bonny Jeannie." He smiled, then shook himself a little as if he, too, was having trouble concentrating.

"Your age?"

"Twenty-seven."

"And is that *Mrs*. Findlay?"

"Miss," she said firmly. Not exactly a fib. It was her maiden name that she'd returned to, and she'd been a Miss when she had it before.

"No husband then?"

"No. I'm an old maid."

That seemed to amuse him but better he be amused than

that he, a banker, should learn who her husband had been
and how he had died.

"And where do you live, Miss Jeannie Findlay? I must
see you safely home."

"I've a flat in the Lawnmarket," she said shortly.

"The Lawnmarket."

The careful tone of his voice told her he knew all about
the Lawnmarket. "I'll catch an omnibus," she said, knowing she wouldn't think of spending the fare on anything
so unnecessary as long as she had two strong legs.

"Nonsense, Miss Findlay. My carriage is nearby. I'll
drive you home." He lifted one hand to stop her protest.
"I insist. The accident was my fault. I feel responsible."
With that, he put an arm around her in a very familiar way
and helped her to her feet.

About to chastise him for holding her so closely, Jeannie
bit the words back. For one thing, her head still felt as
though it would fall off if she nodded. For another...for
another she *liked* the feeling of his arm around her. It was
a strong arm, a capable arm and it made her feel warm
and protected. She couldn't remember the last time a man
had put his arm around her. Her father had never demon-
strated any affection for her or her sister. As for Rory
Douglas, well, he had been no more than a boy when she
married him, no more than a boy when he died.

"You're limping," her escort exclaimed, letting go of
her so suddenly she almost fell. "Did you twist your ankle? You made no mention of your ankle."

She felt herself flush. Drawing herself up as straight as
she could under the circumstances, she said flatly. "I always limp. I was born crippled in the hip." She forced a
smile. "Now you know why I'm an old maid. Nobody
wants damaged goods."

He was silent for a moment, then he settled his hat

squarely on his head and offered her his arm. Hesitantly she slipped her gloved hand into it, feeling an unfamiliar warmth curl around her heart at the hard strength under her fingers. "I'm sorry, Jeannie," he said after a moment.

"I dinna recollect giving you permission to use my Christian name," she said sternly to cover up the flustered way she felt hearing her name spoken with such... tenderness.

"I do apologize," he said at once with another of the wide white smiles she was beginning to watch for.

The hood was folded down on his carriage, the matched gray horses waiting patiently. As he handed her up, Jeannie tried to look as if she were used to climbing into a grand carriage every day of her life. She was abruptly conscious of the worn fabric of her gloves, the shabbiness of her frock. It was a good sturdy green serge and had been given her in part payment of a bill for a French Chip carriage bonnet. She'd turned the fabric painstakingly but it still had a slightly worn look. Och, what did it matter. When she owned her own shop, she'd be able to afford new gowns all the time. She could bide her time. She was a patient woman, Jeannie Findlay.

No coachman, she noted. She had expected a coachman. Imagine Jeannie Findlay driving out with a gentleman alone. Her neighbors were going to have a good gossip over this when they saw her come home, she thought as her companion climbed nimbly up beside her and took the reins. Her reputation, such as it was, would be ruined. The thought didn't worry her over much.

Soon the horses were cantering along, passing a green-grocer's cart, heading straight toward a butcher's van and a cart piled high with barrels of ale coming in the opposite direction. Jeannie closed her eyes, but there was no crash. When she dared to open them, he was looking at her sideways, smiling roguishly, setting her heart to jumping all over again.

"I'd feel safer if you'd keep your eyes on the road instead of on me," she said sharply.

"But I like looking at you, Jeannie," he said without shifting his gaze. "Does it offend you that I look at you?"

She hesitated. "No," she said. "It doesna offend me."

Something flickered in his eyes as he looked directly at her, something she couldn't interpret, and it seemed to her that his breath had caught in his throat just as tightly as hers had done. When he finally turned his attention to the traffic, the smile still played around the corners of his mouth.

"I've been remiss," he said cheerfully after a while. "I quite forgot to introduce myself." He gave her a funny little half bow, made awkward by his position in the driver's seat. "Robert Charles McAndrew at your service. No Sassenach after all, you see, but a fellow Scot, albeit I've lived in London most of my life."

So engrossed was she in watching the interesting curves of his mouth, it was a moment before she took in his words. Then she averted her face and sat up very straight, feeling a definite chill at the back of her neck. "There was a Laird Robert Charles McAndrew lived in Glendarra in the Highlands, some seventy-odd years ago," she said stiffly. "He was known far and wide as Black Robert."

"My great-grandfather," he said cheerfully. "How on earth did a young woman like you ever hear of Black Robert? He's long since dead, of course, but my grandfather still maintains our house in Glendarra. He's there now as a matter of fact—for the deer hunting." He grinned. "Eighty-seven years old and he's out tramping the forest with the best. Only last week he brought down a buck with a fine set of antlers."

"Sins of the fathers, sins of the sons," Jeannie said darkly.

He looked surprised. "You don't approve of killing deer? But it's a grand sport, Jeannie—Miss Findlay."

"Grand sport for the deer, too, no doubt." Anger was tightening Jeannie's stomach into a dozen knots. Her head was throbbing again. "Black Robert," she said, putting every ounce of disgust she possessed into the pronunciation of the hated name. "Seventy years ago, Black Robert evicted my family from their farm in Glendarra, if you could call it a farm, so miserably small it was. Hardly more than a wee strip of land. But Black Robert wanted it back so my family and a hundred other families had to go."

His brow was furrowed. "You're talking about The Clearances?"

"The Clearances. That infamous time when the Highland Lairds decided they could make more money from sheep than from lawful tenants who had farmed the land for generations, making nobbut a pittance as it was, scarce enough to keep body and soul together."

"I agree that it was a terrible thing, Jeannie, but the lairds really had no choice."

So angered was she that she barely noticed his use of her Christian name this time.

"If you've studied Scottish history at all," he began, then hesitated. "Are you…that is, you do read? You quoted Scott earlier…"

"I've a fair education, Mr. McAndrew," she said icily. "My father might not have thought over much of having only daughters, but he sent my sister and me to day school for all that. The Scots set great store by an education, as you should know if you were a true Scot. I know as much history as you do, more truthful history. My family lived it on the *other* side, the poor side."

"But you must surely realize that once Bonnie Prince Charlie was defeated at Culloden and Scottish dreams of independence were killed forever, the lairds could no longer count their wealth in the number of tenants they could raise for their armies. They had to find other sources of income." He smiled his charming smile, his hands skillfully manipulating the reins as the carriage turned a steep corner. "It was a long time ago, Jeannie. Before you and I were ever born."

"Aye, a long time. But Highlanders have long memories. Fine it was to call on your tenants to be killed on battlefields, but when the wars were over, why then what was the use of them?" She darted a challenging glance at him and was pleased he had the grace to look ashamed. "And it wasna just that the lairds had no money," she said emphatically. "They wanted to raise sheep to pay for their grand houses in Edinburgh and London. Did your family not happen to move to London about that time, Mr. McAndrew?"

"Well, I suppose they did, but—"

"With no thought of the evicted families who came near starving, no doubt. And now," she added when he seemed about to interrupt—oh, she'd allow no interruption. She was in fine fettle now, her headache forgotten, her cheeks burning with righteous anger. She'd yearned for years to tell off one of those high and mighty lairds. "Now," she repeated, "those same lairds, or at least their descendants, have discovered a new source of wealth. They've opened their lands to industrialists—rich men who've made their fortunes on the backs of poor workers and who now want nothing more than to decorate their fancy rooms with the heads of poor dumb animals."

"Times are changing, Jeannie."

"Times may be changing for the likes of you, Mr.

McAndrew, but not for the poor. Never for the poor. Only last week I read in the newspaper about a pair of poor crofters not far from Glendarra who were summoned to court in Edinburgh for killing a deer. They proclaimed their innocence and called the local lord and lady to their defense, but the gentry said they would go to court only if the crofters paid their expenses, knowing full well the men hadn't a farthing to their names. Would you care to guess what will happen to the men when they fail to bring witnesses to court?''

His face was very solemn now. "You're right, Jeannie. That sounds like a gross miscarriage of justice. I'll look into it."

"Justice," Jeannie snorted.

"You should be an advocate. No judge would be able to resist those flashing brown eyes. A woman law agent now, that would be something to see."

He was back to his teasing manner, smiling at her in a way that made it hard for her to hold on to her anger. But hold on to it she would—it seemed important that she should.

They were approaching the Lawnmarket now and she gave him the necessary directions. "You canna drive to my door," she informed him. "The streets are too narrow. If you stop by the fishmonger's there, I can walk the rest of the way."

He stopped where she indicated, but insisted he must escort her all the way home. Calling one of the lads who was always lurking at corners, he gave him a coin to watch the horses and promised him another on his return.

Stiff backed, Jeannie preceded him, trying not to limp too noticeably on the cobbles, aware of how the district must look and sound to him who was used to so much better. Housewives gossiping on corners, arms folded; children everywhere; the rag man pushing his handcart and shouting for business; mad Harry who always dressed in full though tattered Highland regalia, playing a lively march on his bagpipes—outrageously out of tune.

She stopped at the door to her tenement. Five floors above, her friend Mhairi Stewart was hanging out of her window, her blond curls as wild as always, talking to old Mrs. Erskine, who was hanging out of hers on the next floor down. Mhairi must have recovered early from her morning sickness today. Both women stopped talking and fixed wide eyes on Jeannie's companion. "I thank you for your courtesy, Mr. McAndrew," she said stiffly.

He was looking around him at the tall crowded buildings and the rubbish littering the close. Nearby the youngest Murdoch boy was running around in nothing but an undervest, his bloated little belly streaked with dirt, his face filthy. His oldest brother was teasing him, holding the half-starved cat that was Will's special pet, hoisting it over his head so it was out of little Will's reach. "You there, Tam, you give yon cat to your brother and stop your teasing," Jeannie shouted, embarrassed. "You get on to school now before the schoolmaster takes his tawse to you." Next she turned on the little one. "Stop your greeting this instant, Will. Go on up and get your breeks on before you catch your death. Away with you both now."

Saucy Tam stuck his tongue out at her, but Will's dirty face was wreathed in smiles now as he clutched his precious kitten. "Och," Jeannie exclaimed, her voice softening. Fumbling in her skirt pocket, she pulled out a peppermint drop and handed it to the child. The sweet quickly bulged the wet young cheek.

"Their mother's a poor thing," Jeannie explained to her companion as Tam and Will ran into the building. "Too many bairns too fast, one of them with a twisted neck from measles and having to wear an iron frame to keep her head straight, poor wee thing. And the mother not twenty-three years old and expecting again. The father drinks, of course.'' She shook her head. '''Tis of no interest to you, Mr. McAndrew, I'm certain.''

He touched her cheek lightly. ''So much indignation in one slender girl. You are even more beautiful when you are angry, Jeannie Findlay. Could you persuade yourself to stop calling me Mr. McAndrew, do you suppose? My friends call me Robert. My mother calls me Robbie.''

''Robbie,'' she echoed before she could catch herself, then felt herself blush like a schoolgirl, remembering the interested gaze of the two women above. Such a fool she was, falling into a daze merely because his hand touched her face. No, it *wasn't* just his hand touching her face, it was the gentleness of it that had touched a part of herself she had thought closed off to all feeling. And he'd called her beautiful.

''I'll see you into your flat, Jeannie,'' he said when she forced herself to turn away. ''I'm not sure you're safe in this quarter.''

''I'm perfectly safe,'' she said, leading the way up to the first landing. Her voice should have withered him with its scorn. She was glad to have an excuse to be angry with him again. ''The rich aye think poor people are all criminals, but it isna so. The people hereabouts may not have two ha'pennies to rub together, but they are good folk for all that. Morally upright folk, all of us,'' she added with a straight glance over her shoulder.

''Jeannie,'' he said in an aggrieved way, but she let the hint stand. There could be only one reason why he was insisting on seeing where she lived—he wanted to return. Married no doubt, with a cold English fish of a wife who didn't see to his needs. Because Jeannie was poor he'd take it for granted her morals were easy. The gentry were that way. Well, he was about to find out differently, as others had before him. Just let him try.

But he didn't attempt to touch her. When they reached the top of the building he stood in her doorway, hat in hand, catching his breath after the long climb, looking around the drab room as she lit the gas—her room was at the back and always dim.

He looked first at the table by the high window. The only bright spot of color, it was laden with fabrics and ribbons and laces and feathers and other trimmings she used in her work. Then he studied the single gas ring on which she boiled her kettle or a pot of porridge when it wasn't cold enough to waste coal on the fire. Her gaze followed his, seeing her scant possessions through his eyes—the rickety washstand in the corner, the cupboard with her few dishes and pans, the narrow box bed built into the wall beyond. The kist for her clothes, the chamber pot—oh, Lord, the chamber pot, empty thank goodness, but there it was sitting where she'd left it after washing it out. And what if it was—it was a fact of her life that she couldn't always go running out in the middle of the night to use the loo she shared with seven other tenants.

The room was spotless, that was the important thing. The wooden floor might be bare, but it had been scrubbed until it was almost white. Jeannie could not abide dirt on her person or in her immediate surroundings.

"I do think you should go to hospital, to be sure you have no serious injury," he said. He reached inside his coat and took out a fine leather purse. "Let me give you something for the bill. I feel responsible."

"I've no need of your money," Jeannie said indignantly. She gestured at her table. "As you can see I have an honest livelihood. If I had need to go to the infirmary, which I have not, I would pay for it myself."

He regarded her in silence for a moment, then he said, "Jeannie, I saw your boots when you were topsy-turvy over that bench. There are holes in them."

"They are no my best boots," she said, feeling the tattletale heat rushing up to her cheeks again. "There was no rain this morn, I had no need of my good boots."

"But it was cold, Jeannie."

She wished he would stop saying her name in that sweet tender way that made her want to melt inside.

She answered defensively. "And so I cut inner soles out of thick wads of newspaper and padded my boots the way my mother did when I was small. It's a poor person's trick, Mr. McAndrew. You wouldn't know of such things, but it's perfectly comfortable in dry weather."

"I'm not leaving until you call me Robert," he said, apparently impervious to her sarcasm. Then he peered behind her and exclaimed, "You have books, Jeannie, you really are a reader."

She looked with pride at the bookshelves she had fashioned herself and the books crowded on them. "I have most of Shakespeare and Sir Walter Scott," she informed him. "Milton, Bunyan and Addison, too, and Galt. Thomas Boston. 'Man's life is a swift thing,' he said, 'Not only a passing but a flying vanity.' Rabbie Burns of course—he lived for a time in the Lawnmarket, did you happen to know?"

There was that smile again. Aye, he was aware of her sarcasm, and amused by it. "I didn't know. But I do know his work. Do you know this one, Jeannie:

'Till a' the seas gang dry, my dear, and the rocks melt wi' the sun; And I will love thee still, my dear, while the sands o' life shall run.'"

What a fine voice he had for reciting. She couldn't take her eyes from his face. Those bold blue eyes looking at her with such sweet attention while he declaimed her favorite poem of all time. How had he known?

"'And fare thee well my only luve,'" she heard herself saying. "'And fare thee well a while.'"

Suddenly feeling shy, she broke off, her voice faltering. He took up where she left off, never moving his eyes from her face, "'And I will come again, my luve, tho 't were ten thousand mile.'"

They stared at each other, then Jeannie shook herself out of her daze and said, "Aye, well, that was very fine, Mr. McAndrew."

"Robert."

She sighed. "Robert." She glanced at the purse still in his hand and tossed her head, wincing as the bump throbbed a warning. "I've no need of your charity," she said stiffly. "The reason I make do with old boots and this poor room is that I'm saving for a shop of my own in New Town. I'm a thrifty woman and I've a fair amount put by."

"You don't keep money here?" he asked with a horrified glance at the mattress. Aye, he was a banker all right.

"I'm no as daft as you think," she informed him. "My money's in railway bonds at five per cent."

An amused gleam appeared in his eyes. "You're an amazing woman, Jeannie Findlay. I'm glad I met you. May I come to see you again?"

She shook her head.

"I'm a banker, Jeannie. Perhaps I could help you realize your dreams a little sooner."

She looked him directly in the eye. "I canna afford the interest, Mr. McAndrew."

She saw him take her double meaning. He nodded and turned as if to go, then he changed his mind and came back to her. For a long moment, he stood looking down at her, then he smiled his crooked smile once more and said, "I like you, Jeannie Findlay. I like you very much. I feel as though I might have known you a long time ago."

"That's no verra likely," she said, though she felt much the same herself.

"I suppose not," he said softly. And then he kissed her, very gently, very delicately, on her closed lips.

A second later, he turned around, put on his hat and left her.

The little room seemed barer than ever, as though all that was good in life had gone with him. Jeannie sat down on her only chair, feeling like a child's rag doll that had lost its stuffing. Her heart was pounding in her ears.

CHAPTER FOUR

THE OFFICES of British Travel Services overlooked Seattle's Pike Place Market and Liz always enjoyed watching the people milling below. Most of them seemed in good spirits as they thronged around the stalls, buying huge bunches of beets, fat mushrooms, oversize cabbages, little plant pots filled with herbs. In the cobbled street umbrella-carrying pedestrians darted in and out of a continuous line of cars that inched along, drivers swiveling their heads in search of a nonexistent parking place. The market was a popular place, even on a rainy Friday morning in September.

There was silence behind her. Her mother was evidently still trying to digest the incredible story Liz had told her. Liz wasn't sure how Catherine was going to react. Her mother was a good listener, she rarely interrupted, and her smooth face had shown nothing of what she was thinking.

What was happening in Seattle in 1888? Liz wondered. It had been a sawmill community then, the forests teaming with loggers, schooners hauling away the lumber as fast as it was cut—a frontier town rapidly coming of age. Until fire wiped it out, started by boiling glue. When? 1889?

"I wonder if there really was a Robert Charles McAndrew," Catherine said at last.

Liz turned around. "I don't think I want to find out," she said.

"But you must admit he sounds rather dishy."

"He was." She hesitated. "I looked up Scotland in the *Encyclopedia Brittanica* and found out the Clearances Jeannie was so upset about were historical fact. That scared me enough to send me scuttling out of the library."

She took a breath, let it out. "Do you think I'm crazy, Mom?"

Catherine reached for an ivory letter opener on her desk and sat back in her swivel chair, studying it as if it were of supreme importance. "I don't know what to think, Elizabeth." Catherine hadn't become in any way Americanized over the last thirty years. Her accent was still as British as the Queen's. "The Duchess," Liz's father called her. Liz's story had affected her, however, even though she looked so much in possession of herself. She called her daughter Elizabeth only when she was deeply disturbed.

Liz studied her for a moment. Except for their slender height, the two looked nothing alike. Liz had inherited her father's copper-colored curls, bright blue eyes and slightly sharp features. Also his tendency to indulge in forbidden foods, balanced in both of them, fortunately, by a metabolism that gobbled up calories before they could become absorbed. Catherine, on the other hand, kept her figure trim with a strict diet and regular massage. She wore just enough makeup to accent her even features and allowed no gray to show in the jaw-length glossy brown hair she wore parted in the center. She was always smartly, elegantly, turned out in business suits or tailored slacks and bow-tied blouses— the latter today, a heavy cream silk and chestnut-brown wool combination. If there was any fault to be found in her appearance, or her personality, it was that she was perhaps too well-groomed, too perfectly in control.

After a minute or two she set the letter opener carefully back in its holder, smoothed her already smooth hair and lifted calm hazel eyes to Liz's face. "I think you should just put the whole incident out of your mind, darling," she said flatly.

"How can I do that?" Liz demanded. "It happened, Mom. One minute I was sitting looking up at the castle, the next I was living a whole other life as Jeannie Findlay. I stayed right there until Edinburgh's one o'clock gun went off and made me jump out of my skin." She grimaced. "How apropos. I felt as if I *was* out of my skin."

"And this story you've told me, these experiences you've had, all took place a hundred years ago?"

"Yes."

Catherine shook her head. "You fell asleep, you dreamed."

"That's what I thought the first time, but can anyone go to sleep jogging around Green Lake? And the incident in Edinburgh—could I dream in that much detail?"

"Why not?"

Liz shook her head. "It didn't seem like a dream, Mom. Besides, it happened again on a minor scale when I was hypnotized."

A tiny frown furrowed Catherine's smooth forehead. "I'm not too keen on this hypnosis business, darling. It sounds rather odd. You may trust this Dr. Matthew Lockwood, but what do you really know about him? The field attracts a lot of charlatans, you know."

"He's no charlatan, Mom. And I'm going to see him again after work today. I have to get to the bottom of this." She was looking forward to seeing Matt for his own sake, she realized, not just because she was anxious to tell him about her experience in Edinburgh.

"What does your father think?" Catherine asked.

"What makes you so sure I told him?"

"You always tell him things before you tell me. You

always did, even when we were still married." She wasn't acting the martyr, merely stating a fact. A true fact, Liz had to acknowledge.

Liz sat down in a chair near Catherine's desk and shook her head. "You know Dad, he always has a theory. He figures I've tuned in telepathically to something that happened a hundred years ago."

Catherine looked surprised. "That's a fairly intelligent idea. I'd have thought Jake would have come up with some insane suggestion about time travel."

"He did." Liz laughed. "But then he decided if it was time travel I would have looked on while the whole thing happened, rather than participating. I did participate, Mom. I was inside Jeannie, thinking her thoughts, feeling her feelings. I *was* Jeannie." She shook her head. "It does sound crazy, doesn't it?" She sighed. "Anyway, neither of Dad's theories explains my childhood obsession with Edinburgh Castle, does it, the way I drew it again and again without knowing what it was."

"I believe I suggested at the time that you must have seen some kind of travel documentary on PBS, or else you saw pictures in a magazine. You were always reading." Catherine nodded briskly. "Better to follow my initial reaction, I think. Put the whole thing out of your mind."

"But I'm curious, Mom. I mean, it scares the hell out of me, but there's a part of me that wants to understand it, and to know what happened next. It's like watching a miniseries on television and missing the last episode. Did Robert come back to see Jeannie? And what were the secrets she was keeping? Because he was a banker, she didn't want to tell him she'd had a husband. Why not? And she didn't want him to know what her other job was."

"Perhaps she was a prostitute."

Liz shook her head. "No way," she said firmly, then frowned. "Now why would I be so sure of that?"

Catherine shrugged. She didn't want to discuss it anymore, Liz realized. The subject made her uncomfortable for some reason, and Catherine Brooks didn't like to feel uncomfortable.

"I picked up my slides of the Scottish trip on the way in," Liz said.

Catherine stood, looking pleased and faintly relieved. "Wonderful! Let's go in the conference room and show them on the projector, see what you have."

As Liz was setting up the slide carousel her mother asked in a neutral voice, "How is your father, anyway?"

Liz laughed. "In great shape. Enthusiastic as all get-out. He's working on a new invention."

"Isn't he always?"

"Ah, but this one's going to help repair the ozone layer. Some kind of chemical pod you shoot from an airplane…"

Catherine held up a hand. "Spare me the details. I lived with your father long enough to know how mad he is."

"He's not crazy, Mom, he's brilliant. He was a great pilot, all those years in the air force, and look at all the stuff he turned out in R & D while he was working at Boeing—he saved the company millions of dollars."

"And then retired and began trying to blow himself up with experiments in the garage."

"Don't exaggerate, Mom. It was only one small explosion."

Catherine laughed. "He did look funny without eyelashes, didn't he?"

Liz studied her mother's face. Catherine had sounded decidedly fond. "Sometimes I wish you two would…"

"Don't even think it," Catherine said flatly.

Liz sighed. "Okay."

LIZ WAS EARLY for her appointment and she had to wait in an outer room. When Dr. Lockwood's patient—client?—came out she gazed at him curiously, wondering if he, too, was experiencing past-life regression. The man glanced with just as much interest at her. He looked normal enough, a middle-aged man in a smart pin-striped blue suit. She was going to have to stop thinking normal and abnormal, she decided.

Again Matt didn't offer to shake her hand. His smile was formal and didn't make it into his eyes. He was all crisp and businesslike in his speech and gestures. He'd had his hair cut, she noticed. It was definitely shorter, not nearly as shaggy, and obviously freshly shampooed. She could smell a faint herbal aroma. Nice. He was wearing a sweater with well-worn corduroy pants this time, a pastel blue cable knit that looked smooth enough to be cashmere. Apparently he was a tactile man, comfortable in soft fabrics. She wondered what had happened to his friendly smile. It certainly wasn't in evidence. He didn't even meet her eyes when he spoke to her. There was something almost chilling in his clinical detachment.

"How was your trip to Scotland?" he asked when she was seated. "Did you go to Edinburgh?"

"Yes."

She was going to let him drag the information out of her, she decided. If he wanted to be Mr. Frigid, she wasn't going to babble her whole story, exciting as it was.

"Did you regress?"

"Yes." She looked at him accusingly. "You knew I would, didn't you?"

"It seemed probable. Location is a powerful trigger."

He turned on the tape recorder. Obviously he was ready for her to tell him about the regression. But maybe *she* wasn't ready.

She wasn't quite sure why she was so annoyed with him. Yet she was. When she had first come to see him he had acted in a very friendly manner. He had seemed to like her. So she'd trusted him enough to let him hypnotize her. She'd also let her guard down and allowed herself to be attracted to him. Enormously attracted. She could have sworn that at their first meeting, he had been attracted to her, too—a certain look in his eyes... Well, hell, a woman knew when a man was turned on by her. Yet for some reason he'd turned off right after the regression. Why?

"Did you play the tape?" she asked. Maybe the answer was on the tape, maybe she'd cussed him out or something and hadn't remembered doing it. "I'd like to listen to it myself."

"I'll have a copy made for you. And yes, I did listen to it, several times."

"You aren't going to tell me what you think?"

"Later perhaps."

Maybe the friendly attitude had only been trotted out in the beginning to sucker her in. "So do you want to hear about Edinburgh or not?" she asked.

He glanced at her, then away. Evidently he'd noticed the sharpness in her voice. "I'd like you to go through it again under hypnosis, if you don't mind. Paraphrasing doesn't always capture the whole experience."

"Okay." She leaned back, letting her feet come up with the chair's footrest. "I guess I'm ready."

SHE WAS SITTING on a bench gazing up at Edinburgh Castle, trying vainly to draw it. Nearby two boys were playing with a ball, throwing it back and forth. Her fingers were getting cold. "Tell me what you see," a male voice was saying to her.

"JEANNIE," that same voice said a long time later. She was sitting on her chair in her flat, feeling limp and exhausted, but excited about her meeting with Robert Charles McAndrew. "Jeannie, can you hear me?"

"Of course I can," she said sharply.

"I want you to come forward a few days. Robert left after bringing you home. Now come forward in time to another day, a significant day."

MHAIRI WAS SITTING on Jeannie's narrow bed, clad in a loose wrapper, which was all she could get into nowadays. She was looking at Jeannie with a sly grin on her pretty face. "It seems to me your business has increased remarkably this past few days," she said. "I think it's time you told me what's afoot."

Jeannie glanced up from her seat by the table. With tiny, almost invisible stitches she was attaching veiling to a black hat of braided Milan straw. She'd already trimmed it with ribbons and flowers and bird wings in this season's fashion. "Nothing's afoot," she said irritably. "My reputation as a milliner is growing, that's all. I'm a very good hatmaker."

Mhairi tossed the blond curls that hung down her back. She hated pinning her hair up now that she was so far along. It made her head itch, she said. Besides, now that she couldn't go about no one saw her except her husband, Davie, who liked her hair down anyway, and the neighbors. "You've been a hedgehog ever since that man came into your life, Jeannie Findlay, prickly needles sticking out all over you." She raised her eyebrows. "You're asking me to believe it's just coincidence, are you—this increase in business that came so close on the heels of your romantic meeting with Robert McAndrew?"

Jeannie sighed. It would be foolish to go on arguing.

Mhairi knew as well as she did that messengers had begun arriving with commissions within two days of her meeting with Robert.

She shrugged. "I suppose he still feels responsible for me getting my head bashed in. As he should. He's only being kind," she added lamely.

"Kind?" Mhairi snorted. "Men are not kind to single women unless they have intentions. And I'm no talking of *good* intentions. You mark my words, Jeannie Findlay, Robert McAndrew wants to toss you in the feathers."

"Mhairi!"

Mhairi laughed and came over to hug Jeannie. "I'm sorry. I canna resist. You blush as easily as I do." She stood back, tenderly rubbing her oversize belly while she looked pensively at Jeannie. Watching her, Jeannie thought of the babe nestled inside her and felt a swift savage pang of envy. Mhairi smiled wistfully. "I'm sore afraid, Jeannie, that you'll be getting your wee shop sooner than you hoped."

"And what would be wrong with that?"

"Well, for one thing, you'd be moving to New Town and away from me. I don't know why you canna just go on working here."

"I can no expect wealthy customers to come to this place," Jeannie explained patiently. "So I have to go to their houses. Which makes me some kind of servant in their eyes. When I have my own shop, they'll come to me instead, and I'll be the proprietor of an establishment, a woman of substance."

"And for another," Mhairi went on as if Jeannie hadn't spoken, "if you move away to New Town, next thing I know you'll be living in sin with Robert McAndrew and I'll be worrying about your immortal soul."

Jeannie scowled at her friend. "I thought you told me

that as I'm a veritable heathen I don't have an immortal soul.''

Mhairi puckered her lips. ''I've noticed for a fact that you're verra inclined to change the subject when I mention Robert McAndrew.''

''Only because you mention him every five minutes.''

''Och, but he's so beautiful, Jeannie. That golden hair and the shoulders on him! I never saw a sweeter carriage in a man in my life. And those blue eyes. How you could resist him is a mystery to me.''

''I didna have to resist, he didna lay a hand on me.'' That wasn't strictly true, but she hadn't told Mhairi about the kiss and wasn't going to. ''You're contradicting yourself,'' she chided Mhairi. ''If you dinna want me to resist Robert, then you canna object to me living in sin. Not,'' she added hastily, when Mhairi began to grin, ''that I'm going to do so, and not that anyone has asked me to do so.''

Mhairi looked up at the passe-partout framed sketch of the castle Jeannie had hung on the wall where she could see it when she was working. ''He hasna sent a message?''

''Not a word. Nor will he. It was a chance encounter, Mhairi, stop building it into a lovers' meeting.''

''Well, I'm disappointed,'' Mhairi said with a pout, returning to her perch on Jeannie's box bed, which was built into the wall. ''Watching him stroke your cheek that day, I thought for certain...''

Jeannie shook her head. ''He didna stroke it, he merely touched it.''

''And your eyes shone like stars.''

''Och, away with you, Mhairi Stewart,'' Jeannie said. She wasn't going to admit to Mhairi that she was disappointed, too. Against all common sense she had hoped Robert McAndrew might return. But he hadn't. And that was that. She made a face at her friend and set the finished hat on a round block on the table. "You'd best be getting away with yourself now, unless you want to stay here alone. I'm going out."

"You're meeting Robert?"

Jeannie sighed, standing and flexing her left hip to ease the cramp. She'd been sitting in one position too long. "I'm away to collect a debt. Angus Macdonald, the baker in the Cowgate, has yet to pay me for his wife's bonnet. I made it for their daughter's wedding."

"I know the Macdonalds," Mhairi said. "They're no a poor family—they have all of three rooms and a kitchen over their shop, with a servant-maid who sleeps under the kitchen dresser."

Jeannie nodded. "Aye, but Angus is a drinking man. It's coming on five o'clock and I want to call on him before he has a chance to spend this week's profits in the Gray Horse Inn."

"You really think he's going to pay now? His daughter was married seven months ago."

"I mind that well," Jeannie muttered, pinning on her hat.

She felt a queer sort of panic, climbing up the steep side steps to the Macdonalds' flat. Ever since she'd left home, she'd had the peculiar feeling someone was watching her—a kind of prickling in the back of her neck. Several times on the way she had stopped and looked over her shoulder, but the narrow wynds of Old Town had been crowded and she'd not been able to pick out any one person who might be taking a particular interest in her. Imagination, she told herself, though it was not her imagination that her errand was doomed from the start. Isobel Macdonald, serving behind the counter in her husband's bakery shop, had told her Angus was at home and she should see him for her pay. But the woman's eyes had slid away from Jeannie's when she said it.

The building had once been a fine one and occupied by gentry, but now it was nearly as shabby as her own. The distempered walls were stained with water and something else she didn't want to examine too closely, the passages littered with rubbish. The prickling feeling in the back of her neck was even stronger now. When she'd stopped a moment in the entry to rest her aching hip, she'd imagined the scrape of a shoe behind her. But when she'd whipped her head around there was nobody there. She stopped again outside the Macdonalds' door. A babe was wailing somewhere, below in the street a horse and cart were clattering by, there was a strong smell of cabbage in the musty passage. Nothing more.

Imagination.

Squaring her shoulders, she tapped on the peeling door with her gloved knuckles. "Is that you at last, Isobel?" a slurred male voice called out. "It's aboot time, you're late wi' my tea."

The door opened and Jeannie's heart sank. She was too late; Angus Macdonald was already drunk. He was a wee bit of a man—his wife would make two of him. Now his narrow shoulders were hunched over as if he could not stand straight, his arms loose, his galluses hanging down over his trousers. He was still wearing his striped baker's apron and cap. His eyes had the glassy look of a man who spent a lot of time staring into a bottle.

His flushed face turned sheepish at the sight of Jeannie. "Good day to ye, Miss Findlay," he said, politely enough. But, och, the smell of him!

"I've come for my money, Mr. Macdonald," she said, resisting the urge to pinch her nose closed. "You owe me for your wife's wedding hat, you'll remember."

"My wife's no at home," he said and made to shut the door.

Jeannie pushed firmly against it, wedging her foot against the wood. "'Tis you that's supposed to pay me, Mr. Macdonald. Your wife told me so. You've put me off long enough."

"Dinna bother me with your blather," he muttered, his face flushing hotter.

"A shilling then," she countered. "To show goodwill. I've expenses to meet, as I'm sure you're aware. And your wife was very happy with her new bonnet. It was Manon brown, you'll recollect, and trimmed with tulle and Ebenier roses to match her gown. We picked the style out together from a fashion plate in *Lady's Magazine*."

Maybe if she inundated him with description he'd forget himself and put his hand in his pocket. But her ruse didn't work. He just stood swaying, his eyes glazing over. "I'm no leaving empty-handed this time," she said firmly.

His head wobbled from side to side. "Awa' wi' ye," he said.

Jeannie made an exasperated sound. "I'm taking you to the law, Mr. Macdonald," she said. "I'm only sorry they closed the debtors' prison six years ago, or I'd have you locked up for robbing a woman of her just dues."

"I'll show ye what's due ye," he said belligerently. His sudden movement took her completely by surprise. He wasn't a violent man, Angus Macdonald, not that she'd ever heard. Isobel, maybe, she'd have believed it of, but Angus was such a wee bit of a man. The whiskey was on him, of course, giving him false courage and the strength of two. But who would have believed Angus Macdonald would punch a woman in the stomach and then shove her tumbling down the stairs?

"ARE YOU ALL RIGHT, Jeannie?" somebody asked. "Do you want me to wake you?" It was a man's voice, with some urgency in it.

"I am awake," she answered sharply.

THERE WAS A MAN looking down at her, a young, smooth-faced, broad-shouldered, stocky man in livery with a cock-aded hat and a sour expression around his mouth as if he'd just eaten a pickle. She didn't think he was the one who had spoken to her. It was all confusing, especially as he looked vaguely familiar to her. Evidently he had taken off his gray coat and placed it over her. "I've sent a lad for the doctor," he said. "I think it's best if you dinna move until he's looked at you."

Jeannie had no desire to move. Every part of her was throbbing with bruises. She felt like a bag of bones some-one had slung down on the stone, all loose and jumbled. "I've seen you somewhere," she croaked, and the memory immediately became clear. Coming out of Angus Macdon-ald's bakery she had glimpsed a man in livery standing next to a lamppost at the corner of the street. This man. And she had seen him earlier when she crossed a street. "You were following me," she accused.

"Lucky for you I was."

"Who are you? Why were you following me?"

"Best you don't try to talk," he said, but she was sure it wasn't concern for her health that prompted the terse command. "The doctor will be here betimes," he added.

"I'm no in need of a doctor," Jeannie said, struggling up to her elbows. "I canna afford a doctor and I didna ask for a doctor."

"Whisht, woman. You don't need to worry. It'll be paid for."

Before she could question this statement, the doctor arrived, a portly, elderly man Jeannie had seen driving around Old Town in his pony trap. He felt her all over, much to Jeannie's embarrassment, and said she had no broken bones. She should stay quiet a day or two and she would be fine.

The man in livery had disappeared soon after the doctor arrived and she thought she'd never see him again, but when the doctor assisted her to her feet she saw him coming down the stairs from Angus's flat, looking pleased with himself. "I had a word or two with Mr. Macdonald," he said. "Some disagreement about a bill, was it?"

"Aye," Jeannie said faintly, clinging to the banister.

"Well, you'll no have any more trouble with Mr. Macdonald. He'll be paying his bill in full the end of next week. I've promised to collect it from him myself."

Jeannie stared at him. "Why should you do that for me? What's your interest in me?"

He shook his head, with a glance at the doctor, then lifted her up in his arms in a swift movement that took her by surprise. "Miss Findlay lives in the Lawnmarket," he told the doctor. "Can you take us there?"

He knew her name!

"I can that," the doctor said, with a curious look at the two of them.

Jeannie was too concerned with holding her aching bones together as the trap rattled along to question the man further, but when he carried her up her stairs, she refused to allow him to open her door until he identified himself. "My name's Jamie Kintyre," he informed her. "I'm groom to Mr. Robert McAndrew."

Robert.

"Why were you following me?" she asked again.

He wouldn't answer until she'd let him open her door. He glanced quickly around the cold, bleak room, taking it all in, no doubt, then placed her carefully on her bed. "I was told by Mr. McAndrew to watch over you," he said. "Not my business to ask why."

Without asking her permission he unfastened her boots and took them off. He'd already placed her hat on top of the kist. She was feeling too bruised and battered to protest this cavalier treatment.

In no time he'd found a box of matches, lit the gas and had a cheerful fire going in the grate. "You don't need so much coal on there," Jeannie protested. "It doesna grow on trees."

"There's someone could sit with you a while?" he asked, putting another lump on, ignoring her entirely.

"I don't need anyone," Jeannie said.

"Then I'll sit here myself," he said, pulling over her only chair.

Jeannie sighed. "You could ask my friend Mhairi. She's in five hundred and three. Mhairi Stewart's her name."

"I'll do that, then." He touched his hat and left before she could collect herself enough to ask him anything about Robert McAndrew. Ah well, she thought, he probably wouldn't have answered her anyway.

Mhairi was there in less than five minutes, wrapped in a shawl, full of exclamations and questions and dismay, not to mention curiosity about Jamie Kintyre. Jeannie pretended faintness to avoid answering. She didn't have to pretend too hard, though she felt better after Mhairi made her some tea and unpinned her hair and helped her into her nightgown and put an old plaid over her.

"I'll need you to ask Davie to go tell Mr. Moffatt I canna work tonight," Jeannie said.

"Nor tomorrow night," Mhairi said stoutly, heading for the door.

Jeannie nodded wearily, trying not to calculate how much silver she'd lose by taking two nights off.

"And are you ready to tell me about Jamie Kintyre?" Mhairi asked the minute she came back. "Is it a new habit you have now, coming home with a different man every week or so?"

Jeannie feigned sleep. Her own mind was whirling with questions, but she couldn't concentrate on them with Mhairi there, and Mhairi seemed disinclined to leave.

It was an hour later that Robert arrived. They heard his firm tread on the steps outside and exchanged a glance that was fearful on Mhairi's part. There was no fear in Jeannie, but there was a sudden strange constriction around her heart. "Robert," she murmured and it seemed to her that the blood sang through her body, taking with it the pain of her bruises.

He came in carrying an enormous basket with a checkered cloth drawn over it. He was dressed in very formal clothing as though he'd been about to go out for the evening, to a concert perhaps, or a play, or his club. He looked splendid, dazzling, elegant, standing there taking off his kid gloves, his golden hair combed just so, his bold blue eyes fixed on Jeannie's face, ignoring Mhairi as if she were invisible.

"I'm not accustomed to receiving a gentleman in my nightgown," Jeannie said, making her voice stern. Her heart was still pounding from the shock of seeing him.

His smile blazed out at her. "You're accustomed to receiving a gentleman in some other garment?"

"I am not," she said indignantly, then realized he was teasing her. "This is my friend, Mhairi," she said weakly.

He recollected his manners at once and bowed to Mhairi in a very elegant way. Mhairi was so overcome she attempted a curtsy, which in her advanced condition was laughable to behold. "May I pour you some tea?" she asked.

Robert accepted gravely, gazing again at Jeannie. "Should I take you to the infirmary, do you think?" he asked.

She shook her head, then, because of the pain, wished she hadn't. "The doctor didn't think it was necessary. And I've no mind to go in a hospital as long as I've breath left to me."

"Hospitals exist to take care of the sick and the injured," he pointed out.

"So they say." She hadn't meant to sound so sharp. "My father died of typhus in a hospital," she explained. "My mother of cholera. I've no faith in hospitals."

There was a clatter from the cupboard. Poor Mhairi was all thumbs trying to get down a cup for him, straining her ears to listen at the same time. After she'd served him, she perched herself on the edge of Jeannie's worktable and stared at Robert, ready to hang on any word he might utter.

Robert glanced at Jeannie, raising his eyebrows in a message of such intimacy that she felt herself blushing as furiously as Mhairi had a few minutes before.

"We won't keep you, Mhairi," she said softly.

"Oh, but I…oh, yes, well then, I'd best be getting Davie's supper," Mhairi stammered, blushing again as she hurried clumsily to the door. "You'll tell me if you need me?" she said over her shoulder.

"Aye," Jeannie promised.

After she'd gone, Jeannie gazed up at Robert for a moment, then forced herself to remember she was angry with him. "You had no right to have me followed," she said, then added as an alarming thought occurred to her, "Did yon Jamie Kintyre follow me all the time?"

"He alternated with my coachman. Just making sure you were safe, until you were settled for the night."

Then Robert no doubt knew where she worked in the evening. But if he wasn't going to mention it, she wasn't, either.

He took her hand and held it, looking down at it attentively, his mouth wry. "I was worried about you. I had to take the train to London and I wanted to be sure no harm came to you."

He had been out of the city. That was why he hadn't come before. Jeannie's heart sang. "Such a long journey," she murmured.

"It's only ten hours by train. And very comfortable. These are modern times, Jeannie."

"You must be thinking I'm forever falling over my feet," she said, for want of anything else to say.

"Running around bill collecting on your own," he grumbled at her.

"Och, I've done it for years, Robert. It was just that Angus had been drinking. He'd never have had the courage else. I'm no a weak woman. I can take care of myself."

"So I see." His tone was sarcastic but she could tell he was pleased she'd taken to calling him by his Christian name.

He let go of her hand and stood. She was afraid he meant to leave, that he'd come only to be sure she was all right. But he picked up the basket he'd brought and started placing dishes out on her worktable. Wonderful aromas filled the air and her stomach let out a rumble that luckily wasn't too audible.

"I've brought some good Scotch broth and bread and a small meat pie," Robert said. He laughed. "You should have seen my cook's face when I told her I was going on a picnic. 'At this time of night,' she said, all scandalized.

'And why not?' I asked.'' He grinned at Jeannie and she felt a weakening in her midsection that had nothing to do with hunger. ''There's cheese and an apple to follow,'' he said. ''And there's an egg for your breakfast and thin bread and butter wrapped to go with it. We need to put the roses back in your cheeks, bonny Jeannie.''

Bonny Jeannie.

The food was as wonderful as it smelled and best of all Robert insisted on feeding her, first propping her up against her chaff pillows, his hands warm through the cotton flannelette of her nightgown. Then he draped a tea towel over her chest against spills, and spooned the soup into her as if she were a bairn. The meat pie melted in her mouth, the cheese was strong and ripe, just as she liked it, the bread rich, the apple crisp and juicy.

Jeannie's usual diet consisted of oatmeal mixed with water for gruel, oatmeal mixed with milk for porridge, oatmeal made into a paste and baked to make oatbread or bannocks, broth with bear grains, potatoes, and only occasionally a bit of herring or mutton. She couldn't remember when she'd last eaten an apple or had butter on her bread.

''That was delicious.'' She sighed when she was done.

He put the dishes aside and looked at her very solemnly. ''I've an idea you don't eat enough, Jeannie,'' he said. ''You're much too thin.''

''Aye, I know. Mhairi jokes I'm the only woman she knows whose stays are loose on her.'' She blushed immediately, realizing it wasn't proper to mention corsets to a gentleman.

He was smiling.

''Will your wife no be expecting you?'' she asked hesitantly when he showed no inclination to leave.

''I don't have a wife,'' he said with a twinkle in his

eye, showing he'd noted the slyness of the question. Then his expression became serious. "My wife died several years ago, in childbirth," he said quietly. "The child, a boy, died with her."

"I'm sorry." There was a silence. "You've not wanted to marry again?"

"No." He laughed softly. "My parents would like nothing better. They're forever trotting pretty young things past me in hopes my eye will light on one."

Jeannie felt fiercely jealous of the pretty young things. She could imagine them in their fancy ball gowns, flounced trains dragging the floor, flowers in their hair. They would look up at Robert from under long flirtatious eyelashes, would touch him coquettishly with their soft hands.

She tucked her own work-roughened fingers under the plaid. "It was kind of you to take the trouble," she said slowly.

"It wasn't trouble," he said. He raised his eyebrows. "I've a present for you."

"No, now, you've done enough...."

"It's not a material present," he said. "I just thought you'd be pleased to know I intervened on behalf of your crofters—the ones who shot the deer."

"They said they didna shoot it," Jeannie reminded him indignantly.

"Yes, well, there seems some doubt about that, but I leaned on a barrister friend of mine in London who owes me a favor and he promised to look into the case. He seemed to feel a little money in the right places would take care of the problem."

"Aye, money does that," Jeannie said, then grimaced, realizing how ungracious she had sounded. "You're a kind man, Robert McAndrew," she said softly. "I'm grateful to you for that and other kindnesses."

"I'd like to do more for you, Jeannie," he said. "As I told you before, I'm a banker. There's capital in Scotland, you know, even though little of it attaches itself to the promotion of specifically Scottish ends. I'm attempting to establish a policy whereby some of that capital will go to small businessmen, and women, right here in Edinburgh. To people who are hardworking and honest and could improve themselves and the city with their enterprise."

"I've no wish to take charity from anyone," she said firmly.

"It's not charity, Jeannie. It's business."

His smile was so winning, so charming, it was hard to resist him. "I'll consider it," she said. "But I can tell you now, I'd prefer to make my own way without getting into debt."

Her voice had weakened, though not her will. She had an idea banks probably made enquiries about a person before lending out money. In her case, enquiries could not be risked. She sighed. The warmth of the food and the fire had conspired to make her sleepy. It was hard even to keep her eyes open.

"You must get some rest," Robert said, lightly stroking his fingers down the length of her hair. Then he touched her cheek. "Are you still in pain?"

Every part of her body was smarting in one way or another, but she saw no point in complaining. "I'll be fine," she insisted, hoping he wouldn't be in too much of a hurry to remove his hand. It felt good against her cheek, warm and comforting. But remove it he did.

"I'll leave you to sleep," he told her. "But I'll be back tomorrow."

"I wanted to thank you," she murmured, rallying herself. "The women in New Town who sent for me to make hats for them. You told them about me, did you no?"

"I told my hostess at a dinner party that I'd heard of a pretty young milliner who made outrageously smart hats. That they were the very height of fashion," he said. "I suppose it's possible she might have mentioned something to her friends."

"Thank you," she said. "It's been a long while since someone was so kind to me."

In the dim gaslit room, his wonderfully handsome face looked almost luminous. It gave her pleasure simply to lie there and look at him. "I'll always be kind to you, Jeannie Findlay," he said. And then he leaned over her and kissed her very gently on the lips, the way she'd been wanting him to since he walked in her door. In spite of her sleepiness, a part of her stirred to that kiss, a part that had lain dormant since Rory Douglas died. A sweet aching numbness seemed to drug her limbs, taking the soreness out of her bruises. Her own mouth moved on his, giving him back the warmth he was giving her. Her heart was beating against her ribs like a frightened bird, but she wasn't frightened, she wasn't frightened at all.

For a long time after he turned off the gaslight and left her, she lay there, half asleep and half awake, reliving the way he had touched her face, the way he had kissed her. She had never thought much about love in her life. Her father had died when she was fourteen, her mother when she was ten. They had probably loved her, she thought, but they had not been demonstrative people. She and her sister had loved each other, but her sister had gone years ago to live in Glasgow where her husband worked on the iron ships.

Then there was Rory. Och, puppy love that, nothing like

the rich warm glow that came over her when Robert Charles McAndrew touched her.

"Robbie," she whispered into the darkness.

CHAPTER FIVE

"I CAN TELL EXACTLY what's going to happen," Liz exclaimed, setting the recliner forward with a thump and glaring at Matt. "It's so obvious, it's pitiful. How can any woman be so stupidly passive?"

She was on her feet a second later, heading for the door, so furious she could barely breathe, yanking the strap of her purse onto her shoulder with fingers that shook. "I don't want to do this again," she said through her teeth as she reached for the door handle.

Matt was on his feet, too, looking astonished, grabbing her arm before she would wrench the door open. "Liz, wait, rest a moment, you're not quite—"

She pulled her arm free. "I have to get out of here."

"I can't let you go like this." His voice was calm but insistent. "You must wait, you're still disoriented." He was stopping her from opening the door, wedging himself between her and freedom and she couldn't let him do that.

"Let me go," she snapped, pushing at him with both hands.

"Hey, no, listen. Hold on a minute." As she struggled to get past him, he put his arms around her, holding her in a grip that felt like a vise. Her whole body was shuddering as though she'd been exposed to extreme cold. "You're taking it personally," he said. "It isn't you, Liz, it's Jeannie. It's not you."

All of a sudden the fight went out of her and she collapsed against him. He held her that way for a full minute, rocking her gently in his arms, murmuring to her, soothing her. She felt slightly stunned in the wake of her anger. The last thing she had expected this afternoon was to find herself body to body with Matthew Lockwood. Not that the experience was an unpleasant one. Her face was pressed against the soft fabric of his sweater, his breath was stirring her hair and she was very much aware of his lean muscular body. She had no desire to move, she admitted to herself, unless it were to let herself relax completely. It seemed as though it would be the most natural thing in the world to let herself melt against him.

She stiffened, realizing how quickly the quality of the embrace had changed. One minute she was a patient being calmed by her doctor, the next she was a woman wrapped intimately in a man's arms.

Abruptly he let her go, lifted her chin with one hand and looked deeply but clinically into her eyes. "Okay now?" he asked.

She nodded mutely, feeling the heat of embarrassment wash up her neck and over her face. Obviously he hadn't experienced any electrical charge. Thank God she hadn't let herself melt. "I'm sorry," she said. "I'm okay now." She put a hand to her forehead. "How long was I out?"

He glanced at the clock above the fireplace. "About an hour."

"It felt like much longer."

"That's a common phenomenon. Sometimes people regress through whole lifetimes in a single session. They are frequently surprised to discover how little actual time has passed."

Liz shook her head. "I don't know what came over me. I was so *angry*." Her voice was shaky, but whether the emotion stemmed from her reaction to the regression or her reaction to him she wasn't sure.

He gave her a wry smile that was at least a partial return to his original friendly manner. "I noticed. Come on, sit down and we'll try to find out why."

She shook her head. "I'll be fine. Truly. I can't think why I acted so irrationally. I'm not usually the hysterical sort." Because she was embarrassed, she was speaking more tersely than usual. Camouflage. No way could she let him suspect she felt so drawn to him. Sexually drawn. He was still standing very close to her, looking down at her, one hand resting on her shoulder. God, even her fingers were shaking. She stuck her hands in her jeans pockets. Be casual, she told herself. Flippant even. She laughed, rather nervously. "At these prices, I can't afford to cry on your shoulder. Maybe we can talk about it another time."

"The clock was turned off five minutes ago," he said calmly. "And now's the best time to explore the reasons for your anger, while the memory's fresh."

She shook her head stubbornly. "I'm not going back in that chair."

"Okay." He studied her face closely for a minute more, then there was an indefinable change in his expression. "Tell you what," he said, "hearing you talk about Jeannie eating that meat pie made me hungry for one. I just happen to know of an English pub/restaurant in the U district that serves steak-and-kidney pie, roast beef and Yorkshire pudding, mulled wine. How about it?"

His voice was friendly again. He had totally dropped the clinical attitude. And his eyebrows had slanted up in the way that was so droll.

"You're inviting me to dinner?"

"That's the general idea."

He'd succeeded in surprising her. Stalling, she looked

down at her blue-and-white ski sweater and jeans. "I'm not exactly dressed for—"

"It's a casual place."

He removed his hand from her shoulder and took a step back, as though he'd just this minute realized how close he was to her. As he moved their eyes met, and she felt a very definite emotional reaction to him again. She could develop a crush on this man real easily, she thought.

How trite. What was it they called it in psychological parlance—transference? Probably she should turn down his offer, keep their relationship on a strictly professional level. She had enough on her plate with Robert Charles McAndrew.

All the same, the thought of going out to eat with Matt Lockwood was extremely appealing. It would sure beat returning to her empty apartment. She'd just have to close her eyes to the effect he had on her. She was a grown woman, after all; repression wasn't that difficult. "Are you sure you want me around?" she asked, forcing a grin. "After the way I just treated you?"

"I've been treated worse. Some people come out of regression with both fists flying. At least I'm bigger than you."

The memory of his arms around her returned in full force, making her nervous again. She was aware of a great deal of tension between them, all of it, she was sure, emanating from her. It was embarrassing to remember how many intimate details she must have given him about Jeannie's feelings for Robert, the way Jeannie had felt when Robert kissed her.

The way she, Liz, had felt. God, the sensations that kiss of Robert's had aroused! She could still feel the imprint of his mouth on hers, the way blood had coursed through her veins in response, the sweet passive languor that had invaded her body.

She had little to say as Matt drove them to the restaurant. He didn't talk, either, but he glanced at her from time to time, as though to gauge her mood. He must think she was a nut—she wasn't even sure what she'd been so angry about.

"I'm usually such a controlled person," she said after they'd been shown to a small table in the corner of a long, rustic-looking room.

"Maybe that's part of the problem," he said.

"You think there's a problem?"

"It was a pretty strong reaction. Something got triggered, that's for sure. Some emotion of your own that resented Jeannie's response to Robert." He broke off to place their order with a pretty young waitress in a tavern-wench outfit.

The restaurant was full, mostly with young people. University students probably, many in couples. They must look like a couple themselves, Liz realized. The thought wasn't at all unpleasing. She had noticed several women turn their heads to look at Matt as they walked by. He was a man women would always look at twice.

What would all these cheerful young people say, she wondered, looking around, if she were to announce that she'd just returned from a visit to the Edinburgh of a hundred years ago. Probably that she must have stopped off at another tavern on the way.

She sipped the glass of mulled wine the waitress brought and felt soothed by its spicy flavor. "Am I losing it, Doc?" she murmured, attempting a jocular tone that didn't quite succeed.

He shook his head. "I'm at fault. Usually I can tell when someone isn't quite...present, shall we say? But you took me by surprise. I'm sorry. In future I'll make sure you're fully prepared to wake up.''

"You told me I'd feel rested and relaxed, just as you did before, I remember that.'' Liz took a deep breath, then let it out. "For some reason it didn't work this time. I was so damn mad.''

"You called Jeannie 'stupidly passive.' Why? Do you know?''

She spread her hands helplessly. "It's such a cliché, you know. Wealthy older man, poor but pretty young woman. Obviously Robert's going to seduce Jeannie. Just as obviously she's going to let him. So then she'll get pregnant—as I recall, women didn't have much birth control going for them in the nineteenth century. So poor vulnerable Jeannie will get pregnant, and Robert will suddenly discover he's urgently needed in London and there she'll be. Stuck. She'll never have her wee shop in New Town. She'll be struggling to raise Robert's bastard.'' Her voice shook on the last word. She was angry again, she realized.

She took another sip of the hot wine, holding the glass mug in both hands to warm them. "Listen to me,'' she exclaimed. "I'm talking as though the story's in the future, when all the time it's in the past. Whatever the ending, it's happened already, right? There's not much I can do to change it.''

He nodded. "But the discovery of it is still in the future for you, Liz. I hope you'll decide to go on. When a past-life memory is this insistent, it's probably far healthier to pursue it.''

"You think it's definitely reincarnation then? You really believe I was once Jeannie Findlay?''

He looked at her levelly. "I think I'm going to let you decide that for yourself. However, you might consider the fact the clothing is correct for the date you mentioned—

September 1888, and the living conditions seem authentic." He paused. "Do you feel there's any similarity between you and Jeannie? Not in looks, but in character, attitude?"

She frowned. "Well, I guess we're both independent, outspoken, inclined to be prickly. Jeannie seems more...fragile than me. She thinks of herself as pretty tough, but I don't think she is really. She's small, for one thing. She thinks of Robert as tall, but he's not really, compared to someone like you for instance. I guess he's average height."

"People were shorter in the past."

"I guess so." She hesitated. "This...regression was very detailed, wasn't it?"

"You evidently opened a floodgate when you visited Edinburgh Castle." He paused as the waitress set their food in front of them. They had both ordered meat pie. Liz tasted hers. It was good. Perhaps not quite as savory as the one Robert had brought Jeannie, but certainly hotter.

She laughed abruptly and Matt glanced at her sharply. "I was thinking that this pie was hotter than Jeannie's," she explained, still laughing. "Then I thought, well, naturally it's hotter—it's a hundred years fresher."

He laughed, too. "When you start analyzing, it gets spooky, doesn't it?"

"Spooky's the word." She shook her head. "This is sure a vivid fantasy I've made up for my own entertainment."

"Do you really believe that's all it is?"

"No." She held up her fork. "But that doesn't mean I believe in reincarnation."

He smiled at her, the light filling his eyes the way it sometimes did. There were star bursts of lighter gray radiating from his pupils, she noticed. How had she not noticed them before?

For a while they ate in silence, then Matt said, "You know, the novels I enjoy the most are mysteries. I like the fact you can never quite predict what's going to happen next. Especially when the novel's well written, with plenty of plot twists."

"You think there might be a plot twist in Jeannie's story?"

"It's possible. Perhaps we shouldn't jump to conclusions."

"You think we should go on with it?"

"Definitely." He hesitated. "If the fee is a problem, Liz, our research department can usually make accommodation for..."

She felt embarrassed again. "I can afford it, Matt. I wasn't quite myself. I've no idea why I was so angry. That was a snide remark about your charges. You're really quite reasonable."

"I'd still like to know *why* you were so angry. There has to be a reason." He hesitated again. "May I ask you a personal question?"

Liz laughed. "I don't see why not. We've gone beyond casual acquaintance."

That was a dumb thing to say, considering that he had held her in his arms less than an hour ago. He was just doing his job, she scolded herself, but she could still feel the soft cashmere of his sweater against her cheek, the warmth of his hand on her shoulder. She looked down at her plate, not wanting to meet his eyes.

"What kind of relationships do you usually have with men?" he asked.

Startled, she did raise her eyes to his face. His clinical expression was fully in place on his lean scholarly face.

God, she had to stop taking this man personally. "Oh, I see," she said slowly. "You mean because something in me reacted so strongly?" She shrugged. "I have several men friends, probably as many men friends as women."

"I was thinking more of lovers."

The word seemed to hang between them. "Oh, well— lovers." She wasn't going to blush. It was Jeannie who blushed easily, not twentieth-century Liz Brooks. "I don't do too well," she said with scrupulous honesty. "I've thought I was in love a couple of times, but I seem to get attracted to men who shy away from commitment. It's made me reluctant to date at all."

She sighed. "Men don't seem to be interested in anything long-term nowadays," she complained. "It's all short-term and lots of passion, not that I've anything against passion, exactly. But I've got to tell you I don't really trust it. It's too easy to lose control of a situation when you…" God, what was she saying?

There was a glint of humor in his eyes, but when he spoke his voice was perfectly even. "Usually when women consistently choose the wrong type of men, and vice versa, of course, there's a deep-seated resistance to commitment on their own part."

"You sound like a *Cosmo* article," she said. "'*Are you shooting YOURSELF down? Maybe it isn't HIS fault after all.*'"

He smiled. God, he knocked her out when he did that. His smile wasn't as bold as Robert's, more wry than brilliant, but it could certainly… Damn, she was acting as though Robert was a real live person.

"I've written articles for *Cosomopolitan*," Matt confessed with a rueful grin.

She laughed. "Now I'm really impressed. *Cosmo*'s my

favorite magazine. I'll watch for your byline. What do you write about, reincarnation?''

"Medical subjects mostly. Some on hypnosis. Childbirth.'' He inclined his head and the clinical expression returned. ''You wouldn't be avoiding my comment about resistance, would you?''

She concentrated on forking up some of the vegetables that had accompanied her meat pie. ''I guess I am,'' she admitted at last. She forced herself to meet his gaze. ''I don't know that I deliberately choose the wrong guys,'' she said earnestly. ''It seems that they choose me. You could be right, though, about me being the one who's afraid of commitment. I'm not in any particular hurry to get married.''

''How's your parents' marriage?''

She grinned. ''Right on, Doc. Classic stuff, huh? My parents' marriage broke up, so I'm afraid of commitment. I should have seen that coming. Yes, my parents are divorced. They quarreled all the time I was growing up. I don't mean knock-down-drag-out fights, just bickering. I think they stayed together for my sake, but I'd probably have been better off if they had separated earlier. They used to wait until I was in bed, then have at it. I heard everything they said to each other.''

She could see herself lying in her bed, clutching a doll, no, a panda bear. Her bedroom had been above the living room and the heat vent had carried their words as clearly as if she'd been present in the same room. ''I suppose they didn't—'' She broke off as a memory knifed across her brain with a sharpness and clarity that astonished her.

''What?'' Matt asked.

She didn't answer him. It was a minute before she realized she was staring at him openmouthed, her fork suspended halfway to her lips. ''Nothing,'' she said shortly. ''I thought I had something, but it...went away.''

That was an out-and-out lie, but she just couldn't bring herself to put the sudden flash of insight into words, even though it probably explained completely her irrational reaction to Jeannie and Robert's embrace. No, this was something she had to think about when she was alone. This was not something to talk about in the middle of a crowded restaurant.

Matt was looking at her skeptically, but he didn't question her further. ''You will go on with it?'' was all he asked.

''Oh, yes. I have to now, just to prove to you that men are rats and always have been.''

''You really believe that?'' he asked. He had his clinical look again.

She shook her head. ''I've known several nice men,'' she said, thinking of Allen. She sighed. ''It's true, isn't it? Nice guys finish last.''

''Not always.''

''What about you?'' she challenged. ''We're not in your office now. This conversation's too one-sided. Confession's as good for your soul, too. You're a nice guy. How are your relationships?''

''I didn't do too well, either,'' he said flatly.

She was embarrassed. ''Oh, Lord, me and my big mouth. I forgot. Erica told me you were divorced.''

He nodded. ''Don't worry about it. It was long enough ago that there's no pain left, just some residual regret that it had to happen. It was inevitable, though, not just because of my change of occupation. I married Meredith for all the wrong reasons, mostly because she looked something like someone else. Someone I knew...''

''Your first love?''

"I guess you could say that." It was his turn to avert his eyes.

Meredith, she thought. The name sounded cold. Sexless. "Would you like some dessert?" he asked after a moment's silence.

Diverting tactics, she decided, being an expert at them herself when anyone came close to secrets she didn't want to reveal. "I'd love dessert," she said obligingly.

From then on he led the conversation into safer areas, discussing her déjà vu reactions to Edinburgh. "Déjà vu is perhaps the most common phenomenon there is," he told her. "Everyone's had the experience of feeling they've been to a place before, or experienced a certain situation before. If you believe in reincarnation, there's nothing mystical about it. You've been to this place in a former life so naturally you remember it. The same applies to your experiences as Jeannie. Once you accept the theory of reincarnation, regression loses all spookiness. You are simply remembering, just as you sometimes remember incidents in your childhood."

"You make it seem very reasonable," she said.

"Only because it is."

His voice was soft. Their eyes met. Liz could hear her pulse pounding in her ears as loudly as it had pounded in Jeannie's when Robert kissed her. Matt had dropped the chilling professional manner altogether now, she realized. His friendly side was back. More than friendly. Was he remembering that he had taken her in his arms when she became so upset? Did he think of his action as merely a way of restraining her hysteria, or had it affected him? Actually she wished he'd hung on to at least some of his distant manner, because the way his eyes followed her now was very disconcerting.

As though aware of her discomfort, he began talking

more generally, mentioning Seattle Opera's latest performance, the play at the repertory theater, sailing on Puget Sound, skiing in Snoqualmie as compared to Crystal Mountain.

She could imagine him skiing. He wouldn't be a hot-dogger, trying to impress everyone. He'd carve nice long loopy turns in fresh powder, making it look easy. He'd look terrific in a ski suit, especially the close-fitting kind.

Feeling unnerved all over again by the turn her thoughts were taking, she reminded herself sternly that this man was her doctor. Well, not exactly her doctor, but he was certainly out there in a professional capacity somewhere.

He drove her back to the institute so she could pick up her car, still talking lightly about the Pacific Northwest and the wonderful outdoor and cultural activities it offered. But when he parked the car, he was abruptly silent and she felt tension—constraint—spring up between them again in the confines of his compact car. "I enjoyed the evening, Liz," he said slowly. "You're a good listener. I'm afraid I talked too much."

"Not at all." Her voice sounded stiff. Why? Because she was still very aware of him as a man and it had been a long time since she'd experienced that feeling. Excepting Robert Charles McAndrew, of course.

"Something funny?" he asked.

"Just a stray thought," she said hastily. "Same time next Friday?" she asked.

He hesitated, surprising her. He was the one who'd insisted she had to go on with this thing. Was *he* getting cold feet now? *Had* he noticed her reaction to him? She would die of embarrassment if he decided he couldn't go on with her because of that.

"It's an absorbing regression," he said after a moment.

"I'm looking forward to pursuing it to its natural conclusion."

"The rate it's going it could take years," Liz said.

He laughed, then turned to look at her. "At the prices I charge, I can stand it," he teased. "How about you?"

His smile had faded as he looked at her again. There was something showing in his eyes that had flickered there once or twice before. As though he had spoken his feelings aloud, it was suddenly clear to her that all the sexual tension she'd been aware of this evening wasn't as one-sided as she had believed. If he were to lean over and touch her, she just might explode.

He didn't lean over. Liz took a deep shaky breath. It seemed important to be very honest with him. "Something's happening here, isn't it?" she said.

His eyes darkened. "It looks that way," he agreed.

"I don't think I can handle it," she said worriedly. "I mean, I'm already halfway hung up on Robert Charles McAndrew." Maybe a little humor would help the situation. "I'm strictly a one-man-at-a-time woman, Doc."

It didn't help. If anything the tension increased. At last Matt averted his eyes. "It's getting late, Liz," he said quietly. Then he got out of the car and she had no choice but to follow.

"How's your mom?" Jake Brooks asked.

Sooner or later, whenever Liz visited her father, he asked that question. Liz wasn't quite sure if he was concerned about the answer, or just asserting her right to call her mother, Mom. Catherine had wanted Liz to call her Mummy in the English way, but Liz had never managed to get her tongue twisted around just right. Jake had always supported her.

As usual he was puttering around in his garage, wearing

his favorite dungarees and plaid flannel shirt. Jake's clothing had been another source of discord between Liz's parents. "I don't care if you want to wear those disgusting overalls when you work in the garden," Catherine used to say. "But when you take me shopping, you could try to dress like a human being."

Catherine had never forgotten, or let Jake forget, the time they had gone to vote together. She had looked at the bottom of the polling-booth curtain and seen that Jake was wearing dirty work boots. It wasn't worth their time going to vote anyway, she'd say after retelling this story. Their votes canceled each other out.

Liz watched as Jake attached some wires to some kind of capsule, amused at the way his wide mouth tightened and relaxed in rhythm with his work. "Is that thing really going to do any good to the atmosphere?" she asked.

He grinned. "It works on paper. Anyway, the fun is in the doing, not the succeeding."

No wonder he and Catherine had broken up. Their philosophies were exactly opposite.

He worked in silence for a while, then put away his tools in his usual neat fashion. "So it's definitely reincarnation, is it?" he said with another grin.

Liz had waited patiently for a comment after she'd told him what she'd come up with the previous day. Jake was not one to respond hastily to anything. He liked to mull things over before making a statement.

"Not in my book," Liz said.

He ran a hand through the tight carroty curls that were so much like her own except for a sprinkling of gray, then shook his head. "Well, I guess I don't know enough to say one way or the other. You know how I am for book reading—I'd much rather use my hands than my head. I might just read up on it a bit, though. Couldn't hurt. I'd like to think I've an open mind.''

He came over to where she was perched on a stool and ruffled her hair. ''Come on in and have dinner. I had a feeling you'd be by. I've made you slumgullion.''

Liz grimaced as she followed him into his tiny kitchen. Her father had always cooked what he called slumgullion for them both when he took her on camping trips as a child. She'd never had the heart to tell him she hated the mixture of ground beef and onions, rice, peas and carrots. Having downed it all these years with an apparently hearty appetite, she was doomed to eat it forever, she supposed. *The things we do for love,* she thought as he shoveled great helpings of the odorous mess onto two plates.

They sat at the island counter, looking out at Lake Washington. The small cottage was an anomaly in this particular area. Jake had inherited it from his grandfather and rented it out for years. Out of sentiment, he'd refused to sell to the many developers who had made outrageously generous offers for the property. Now the house squatted incongruously between high-rise condos. Jake didn't care. After the divorce, he'd moved into it and professed himself happy.

''What's this Dr. Lockwood like?'' Jake asked.

''Nice,'' Liz said carefully. ''Very professional, not at all peculiar.''

He raised his somewhat bushy eyebrows. ''But you still don't believe what he's telling you?''

Liz sighed. ''There's something weird going on, that's for sure. And so far I haven't come up with a better explanation than his. I guess all I can tell you is the jury's still out. Maybe the answer will hit me on the head when I'm involved in one of Matt's—Dr. Lockwood's—regressions.''

"You tell the duchess about it?"

He always brought conversations back around to Catherine somehow. Interesting. Especially as he was concentrating with unusual intensity on his plate.

"Yes," Liz said.

"That's good. She doesn't like to be left out."

"I know." She studied his face for a minute. Was now a good time? "I have a question for you, Dad."

He looked up, evidently surprised by the serious note that had come into her voice. "Sounds ominous."

"Not really. At least I hope not." It was harder than she'd expected to get the question out, but she had to know. "Was Mom pregnant with me when you married her?" she managed finally.

He set down his fork and pushed his plate away and stared at her. "Why on earth would you ask a thing like that after all these years?" he demanded.

"It came up while I was...seeing Dr. Lockwood. I came out of the regression feeling furious about something. Later I connected it with something I heard when I was a little kid. I buried it deep down, but it was always there and it finally surfaced." She watched several robins hopping across the lawn outside the windows. It had rained earlier and the robins were harvesting a bumper crop of worms, dragging them right out of the ground.

"You and Mom were arguing," she went on. "I was in bed but I wasn't asleep, and I heard you shout, 'Why the hell did you marry me then?' And Mom said, 'What else could I do? I had to marry you. My father would have killed me if I'd had an illegitimate baby.'"

"Oh."

He busied himself clearing away the dishes, clattering them into the sink and turning on the hot water full blast so he wouldn't be expected to talk. She gave him five minutes, then said, loud enough to be heard, "You didn't think it was something I should know about?"

He turned off the water, straightened, then shook his head, his back still to her.

"You told me I was premature."

"It seemed easier," he said defensively. "You know how the duchess is. She was ashamed. She was only a few weeks pregnant," he added, as though that made a difference. "She'd only missed one period."

"But you *had* to marry. Because of me. That's what made me so angry, I think, after the regression. It looked to me as if Robert was probably going to end up seducing Jeannie and making her pregnant. The way you did Mom."

He turned around at last, looking mildly offended. "I wouldn't say I seduced her exactly, Liz girl," he said defensively. "Lovemaking's a two-person activity, as I'm sure you know."

"All the same, you had to get married."

He nodded. "But I would have married her anyway. I was crazy about her." His face had taken on a reminiscent, faraway expression. "She was so cool and untouchable, so remote. So ladylike. I was amazed to find she was just as hot underneath as—" He broke off sheepishly, evidently deciding it wasn't quite proper to talk to his daughter about her mother's passion. Liz couldn't imagine her mother in the throes of passion and didn't want to try.

"Would she have married you?" she asked in a softer voice.

He thought that over for a while, folding up his dish towel just so, then refolding it. "I think so," he said finally. "We were very much in love, Liz."

"So what went wrong?"

He shook his head. "Time. Circumstances. All those

years I was flying, gone all the time. Your mother having to cope with broken washing machines and diaper rash. She got to be so capable, with her own way of doing things. And when I retired from the air force, went to work at Boeing and was home more, well, I suppose it was natural she'd resent my wanting to do things my way. We're both strong-willed people, Liz. We can't seem to meet any way but head-on.'' He grinned. ''You may have noticed.''

Liz laughed shortly. ''I certainly have.'' She looked at him curiously. ''You still love her, don't you, Dad?''

He turned around and started attacking the dishes again. ''Love's a hard habit to break,'' he admitted finally.

CATHERINE'S RESPONSE was not as different from Jake's as Liz had expected. Liz waited until Monday, over lunch at Catherine's favorite downtown restaurant. She gave a fairly complete rundown of what she'd discovered during the most recent hypnosis session, omitting only her own anger and the reason for it. Somehow, faced with her mother's serene coolness, she couldn't quite bring herself to talk about possibly unwanted pregnancies.

''Interesting,'' Catherine said, daintily sipping a spoonful of the clear soup that was all she allowed herself for lunch. Liz bit into her hamburger and waited.

''Perhaps I should consult Dr. Lockwood,'' Catherine said.

Liz's immediate negative reaction to this suggestion surprised her with its ferocity. ''I don't think that's a good idea at all,'' she said emphatically.

Catherine raised her smooth brown eyebrows. ''Why not? You want to keep him all to yourself?''

This was so close to the truth that Liz couldn't reply for a minute. ''I just can't imagine why you'd want to, that's all," she managed finally. "You're not the one having weird experiences."

"But I have had," Catherine said, surprising her. She moved an impeccably manicured hand in a dismissing gesture. "Oh, nothing like yours, I'll grant you. But strange, unexplainable. I wanted to tell you about it when you first raised the subject of reincarnation, but it didn't seem quite proper to admit to such an experience."

Setting her soup bowl to one side, she put her elbows on the table and rested her chin on her clasped hands, not looking at Liz. "It was before I met your father. I had to travel several times a week between hotels in Hayes and Uxbridge. I didn't drive then, so I took the tube. On the way there was an American base, right next to the railway. Guards were posted at each corner of this huge building and I would look at them in the morning on the way to Hayes and in the evening on the way home and I'd get this odd feeling that I had once lived in America. More than a feeling, actually. Looking in the train window, I could see myself in colonial dress—you know, puritan style with the apron and white bonnet. It became almost an obsession, looking at those guards, seeing myself superimposed in that old-fashioned costume. I felt I *had* to sit on that side of the train, so I could see them and get the feeling again."

"Did the feeling ever go away?" Liz asked, almost afraid to speak. She was amazed that her practical mother could have experienced anything so…surrealistic.

Catherine shrugged. "I changed jobs. I went to work on the front desk in our hotel in Iver and I took a bus instead of the train. However…" She paused and a reminiscent expression, similar to the one that had crept over Jake's face the previous day, appeared on her even features. "I've often thought that was why I was attracted to your father.

The fact that he was an American. So it seems to me it might be interesting to have myself regressed—to find out what the old experience was all about.''

''Wow,'' Liz said softly. ''Looks as if this whole family's weird.''

Catherine shook her head. ''Other people have similar experiences, darling. I know many people who say quite openly they believe in reincarnation.''

Liz shook her head. ''It's all up there with UFOs if you ask me.''

''Some people believe in them, too, dear.''

Liz made a face. ''I'd really rather you didn't go to Dr. Lockwood, Mom, all the same. I'd feel…funny about it.''

''I'll respect your wishes, of course,'' Catherine said at once. Then she sat very straight in her chair, compressing her mouth in a way that was all too familiar to Liz. A lecture was forthcoming, obviously.

''I understand you know that I was pregnant when I married your father,'' she said. ''Jake rang me up last night. He said you were quite upset about it.''

Liz was furious. ''Dad had no business telling you. I can't tell either one of you anything without you babbling to each other.''

''We do both love you,'' Catherine pointed out. ''If we were still married and living together, you'd expect us to discuss you, wouldn't you? Why should it be different just because we live separately? You are still our only child.''

Liz took a deep breath and let it out slowly. For some reason the subject of her mother's pregnancy aroused all kinds of deep-seated animosities in her. Because she'd heard about it as a small child, she supposed. ''I'm sorry, Mom,'' she said quietly. ''I know you both have my interests at heart. And I'm not really upset, not anymore. It was just a gut reaction after the regression. Dad told me you'd have married each other anyway. Do you agree with that?''

Catherine inclined her head to one side. "I suppose I would have, given my miniobsession with Americans." She laughed shortly. "Goes to show how misleading psychic experiences can be, doesn't it? But yes, I do think I'd have married Jake even if I wasn't pregnant. He was so...vital, you see, not at all like anyone I'd ever known before. My family was so terribly well-bred, so afraid of doing the wrong thing they never did anything. And so dreadfully stuffy. Jake was like a breath of fresh air."

There was an almost dreamy smile on her face now. Always attractive, she looked decidedly pretty, with a glow in her hazel eyes that wasn't often there. After a moment, she picked up her coffee cup. "I do want you to rest assured there wasn't a moment when I didn't want you," she said with a loving glance at Liz. Then she shook her head. "Enough of that. You've told me this enthralling story and I haven't even commented. Tell me more about it. How did it feel being hypnotized? Are you going back to Dr. Lockwood for more of the same?"

An image of Matt Lockwood appeared in Liz's mind. He was smiling his easy, friendly smile, standing looking down at her with his hands in the pockets of his disreputable-looking cords. Yes, she was going back. She could hardly wait for the week to pass so that she could go back.

Which was she most anxious about, she wondered—the continuation of Jeannie and Robert's story, or possible further developments between Matt Lockwood and Elizabeth Brooks?

CHAPTER SIX

MATT'S SECRETARY was a pretty young woman with long flaxen hair and green eyes. Until now she had treated Liz with great friendliness, but at the moment her fairly generous mouth was set in a straight line and her hands were clenched at her sides. "I can't do anything about it," she said adamantly. "Dr. Lockwood said to tell you to see Dr. Demetrius this time. Right over there in A-3, beyond the duck pond."

"But I don't want to see Dr. Demetrius," Liz said for the third time. "My appointment was with Matt—Dr. Lockwood. You say he's not sick and you didn't mix up the appointments, so why can't I see him?"

"He said to tell you to see Dr. Demetrius," Sally repeated sullenly.

Liz took a deep breath, let it out and accepted defeat. Maybe Dr. Demetrius—whoever he was—could tell her what was going on.

Dr. Demetrius was a woman—gray-haired, bespectacled, decidedly chubby, wearing a pink sweat suit and sneakers. Something in her attitude reminded Liz of Dr. Ruth on television. She had a wonderfully kind smile and she was certainly friendly enough, though she had a disconcerting habit of darting glances at Liz's face as if she were surreptitiously studying her.

"Dr. Lockwood asked me to regress you this time," she

said in answer to Liz's immediate question. "He gave me all of his case notes."

Liz didn't want to be thought of as a case.

"He thought it might be interesting to get my reaction," the doctor went on.

"But I would much prefer—" Liz broke off. If there was some reason for this change she'd just have to accept it, but she was really very disappointed. She'd been looking forward to seeing Matt again. Silly to feel rejected, but that was exactly how she felt. "Okay," she said abruptly.

Dr. Demetrius's face was immediately wreathed in smiles. Gesturing toward a couch, she had Liz lie down so she could hypnotize her. Liz was quite sure the experiment wouldn't work—the doctor's methods of induction were totally different from Matt's. She had Liz work at relaxing her body from the feet up, muscle group by muscle group, and then there was a lot of stuff about Liz not being able to open her eyes even if she wanted to, which made Liz feel rather nervous. So it was with a feeling of great surprise that she felt the familiar lethargy stealing over her. Within a few minutes she was totally relaxed.

But when Dr. Demetrius asked her to go back in time to September 1888 in Edinburgh, nothing happened. No pictures shimmered behind Liz's closed eyelids. No shadows appeared in her mind. There was only darkness.

The doctor tried several approaches, but it was as if Robert Charles McAndrew and Jeannie Findlay had never been.

When Liz was awakened she felt a surge of panic. What if she had lost them forever? What if Dr. Demetrius had driven them away?

Somehow she managed to convince Dr. Demetrius that she wasn't upset by this lack of communication. But as she left the building she felt as if someone she loved very much had died. If anyone were to look cross-eyed at her she would burst into tears, she thought despairingly.

The sound of a car engine broke through her reverie as she walked around the duck pond and she glanced up to see Matt's secretary driving a rather decrepit Mustang out of the compound.

Without planning on doing any such thing, she found herself changing direction, walking toward Matt's building. The outer door was unlocked and there was a faint line of light showing under Matt's office door. She didn't hesitate. It was only afterward that she realized he might have been regressing someone. Luckily he was alone, sitting on one of the sofas that bracketed the fireplace, apparently gazing at the flames of the log fire burning there.

He jumped up immediately. "Liz, what on earth...is anything wrong? What happened?"

"Nothing," she said, her voice trembling. "Nothing at all. I couldn't find Jeannie or Robert."

"Ione couldn't hypnotize you successfully?"

"She managed that all right. But there was nothing there."

He frowned. "That's too bad. I was hoping she could take over...."

"I wish you'd tell me what I did," Liz blurted out.

He looked at her, obviously bewildered. This evening he was wearing a wonderfully soft-looking tweed jacket with a blue polo shirt and his gray cords. The jacket was a lovely misty color, almost the exact shade of his eyes. She wanted to touch it, wanted to touch him.

"You're probably going to think me naive," she said flatly. "But I've never learned how to play games. I put my cards on the table and I expect everyone else to do the same."

She took a deep breath. "When I first came to see you,

I was really scared about the odd things that had been happening to me, and afraid of being hypnotized. But I couldn't stay scared when you were so…normal about everything, so matter-of-fact, so friendly. Then after the regression you changed. You were suddenly all stiff and distant. You stayed that way until you took me out to dinner after the next session. Then you were friendly again and I relaxed, sure we were friends after all. That feeling in the car, between us, you agreed it was there. I figured you left so quickly because I was disturbed, confused about my reaction to Jeannie's Robert.…''

"We are friends, Liz," he said softly.

"Then why did you pass me off on Dr. Demetrius? Is the story too boring for you? All this romance stuff. You'd prefer murder and mayhem?''

He smiled faintly. "I get my share of that. Jeannie and Robert's story is a welcome change of pace, believe me.''

"Then why?''

She was behaving like a child, standing there with her hands raised helplessly. But she couldn't seem to prevent herself from pleading with him. "I didn't feel I could relax with Dr. Demetrius," she said. "She did hypnotize me, but I couldn't find Jeannie again. I'm afraid I've lost her altogether. I've lost her and Robert.''

"And that distresses you?''

He was once again looking at her in a clinical way and all of a sudden she couldn't bear it. Turning on her heel she headed for the door, then stopped, her head drooping. She supposed she'd asked for that. All her scoffing about reincarnation. How could he possibly be expected to believe she identified so closely with Jeannie, so much so that she was halfway in love with Robert Charles McAndrew herself.

"Look, just forget it," she said tiredly without turning

around. "I can't seem to cope today. If you don't want to deal with me, I'll go back to Dr. Demetrius next week and try again."

She hadn't heard him come after her, but he was suddenly there, standing next to her. "Please don't go, Liz," he said, and as she turned and looked up at his face, moved tremendously by the gentle note in his voice, he groaned. Then his arms went around her and pulled her close.

The tweed jacket was as wonderfully soft as it had looked, smooth and sensuous to her touch. She moved her fingers over it to his shoulder, which felt even more solid than she'd expected, then lifted her hand to touch his face uncertainly. There was a stern cast to his mouth that she hadn't seen before. His lean features seemed shadowed, almost grim. But a second later his mouth met hers and it wasn't stern at all, just firm, yet remarkably gentle, brushing softly against her lips with patient movements as though he wanted to give her time to adjust to this abrupt change in their relationship. Once again she was conscious of a desire to let herself melt against him, and she let it happen until she was as close to him as it was possible to be. Her hands had somehow found the back of his collar, then they moved up to the back of his neck, to the crisp shaggy hair that she had subconsciously wanted to touch since the day he walked into her life.

Her mouth parted softly, wanting more from him, and she heard the swift intake of his breath, felt the steely strength of his arms as they tightened around her. Felt the dizzying sensation of his tongue touching her lips and the sweet taste of his breath in her mouth. His fingers tangled in her hair and tightened, sending a message to her of the intensity of his feelings. He was strong, insistent. Nothing tentative about this man. What he wanted, he went after. Not with force—she couldn't imagine him ever using force. But he wasn't treating her like a delicate flower, either. And she appreciated that. She had always appreciated equality. She pressed closer and felt the unmistakable pressure of his erection against her. And still she wanted more.

"Liz, this isn't very smart," he said hoarsely, setting her away from him slightly. He looked stunned, but not as sorry as his words implied. "Do you understand now why I asked Dr. Demetrius to see you?"

She couldn't answer for a moment. She felt as though she had just slid down a hill on a toboggan. Finally she managed to nod. "I guess I do. This is like a doctor/patient relationship, isn't it? Unethical to get involved in any way. We are involved, aren't we?"

He groaned again, in agreement, she supposed, and filled both his hands with her hair again, looking at it, smiling ruefully. "You have the most marvelous hair," he murmured. "I told Ione it looked like a forest fire." He took a deep breath, let it out and looked at her very directly, his eyes smoky gray, mist over the sea. "I've wanted to take you in my arms, kiss you, hold you, since you first walked into this room. I thought I could handle my feelings, keep a professional distance, but I couldn't. I can't. That's why I turned you over to Ione."

She grinned wryly, her fingers tracing the line of his mouth. "You sure gave it a good try. Mr. Frigid. I thought I'd offended you, couldn't think what I'd done."

"So you'll settle for Dr. Demetrius?"

She shook her head. "I can't do that. I'm convinced you're the only one who can recall Jeannie and Robert for me."

"That's not so, Liz. They are there in your memory. Any qualified hypnotist…"

Stubbornly she shook her head.

"Don't you see," he persisted, his hands coming up to her shoulders as if he were going to shake her. "It's only because you decided it wouldn't work that the session was unsuccessful. I planted the suggestion, remember, that you wouldn't regress unless you wanted to."

"I was willing to give it a try."

"Consciously maybe, but not subconsciously."

He kissed her again, hungrily, arousing her to fever pitch, then he set her away again. "We have to choose, Liz. You're a very desirable and attractive woman. Apparently I've no defenses against that fact. In which case I cannot work with you in a professional capacity."

She stood back and looked at him. His eyes were very intense, shadowed, his mouth stern again. "You really mean that, don't you?" she said.

He nodded, lifted one hand as if to touch her, then dropped it again.

He was an honorable man. The knowledge of that filled her with pleasure, admiration and frustration. She took a deep breath. "In that case, I guess we have to set aside our...feelings," she said flatly.

His mouth was wry. "You think we can do that?"

"No. But I'm willing to try." She sighed. "I remember thinking fairly recently that repression isn't all that difficult." She was suddenly very serious again. "It's important to me to find out the rest of Jeannie's story, Matt. I'm not sure why it should be so, but I have to know all of it. For the sake of that, I'm willing to sacrifice my personal feelings, I guess. I mean we could think of it as a postponement rather than a cancellation, couldn't we?"

He grinned. "An adjournment?"

She laughed, still feeling breathless but starting to recover her equilibrium. "We could issue rain checks," she suggested.

"It rains a lot in Seattle."

"Uh-huh."

He took a deep breath. She felt it a compliment that the breath was obviously shaky. "Shall we roll time back then?" he asked, moving away from her, back to the sofa. "Here I am, sitting gazing into the fire, thinking about one Elizabeth Brooks…"

"You were, really?"

He went on as if she hadn't spoken, "…wondering how she's getting along with Ione Demetrius, if she's here in Seattle, or back there in Edinburgh in 1888. You have just walked in, very calmly, to tell me the regression didn't work."

His voice had become steady as he spoke and she took her cue from him. "I've nothing against Dr. Demetrius, but I'd rather you would regress me, Dr. Lockwood," she said.

"I'd be happy to, Miss Brooks." He gestured toward the recliner. "Shall we begin?"

"I SHOULD NO have taken another day off," Jeannie said complacently, looking up at Robert. "But I'm awfu' glad I did. This is the happiest time I've ever had in my whole life. I feel I want to hold it tight in my hands so it will never get away."

They were sitting on a tartan blanket under a tree at the top of a small hill in the most beautiful park Jeannie had ever seen. It belonged to a friend of Robert's, a Lord somebody whom Queen Victoria had liked to visit when Prince Albert was still alive and they were staying in Scotland.

"It isna right that one man should own an entire park," Jeannie had said, outraged, when Robert suggested the outing.

"His family created it," Robert pointed out. Then he

had smiled wistfully. "Could we not worry about who owns what and who doesn't, just for today, Jeannie?"

Easy for the rich not to worry about such things, she had thought, but then had determined to enjoy herself, and pretend that, just for today, she herself was rich. Which indeed she felt, looking at the extensive grounds all around her, filled with trees that grew right down to the sea. Robert had pointed out the fine view of the Forth, the Isle of May, the Bass Rock, and she had seen the astonishing view of Edinburgh on the way in. They were a long distance from the house, which suited Jeannie just fine. One glimpse of its castellated towers had been enough to intimidate her.

She had taken off her sailor hat and set it carefully inside Robert's carriage. She had made it for a lady in New Town, but as it wasn't due to be delivered until the next day had taken the liberty of borrowing it for herself. Her dress was new, in a way; she had taken the tartan sleeves and skirt from one she'd bought secondhand and attached them to the plain green bodice from another, creating a gown that was the height of fashion and suited her own coloring perfectly. She had also borrowed Mhairi's prized paisley shawl, which so far she hadn't needed.

The beautiful weather was like a gift, a temporary return to summer. The sky was clear except for small fluffy clouds. Best of all, there were no other people anywhere in sight. That was a big advantage the rich had, she thought. They could get away from people at least some of the time.

"We might be the only man and woman in the world," Robert said contentedly, as though she had spoken her thought aloud.

"Adam and Eve," Jeannie said. "Enjoying a beautiful day in the Garden of Eden."

"Halcyon days," Robert commented.

The imp of mischief that never left her long alone, prompted her to show off the education he had questioned when they first met. "Oh, aye, now that would be the time in autumn when the Ancient Greeks believed the gods calmed the seas and gave some good weather borrowed from the summer so that the mythical halcyon bird could incubate its eggs."

He was obviously impressed. "The Americans call it Indian summer," he said.

It was her turn to be impressed. "You've been to America? All that way?" She could not conceive of such a long journey. Their carriage ride today was one of very few times she had left the city.

She was lying on her back on the tartan blanket now, trying to make animal shapes out of the clouds, the way she had when she was a wee child. Her stomach was full of delicious food and wine, the sun was warm on her face and her body, soothing to her still-bruised flesh. Any minute now, Robert was going to kiss her. She was truly content.

Robert leaned over her. "You're smiling, Jeannie," he murmured.

How blue his eyes were in the sunlight, as though they had trapped all the color from the sky, just as his hair had stolen its gold from the sun. "There's much to smile about here," she said softly.

"There is indeed," he agreed, looking directly into her eyes.

Then the sun was blotted out as his head came toward her. He held her face in both hands and covered it with soft light kisses, each as delicate as the touch of a feather. Finally his mouth covered hers and his kisses grew more demanding. A shiver ran through her body, but it was not caused by fear. When his tongue tentatively explored inside her mouth, she made a small sound of surprise, then instantly decided she liked this totally new sensation and met his increased ardor with her own. Other sensations were crowding in on her—the pointed tips of her breasts had begun a sweet aching and there was a swollen tightness in her lower body that made her want to lift herself against him.

Robert raised his head. His eyes dazzled her. "I love you, Jeannie Findlay," he said softly and it seemed to her that her soul soared.

"Och, now why would you be loving a bag of bones like me?" she asked. "Especially when not all the bones are straight."

"I love every part of you," he countered. "You have one small part of your body that didn't develop correctly, through no fault of your own. I could wish you perfect for your own comfort, but for me that small imperfection is just part of the whole wonderful woman. I love the strength of you and your independence and the way you speak your mind. I love you for your ambition and your willingness to work hard. The women I've known think themselves hard done by for running a household, and I've no doubt it's hard work for a woman who's raising her children and scrubbing the floors herself. But the women I've known have nannies and maids and kitchen help and cooks, and nothing to do with themselves but look pretty and gossip and take tea with one another. You're different, Jeannie, and I love your differentness."

He grinned at her. "I love you not only for all these things but also for your bonny brown eyes and your auburn hair and your smile that warms my soul."

Awed, she gazed up at him. "I love you, Robert," she said, though it didn't seem nearly enough to say.

She did not protest when his fingers began undoing the buttons of her bodice. She had known what would happen the minute Robert spread the tartan blanket on the soft green grass beneath this magnificent beech tree. And had known, too, that she would do nothing to prevent it.

She heard him draw in a breath suddenly and saw that he was looking down at a great bruise on her right shoulder. His eyes had darkened and she thrilled to the anger in them. "Jamie should have beaten the man who used you so," he said. "I may yet do so myself."

"Och, he was drunk, Robbie," she said. "Dinna waste your breath worrying about that poor wee man. He's not worth the trouble."

Her use of his mother's name for him made him forget his anger. His eyes cleared at once and he began concentrating on undoing the front clasps of her stays. "It would seem you know your way about a corset," Jeannie teased him.

He grinned. "Only enough to know relief that you've such a simple one."

And then his fingers were touching her bare skin where no man's hand had touched since Rory's death. Och no, she would not think of poor Rory's fumbling at such a time as this.

"I have dreamed of touching you here, Jeannie," Robert murmured as his hand moved silkily across first one small firm breast and then the other.

She loved the deepened texture of his voice, proof that he was affected by her nakedness. Vowing she would remember every word he said, every touch, she knew at the same time that she would forget, for already her mind was clouding as thought gave way to emotion. Her hands were pulling at the complicated knot of his tie, unraveling it, but she could not work out the stiff fastening of his collar.

At last he came to her assistance, laughing as he stripped off his clothing, commenting how glad he was he'd dressed in sporty fashion in a simple Norfolk jacket and knee breeches. Next he removed her clothing, taking time between the untying of a tape or the rolling down of a stocking or a layer of petticoat to touch or kiss the flesh exposed. Jeannie's excitement increased until she felt she was in a frenzy of love, fretting when his hands were busy elsewhere, feeling bereft when his mouth was away from hers.

Soon her clothing and his were gone and she reveled in the unaccustomed feeling of the sun's heat on her naked body. Robert murmured over every bruise and kissed each one tenderly. He unpinned her hair and ran it through his fingers, exclaiming over its softness. Again he touched each part of her body, his fingers almost reverent on her, while her own fingers and mouth searched out his secret areas. She felt no shame at her unaccustomed wantonness. It seemed right to her that she and Robert should be making love on a blanket with nothing over them but the sun. There seemed no hesitation between them, no strangeness or awkwardness, as though this was not the first time they had lain together.

Her only worry, as he slid his body over hers and began to move slowly, sensuously above her, was that he would be dismayed to find she was not a maiden.

But he was inside her before she quite realized it and he seemed unmindful of her condition, still covering her with kisses wherever he could reach, moving slowly, patiently, his eyes glowing bluer with every minute. They strained together, touching, kissing, murmuring incoherently, moving, always moving.

And then there came a time when a great stillness came over her, one she hadn't ever experienced before. Lost in wonder, she gazed up at his dear beautiful face as pressure built and built inside her. She was seeing the sky and the clouds through the branches of the tree above him with great clarity. Never in her life had all her senses seemed so alive. She could feel the cool dampness of the ground through the warm blanket, the heat of Robert's body held close in her arms, the moistness everywhere her body touched his. She could hear the soft whisper of the warm breeze through the trees, the occasional snorting of the gray horses who were patiently grazing some distance away, and she could taste the sweetness that surged through her suddenly, as the pressure inside her exploded and the sky and clouds and sunlight splintered into lozenges of light.

And now Robert was calling her name and moving more rapidly. There was a look on his face that was more intent than any she had seen before. Then he called her name once more and collapsed on her, holding her so tightly she thought she might never breathe again.

A second later he rolled with her so that they were lying side by side, still sweetly joined, arms clasped around each other, faces so close his features seemed blurred. All that was clear was the intense blue of his eyes. A woman could drown in all that blueness, she thought.

"Sweet Jeannie," he whispered. "I have never loved anyone as I love you."

Extravagant words. She moved uneasily. "Och, Robert, you hardly know me," she protested. "If you knew all about me, you might regret those words."

"Never." He smiled into her eyes, one hand playing in her tumbled hair. "I know you, Jeannie. You are the other half of me."

She laughed, delighted. "You sound like a poet."

"Do you remember our poem, Jeannie? 'And I will love thee still, my dear, while the sands o' life shall run.'"

Her heart seemed to turn, constricting in her chest as she remembered the next line that other Robert had written, "And fare thee well, my only luve..."

"'Tis foolish to talk of knowing when 'tis not so," she said a while later. She had gathered up enough hairpins to fasten her hair fairly neatly, and she and Robert were both dressed respectably again.

"You don't think you know me?" he asked, taking her hand and kissing the palm of it so that she shivered with a return of passion.

She looked at the concerned expression on his handsome face and the clear truth in his blue eyes and sighed, surrendering. "I know you to have a pure heart, Robbie," she said. "That's all that matters to me. I know you would not use me ill, and that's important, too. But there is still a fear in me."

"Of what?" He was kissing her wrist now and it was difficult to keep her thoughts in order. Must she tell him the truth about herself, even if it meant losing him? "I'm not what you think," she said. "There's something you don't know about me. Something I must tell you myself before you hear it from others."

He had appeared puzzled, but now his face cleared and he smiled in a teasing way. "Oh, you mean the fact you work in the evenings at a public house? What is it called, the Horse and Hounds? One William Moffatt, proprietor?"

She sighed resignedly. "Jamie Kintyre told you I'm a barmaid as well as a milliner? I thought he most likely would."

"He told me. My coachman confirmed it."

"And you think no less of me for it?"

He shook his head. "Why would I, Jeannie? I would

wish you didn't work in such a place, and I've worried about your safety ever since I knew the truth. But it's clear you've had to earn money to keep yourself alive. How could I justify sitting in judgment on you for something that's necessary to you?''

''I'll no be working there much longer,'' she said. ''I've saved every penny I made there. All for my wee shop. Soon, maybe one more year, I'll have enough for a start.''

She leaned against him, knowing now was the time to tell him her work as a barmaid was not what she'd meant to confess. She'd already reasoned he knew about that when she found out Jamie had followed her.

This secret was far more serious and she should tell him now while he was holding her close again and she didn't have to look at his face.

But somehow, after all his wonderful declarations, she couldn't bear to bring ugly truth to spoil this day. One perfect day, she thought. Surely Jeannie Findlay could not be begrudged one perfect day.

LIZ HAD GONE through the requisite slow awakening and was feeling much calmer than before, relieved that she had been able to summon Jeannie and Robert again after all. She felt embarrassed, too, however. Matt must have felt like a voyeur, listening to her tell of making love to Robert. *Jeannie, not her, Jeannie.*

But it had *felt* like her. There was a certain lassitude in her limbs, that wonderfully lethargic, satisfied sensation throughout her entire body that only came after truly excellent sex.

She couldn't quite bring herself to look at Matt. He was a doctor, she reminded herself. He was used to hearing all kinds of personal confidences. All the same, considering her attraction to him, the thought of making love to Robert in his presence seemed...

Think of something else, she instructed herself.

"I wonder what this secret is that Jeannie's holding back?" she murmured. As she became more fully conscious, she felt frustrated by Jeannie's secrets. She'd had no idea Jeannie worked part-time as a barmaid, and was glad to have that cleared up. But now she wondered what else there could possibly be that might come between these two. She wanted them to have a happy ending, she realized. That's why she had been so insistent that Matt hypnotize her again.

She realized Matt hadn't answered her and glanced across at him. He was still sitting near the fire, shadows flickering across his lean face as a flame flared up and then died down. He seemed lost in his own thoughts and she wasn't sure he'd heard her. "What do you suppose Jeannie's keeping from Robert?" she asked.

He gave her the steady, serious look she'd decided was his trademark. "What makes you think I would know?" he asked.

She laughed at her own foolishness. "I guess I just think of you as my personal guru, all powerful, all knowing."

He shook his head. "Perhaps we'll find out later." He looked at her again. "How do you feel about this particular session?"

She almost blushed. Averting her eyes, she tried to keep her answer light. "Well, it wasn't unexpected, I guess. If you'll remember I decided last time it was inevitable. I just hope Jeannie isn't pregnant." Her voice was a higher pitch than usual. The remembrance of what had happened between Robert and Jeannie was heavy in the flickering shadows of the firelight, thickening the air.

Trying again to make a joke of it, she said, "Wouldn't

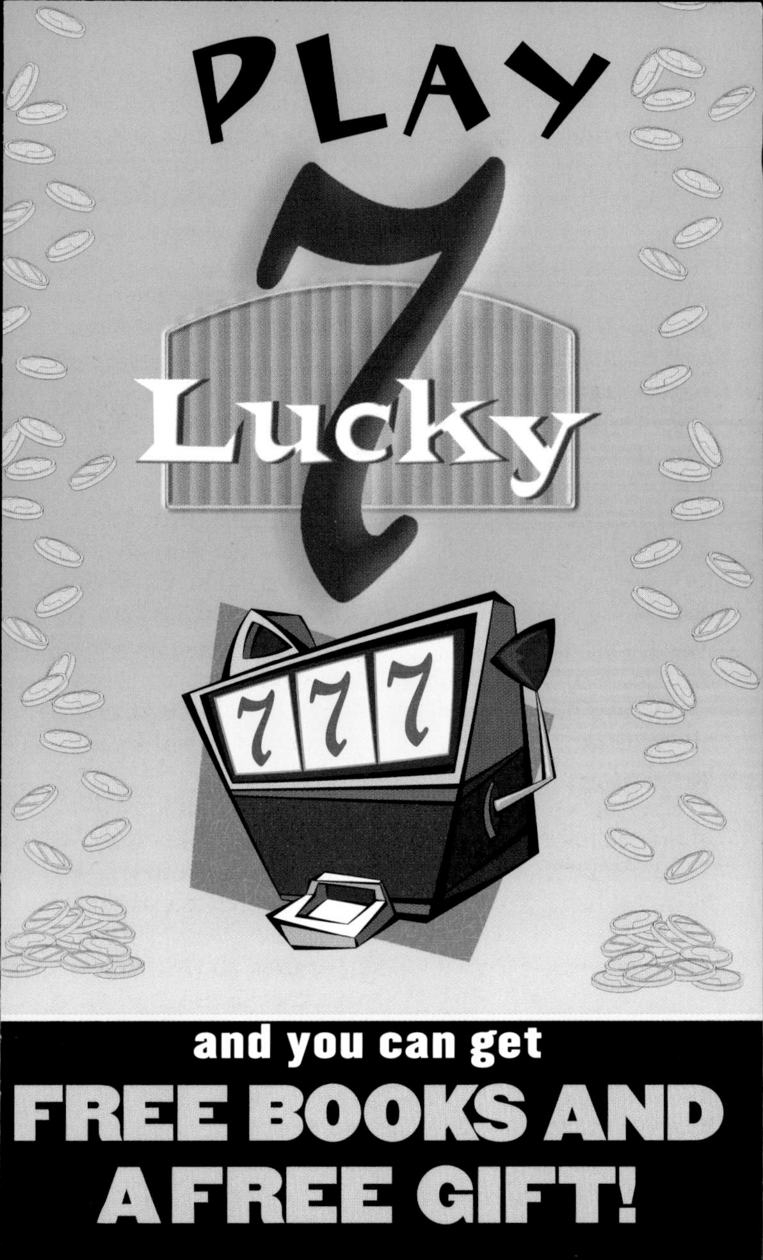
PLAY
Lucky 7
and you can get
FREE BOOKS AND
A FREE GIFT!

NO COST! NO OBLIGATION TO BUY!

NO PURCHASE NECESSARY!

Scratch off the gold area with a coin. Then check below to see the gifts you get!

Lucky 7

YES! I have scratched off the gold area. Please send me the 2 Free books and gift for which I qualify. I understand I am under no obligation to purchase any books as explained on the back and on the opposite page.

345 SDL DNKU   245 SDL DNKP

FIRST NAME   LAST NAME

ADDRESS

APT.#   CITY

STATE/PROV.   ZIP/POSTAL CODE   (S-IMB-04/02)

Worth **2 FREE BOOKS** plus a **FREE GIFT!**

Worth **2 FREE BOOKS!**

Worth **1 FREE BOOK!**

Try Again!

Offer limited to one per household and not valid to current Silhouette Intimate Moments® subscribers. All orders subject to approval.

DETACH AND MAIL CARD TODAY!

The Silhouette Reader Service® — Here's how it works:

Accepting your 2 free books and gift places you under no obligation to buy anything. You may keep the books and gift and return the shipping statement marked "cancel." If you do not cancel, about a month later we'll send you 6 additional books and bill you just $3.80 each in the U.S., or $4.21 each in Canada, plus 25¢ shipping & handling per book and applicable taxes if any.* That's the complete price and — compared to cover prices of $4.50 each in the U.S. and $5.25 each in Canada — it's quite a bargain! You may cancel at any time, but if you choose to continue, every month we'll send you 6 more books, which you may either purchase at the discount price or return to us and cancel your subscription.

*Terms and prices subject to change without notice. Sales tax applicable in N.Y. Canadian residents will be charged applicable provincial taxes and GST.

If offer card is missing write to: Silhouette Reader Service, 3010 Walden Ave., P.O. Box 1867, Buffalo NY 14240-1867

BUSINESS REPLY MAIL
FIRST-CLASS MAIL   PERMIT NO. 717-003   BUFFALO, NY

POSTAGE WILL BE PAID BY ADDRESSEE

SILHOUETTE READER SERVICE
3010 WALDEN AVE
PO BOX 1867
BUFFALO NY 14240-9952

NO POSTAGE
NECESSARY
IF MAILED
IN THE
UNITED STATES

you know that after throwing cold water all over the two of us, I'd come up with the hottest love scene since Scarlett and Rhett?'' She laughed nervously, then glanced at him, feeling unbearably awkward. ''I suppose you got all of it on your tape recorder?''

He raked his hair with his fingers, then grinned, his teeth very white against his shadowed face. ''The complete and unexpurgated version.''

Evidently he wasn't embarrassed at all, which made her feel better about the whole thing.

''Why do you suppose I'm going through this?'' she asked seriously. ''I mean, why now? If this is reincarnation—''

''If?'' Those expressive eyebrows of his slanted upward. ''You're beginning to think it might be?''

''I'm not saying that. But if it was—'' She ignored his grin and plunged on. ''Why are Jeannie and Robert so clear to me now when I knew nothing about them all the years I was growing up?''

''It's hard to tell,'' he said, sobering at once. ''Obviously when you started planning your trip to Edinburgh, the memories were triggered, then your actual visit brought it all to life.''

''Is it your belief that it was all planned that I'd make the trip to Edinburgh?''

''Fate, you mean?''

''Whatever.''

He shook his head. ''I've an idea we make our own fate, Liz. I don't think we're mere pawns on a chessboard. We may make our decisions subconsciously, but I believe we make them ourselves.''

''You're saying there must be a reason why I chose to go to Edinburgh, a reason why I started recalling Jeannie's and Robert's lives?''

"I would say so. Maybe you are just...ready at this stage in your life."

Ready. The word seemed to hang between them. Ready for what, she wanted to ask him, but she was pretty sure she knew the answer.

"I didn't want to leave again," she admitted. "It always comes to a close before I'm ready." Again she felt embarrassed heat rising to her face. What was she saying—that she'd wanted to make love to Robert again?

He grinned. "I think you've probably had all you can manage this time."

Keep it light. Make a joke of it. "We couldn't take a quick look just in case they're still there?"

He laughed. "Next Friday."

She sighed. "I'm off again, I'm afraid. I have to go to Boston for a travel show. Then I'm doing a series of seminars in Florida and Texas, promoting the Prince chain. I'll be gone a month."

"A month!"

He appeared taken aback, maybe even upset. Which was good, she thought. She wanted him to miss her. They might have an "adjournment," but it was nice to suspect that when all of this regression stuff was ended and she'd elicited all of Jeannie and Robert's story that she could, they might be able to take up where they had left off. *I am not promiscuous,* she scolded herself when the thought occurred to her. *That was Jeannie making love to Robert, not me.*

"When do you leave?" he asked.

"Monday." The weekend suddenly seemed to loom ahead, empty and echoing with loneliness. "Are you busy tomorrow evening?" she asked on an impulse.

"You want another session? I suppose it's possible. I'm not sure, though, that..."

"I was thinking of dinner. My treat. My apartment. Do you like Italian food?"

"I love Italian food, but—"

"Fresh pasta with garlic and oil. Veal parmigiana and salad. I'd like to talk some more about reincarnation, pick your brain without it costing me forty-five dollars an hour."

He laughed. "How can I resist such a generous invitation?"

Laughter was good, Liz thought. With laughter they could make it through all this awkwardness. Possibly.

CHAPTER SEVEN

MATT KNEW he was in trouble the moment he rang Liz's apartment and heard her voice telling him she was buzzing him in. He always had been susceptible to women's voices that had a certain husky note. Liz had a mellow, sensual voice that evoked candlelit rooms, full-bodied wine, soft music.

Going up in the elevator, he remembered Ione telling him, "The ethics of this situation are perfectly clear." Hell, he hadn't needed Ione to tell him that. He *knew* he had to maintain his distance if he was going to keep seeing Liz on a professional basis. Doing it was something else. Obviously. Had he ever visited any other patient during a regression treatment? He had a certain professional curiosity about her life-style, he had told himself after accepting her invitation. Some rationalization.

He took a deep breath before ringing the doorbell, then found himself holding it when she opened the door. He hadn't seen her in a dress before. While he was no male chauvinist he did appreciate a woman in a dress. Not that her dress was in any way provocative. Made of lightweight blue woolen material, it seemed to float around her long and exceptionally fine legs, but it was buttoned chastely at her throat and wrists. Blue was obviously Liz's color, contrasting vividly with the mass of copper curls frothing around her face and shoulders, complementing her glowing blue eyes. Looking at her, admiring her, he was reminded abruptly of how she'd felt in his arms—slender, sexy, utterly feminine. *Play it light, Lockwood,* he instructed himself. *Play it light or you're dead in the water.*

"I knew I should wear a tux," he said, stopping dead on the threshold.

Her gamin smile flashed out at him. "I can't imagine you in a tuxedo," she said, eyeing his gray tweed jacket. "You're like my dad, I think, you like your comfort."

"I did wear a tie," he pointed out. "Is that enough to get me invited in?"

She held out her right hand. "It's nice to see you again, Dr. Lockwood."

He took the hand and looked at it. Creamy smooth skin, fragile bones, long fingers. He cleared his throat. The air was alive between them. He could almost hear it crackle.

"This was probably a mistake, huh?" Liz said on a long breath.

He shook his head and let go of her hand. "Not at all. I've got my professional aura wrapped tightly around me. Can't you see it?"

She shook her head.

He tried for humor again as he followed her into the apartment. "You insulted me, you know," he informed her. "It happens that I do own a tux. I get called upon to attend banquets from time to time."

What would be her response, he wondered, if he were to say: "I used to wear a morning coat most of the time, remember, with striped trousers and a silk top hat. Considering the discomfort of Robert's high starched collars and tight waistbands, is it any wonder I opted for comfort this time around?"

She'd want to have him committed, no doubt, convinced he was either out of his mind or some kind of con man putting the make on her.

"This is nice," he said, looking around. "What do you call it?"

She laughed. "Cottage Victorian. Cluttered, isn't it? My mother has a fit whenever she comes over. Her taste runs to glass and chrome and white carpeting. I agree with her that my stuff doesn't really fit this modern building, but I've always felt at home with nineteenth-century country antiques." She made a face at him, looking absolutely adorable. "I suppose you think that's significant."

He didn't answer, having caught sight of the Persian rug covering the living room floor—a beautiful and ancient Sehna, velvety smooth, its once vibrant blue-and-yellow pattern faded to muted pastels.

"I found it in a flea market, can you imagine?" Liz said, following the direction of his gaze. "I wasn't able to find out how old it is, but I think it's probably been around a while."

He nodded, feeling tremendously moved, wishing he could put his arms around her and explain it all to her. The evidence was all here, if she only knew it—the Victorian atmosphere, the Persian rug. The fabrics of cushions and chair covers were woven, and there was a woven hanging on the dining room wall. "Scandinavian," she told him. "I guess it's a bit of a mixture, but it seems to work."

Because it's *your* mixture, he wanted to tell her, the warp and woof of other places, other lives.

They stood on Liz's small balcony while the water heated for the pasta, companionably sipping rosé while looking out at the space needle and Lake Washington and the traffic on I-5 coming into the city for Saturday evening activities. It had been Matt's suggestion they come out here. There was an intimacy to Liz's small apartment that had caused him to doubt his ability to remain aloof. Out here at least the subtle fragrance of her perfume wasn't quite so dangerous.

"There are only two things I like about this apartment," Liz said. "The view and the fact I can walk downtown through Freeway Park. I'd really like to own a cottage like my father's. Or even better, a house—an old one with a round tower and stained-glass windows and lots of niches. Do you live in an apartment, Matt?"

Matt, who owned a house remarkably similar to the one she had just described, shook his head but refrained from comment.

"Have you ever regressed to a past life?" she asked out of the blue.

He was so startled he slopped some of his wine over his hand and had to go in to get a napkin, discovering as he did so that the pasta water was ready.

But she came back to the subject when they were seated at the round oak table beside the window. There were no candles, he was relieved to see. Evidently she was trying to play fair. "Have you done your own regressions, or does somebody else do them for you?" she asked.

"Both," he answered. "Ione has helped me out. For some reason, when anyone does their own regression using self-hypnosis, they don't talk their way through it, they just experience it. If someone else is questioning them they come up with a record for the tape recorder."

"So what kind of life did you have, Doc?" she asked.

She was really trying to keep their conversation going, he realized, and he was grateful to her for her efforts. Looking around at the wonderfully evocative furnishings and that glowing Persian rug, he kept relapsing into silence, afraid to speak in case he said too much and frightened her out of his life forever.

He considered how he should answer her. He certainly

couldn't talk to her about Scotland. Not yet. "I was once a fisherman in Denmark," he told her, watching her face. "Another time I was a monk in a Cistercian monastery in Spain."

She put down her fork and stared at him, her lips parted, looking so scrumptious he wanted to reach across the table and gather her into his arms. "You mean you remember more than one other life?"

"Several, yes. I'm sure you've had more than one, too."

She tapped her forehead. "There are other people up here, besides Jeannie and Robert?"

"A whole bus load."

"Good grief, I hope they don't show up. I've got all I can handle with Jeannie."

Just as Matt was congratulating himself for diverting her attention from himself, she came right back at him again, laughing delightedly. "I cannot imagine you as a monk. What did you do?"

"You couldn't imagine me in a tuxedo, but I have one," he pointed out. Then he smiled. "I transcribed manuscripts. Almost lost my eyesight doing it, too."

Her face glowed. "You mean you worked on those marvelous illuminated manuscripts? What a lovely thing to do. All that embellishment, and the wonderful little pictures in the capital letters." A mischievous glint appeared in her eyes. "Were you celibate?"

"Totally."

"What a waste. But I suppose then you could concentrate all of your libido on your art."

"That was the idea."

She stood to fetch the second course from the kitchen. The pasta had been exceptionally good, heavily laced with garlic just the way he liked it. "I have a lovely medieval book of days," he told her when she sat down again. "I'll show it to you sometime if you really like that kind of thing.''

Her wonderful eyes brimmed with mischief again. ''Did you carry it through the centuries with you?''

He laughed. ''I bought it in a flea market, just as you bought your rug. Only my flea market was in London.''

''London? You've visited Britain? Did you go to Edinburgh while you were there?''

''Briefly. Yes.'' Hastily he brought the subject back to his book of days. ''I was thrilled to find the book. I'd always wanted one. Naturally.''

Again Liz set her fork down. ''Whoa. Wait a minute here. What do you mean, naturally? Are you saying a person likes the same things in every life?''

''Not exactly. And I'm certainly not talking about every knife, fork and butter dish. But it makes sense, don't you think, to believe that if we are repelled by something it's because it has bad memories for us, and if we're drawn to something it's because it was familiar to us, or loved by us in a prior life?''

At least he'd got her away from the subject of his reincarnations. He watched her face, enjoying the play of emotions across it as she struggled to assimilate the things he was telling her—denial, derision, doubt, ending with uncertainty. ''You do think my furnishings are significant,'' she said flatly at last.

He nodded.

''What about my Persian rug then?''

With effort he managed a casual shrug. ''Perhaps you lived in Persia once.''

''Wrapped up in a black veil? God, what a horrible thought.'' She sat back in her chair, staring at him wide-eyed. ''I'll never be able to buy anything again without wondering why I'm buying it. You see significance in almost everything, don't you?''

He nodded and she smiled suddenly, brilliantly. "I like that." She held up a hand. "I'm not saying I'm a believer. But I'd like to believe everything in life is significant in some way." Her face softened as she thought for a moment. "Yes, I do like that," she murmured again. He couldn't take his eyes from her vivid face.

He insisted on helping her load the dishwasher, which was a mistake. Working closely together at the sink in her small galley kitchen, taking the rinsed dishes from her to put in the machine, he was closer to her than he'd allowed himself to get all evening.

She worked in silence, evidently thinking over everything they'd talked about. She was wavering in her disbelief, he suspected; he must be very cautious from now on.

"I wish I wasn't leaving on Monday," she said as they carried coffee cups into her living room. "I can't wait to visit with Jeannie again." She glanced at him sideways. "I don't suppose you could..."

"No way," he said firmly. "We do regressions only in the office. No house calls."

She laughed.

They sat and talked for a while. She told him about her parents, how different they were from each other, but how she thought they really did love and miss each other if they'd only own up to it. After a short silence she told him about remembering the argument between Jake and Catherine and figuring out why she'd been so upset when she thought Robert might make Jeannie pregnant.

"Robert didn't exactly seduce her, did he?" he said, watching her face. "Jeannie was willing enough, seemed to me."

"Ah, but seduction has to start somewhere," she pointed out. "It was Robert who pursued her, not the other way around." She cocked her head to one side and looked at him. "My father said the same thing about my mother, that he didn't seduce her. Smacks to me of Adam blaming Eve for tempting him—men always try to get themselves off the hook."

"I worry about the kind of men you've been involved with," Matt said. "You've a jaundiced view of us all."

"I told you I always get mixed up with the wrong type," she reminded him, then colored slightly. "I didn't mean anything by that," she said hastily, then asked a quick question about his parents.

He told her his mother had grown up in Phoenix, Arizona, coming to Seattle when she married his father. She was the kind of woman who could be happy anywhere, he told her, but when his father retired from the insurance business, she'd confessed she really missed the heat.

Matt visited them when he could, usually in the winter months. "I once made the mistake of driving down in July," he said. "I hated it. Everybody would run from the air-conditioned house to the air-conditioned car, to the air-conditioned stores. All that sunshine and it was too hot to sit out in the yard."

"I *love* Washington's climate," she said softly. Then she sat silently for a while. He loved the way she inclined her head when she thought, her gaze sliding sideways and down to the right. Hadn't he read somewhere that the direction of gaze while mulling things over was opposite to the dominant side of the brain? Which would make her left-brain dominant, the side that governed logic, analytical reasoning, rational thinking, organizational ability. Right on as far as Liz was concerned.

He'd never quite managed to catch himself while lost

in thought, to check his own direction, but he was pretty sure he was right brained—intuitive, subjective, creative, visual.

The soft fabric of her dress molded itself over her firm breasts and slender waist. The long sleeves exposed only her graceful hands. Her mass of curly hair shone with a thousand copper highlights.

"I suppose Washington's climate is quite similar to Scotland's," she said at last.

So that's what she had been mulling over.

"Significantly so," he said to make her laugh.

He loved the way she laughed, too, her eyes crinkling, shining—the laughter itself as musical as water tumbling over pebbles in a stream.

He took a deep breath and stood. If he sat watching her much longer he was going to forget all his good intentions again. "I really should go," he said.

"Do you have to?" Her voice was regretful.

"I have to," he said, then wished his voice hadn't sounded quite so emphatic. That imp of mischief was back, dancing around her eyes and the corners of her mouth.

"But I still have eight hundred and sixty-eight questions," she protested.

"There are books, you know."

She stood, her skirt swirling around her legs again. "You're sounding distant again. Did I annoy you, or is it self-protection?"

He didn't trust himself to answer. He simply looked at her.

"I'm sorry," she said at once. "But we've managed rather well, don't you think?"

He meant to agree but found himself saying, "Speak for yourself," instead.

She nodded solemnly. "It is difficult, knowing how

good it was between us when you…well, you know what I mean.''

"Yes.''

"And it's going to be a whole month.''

"Liz,'' he said desperately. "Are you sure you couldn't consider regressing with Ione's help?''

Her eyes glowed and a wry smile hovered around the edges of her mouth. "My mind is producing all kinds of trite excuses,'' she confessed. "This thing is bigger than both of us. I can't fight myself. We were meant for each other. We're only human.''

"Trite things become trite because they are true,'' he said.

She was trembling. He knew that all he had to do was take a step forward and she would be in his arms. For a full minute they stood looking at each other, then he took the step.

HER BEDROOM was furnished in a Victorian manner also, with a stately but comfortable-looking bed. The blue fabric swathing the wall at its head matched the swags on the window draperies. Yes, she had recreated the period in loving detail. He shouldn't be here, he thought, even as he helped her lift her dress over her head. He had meant to wait until she remembered everything, knew everything. But he had reckoned without his own body's impatience. He wanted her now.

She emerged flushed and smiling shyly from the woolen fabric, wearing only dainty lace and silk that clung to her creamy flesh. He reached for her, but she set his hands aside and helped him shrug out of his jacket, stroking it gently as she laid it on a chair. As her fingers fumbled with the knot of his tie, he wondered if she remembered

Jeannie trying to help Robert undress. Liz had let her dress fall in a pool of blue to the floor.

"Now you," he murmured after he'd pulled off his shirt. She laughed softly and slid out of her half-slip, slowly, gracefully, making a teasing game out of it. He removed his trousers and shorts together, kicking off his shoes and socks at the same time. She tugged down her panty hose. Then she removed her bra and stood before him, straight and tall, in the light from the hall. She was so incredibly slender he was almost afraid to touch her.

"You look like a statue," he said. "An ivory statue."

She reached to switch on a lamp beside the bed. The lamp had a pink shade that cast a rosy glow over her beautiful skin and accentuated the glory of her hair, bringing her to life. Then she took his hands and lifted them to her breasts. "Do I feel like a statue?" she asked.

After a long silent moment, his thumbs gently brushed the erect nipples. "I want to take a long time making love to you," he said softly. "First I want to look at each part of you, then I want to touch and kiss each part of you."

A shiver ran through her body as she nodded, but there was a mischievous glint in her eyes. As he slowly moved his hands over first one creamy breast and then the other, she reached for him, her hands moving rapidly, strongly, up his arms to his shoulders, pulling him toward her.

He couldn't get enough of her mouth. He could kiss her for an hour and not get tired of the softness of her lips, the sweetness of her breath. Her lips moved under his experimentally, with curiosity, tasting him, teasing him with her tongue and teeth, first surrendering to him, then asserting her equality. And all the while his hands moved over her, exploring her, possessing her.

And then he was with her on the bed and there was a sudden wild impatience in him to possess her utterly, im-

mediately, rapidly. Rolling with her, lifting her, he entered
her and found she was ready for him. His heart had never
beat so rapidly or so unevenly. Holding her, his mouth
now harsh on hers, met by an answering harshness, he
moved steadily, reveling in her wildness, the soft almost
guttural sounds that came from her throat. "Now," she
told him, clasping him tightly against her. "Now, now,
now." A second later the pink light from the shaded lamp
exploded brilliantly and fell in sparks all around.

"I'm sorry," he said quietly a little later. "I meant to
wait, to go slowly, but..."

"How could you wait? You're only human."

He laughed, then he wound his fingers in the glorious
hair that lay tumbled around her head on the pillow. It felt
alive under his hands. Kissing her gently, he began the
slow exploration he had intended earlier. There was all the
time in the world now, time to make the discoveries he
had longed to make. Moving down her body and back up
again, treating every part of her with loving attention, looking at her, he nourished himself on the beauty of her. She
lay still for a while, her blue eyes shining up at him, a
faint flush across her high cheekbones, her skin translu-
cent.

For one split second her image seemed to dissolve and
he was looking back through the years, so many, many
years, seeing Jeannie's sweet heart-shaped face raised to
his, her alert brown eyes watching him with profound pleasure.

Then Liz began to move again, setting out on a journey
of exploration of her own, drawing erotic designs on his
flesh with fingertips and mouth. He was suddenly glad that
he'd spent so many hours playing squash, or jogging
around the Institute compound. His only motivation had
been to keep himself physically fit, considering his sed-

entary occupation. The bonus was that he didn't have to worry about how he looked and felt to her.

For a long time there was only the sound of their breathing as they came together and parted and touched and kissed. This time he entered her slowly and tenderly and with the greatest restraint.

A low moan of pleasure trickled out of her throat, and he smiled and bent his head to her as he began to move over her. Heat was spiraling through him, but it was a patient heat, not to be compared to the brushfire that had raced through him a short time before.

Liz's eyes were closed now and there was an intent expression on her face as she moved with him, matching his rhythm, lifting herself with every thrust of his body. Then she opened her eyes and looked at him, her blue eyes smoky with passion, a small sensual smile curling the corners of her mouth. He smiled at her, then felt the unmistakable surge that meant he could no longer hold back. But he did hold back, waiting for her, waiting until her body lifted hard against him and her eyes went dark, her lips parting. As spasms shook her body, he lost what little control he had left. Faster and faster, holding tightly to each other, they climaxed together, then began the long silken slide down to fulfillment.

"Robbie," Liz murmured tenderly.

As he stared at her in shock, his heart accelerating madly while his brain told him she couldn't have, couldn't possibly have said that name, her eyes focused on him and her face twisted with horror. Flailing at him with her hands, she tried to pull away from him, twisting under him to free herself.

He took hold of her hands and held them tightly, keeping his body firmly over hers so that she couldn't slide out from under him. "It's all right, Liz," he said over and over. "It's all *right*."

"No, it's not. You don't understand." Her head was rolling from side to side on the pillow, her eyes squeezed tightly shut.

"Tell me, then, tell me." Somehow he managed to keep his voice calm though his mind was reeling. And after a moment she responded to his calmness by becoming less agitated herself. When he was sure the sudden storm was over, he rolled to his side, pulling her with him so that she was held securely in his arms. "Tell me," he repeated.

All the color had left her face. Her eyes looked huge, luminous, shadowed underneath. Her cheekbones stood out in sharp relief against her pallor. Burying her face against his shoulder she took a series of breaths, then managed to choke out, "I saw his face. Robert's. When I looked at you."

He swallowed hard. "That's not too surprising, Liz," he said carefully, conscious that he must tread very gently here. "You've been thinking about Robert a lot lately. You were there when he made love to Jeannie."

She nodded against his shoulder. "That's how it started," she said. "You were making love to me and it was wonderful and then I was remembering Robert making love to Jeannie and it seemed as though *he* was making love to me, just like before, when I was under hypnosis. As though I'd become dislocated in time and space. I could feel the blanket under me and the sun..." She shook her head. "Then I opened my eyes and looked at you and saw Robert. I was awake, Matt, fully awake. And I saw Robert instead of you. Don't you see what this means?"

He was almost afraid to speak, not even sure he could. Shifting a little, but still holding her close, he said, "Why don't you tell me what *you* think it means?"

She laughed a little then. "Doctors always answer a question with another damn question," she muttered. "You're always making me say what I think, leaving decisions up to me."

She sniffled a little, then pulled away from him, not abruptly and not far, just enough so she could look at his face. "It means Robert's really haunting me," she said. "He's become some kind of obsession, along with Jeannie. I'm beginning to think he's real. So real that my mind became confused and produced the image of his face instead of yours."

His breathing had started up again as she spoke. She was so far from the truth. How ingenious her mind was to come up with such a believable explanation. How much more likely she was to believe it than if he had invented it for her.

Evidently she wasn't ready yet to face the truth. Not yet. He felt disappointed, but not surprised. Her mind still had prejudices to overcome, knowledge to gain. When she was ready, the truth would come to her. He hoped. He sighed inaudibly, then brushed his lips across her cheek. Unfortunately there were no guarantees.

"It was such an awful thing to do to you," Liz whispered. "Saying another man's name, when all the time it was you—" She broke off. For a second he thought she was going to say something more, but she shook her head slightly and tightened her mouth. She was still very pale.

"It's okay, Liz. It's perfectly understandable. Past-life regressions are often traumatic. Occasionally there's some initial confusion. It won't last."

"God, I hope not." She looked up at him and managed a smile. "I can see it's you now."

"I'm glad." He hesitated. "It was really me all along, Liz."

"I know."

He touched her face. "Making love to you was as wonderful as I always knew it would be."

"Always?"

He'd slipped there. "*My* trite saying for today—I've waited my whole life for you." If she only knew how true that was.

She smiled. Her color had returned. "How about—making love to you is like coming home to a warm fire and a light shining in the window."

How close she was to the truth, and yet how far away. "That's not trite," he protested, purposely keeping his voice light.

"I know," she said, her eyes glowing.

He grinned at her. "How about a shower?" he asked. "Or doesn't your bathroom run to one?"

"Of course it does," she said, and climbed out of bed.

"I thought you might have gone in for Victorian plumbing, too," he teased, following her into the obviously contemporary room. "I'm glad to see you restrained yourself."

"And what would a Cistercian monk know about Victorian plumbing?" she asked as she opened frosted doors and bent to turn on the water in the tub.

He'd goofed again. Stepping into the tub with her, he slid the doors closed, then put his arms around her from behind and held her close while the warm water drummed on their bodies. "You did tell me about Jeannie's chamber pot," he reminded her, glad she hadn't turned to see the dismay that must have shown on his face.

She laughed merrily. "Some things are better in this century," she conceded.

He turned her around under the stream of water, then cupped her face in his hands. "Many things," he said.

They soaped each other lazily, making a game of it, arousing each other so thoroughly that after a few minutes they toweled themselves dry and returned to bed, pausing only for Liz to wrap a towel around her head and for Matt to bring a couple of glasses of wine from the kitchen.

Solemnly she toasted, ''To the twentieth century.'' Then he took her glass from her and set it down with his on the marble-topped nightstand.

Her mouth was warm against his once more. Immediately he felt himself hardening. ''Again?'' he murmured.

''Again and again and again,'' she said, laughing against his mouth.

And this time it was tender and gentle and easy, and there were no ghosts present.

CHAPTER EIGHT

THE YOUNG WOMAN in the next booth at the travel show kept looking across at Liz. Eventually, after Liz returned from a lunch break, she walked over. She was younger than Liz, maybe twenty-two or -three, dark haired, plump and pretty. "Do I know you from somewhere?" she asked.

She looked familiar to Liz, too. "I'm staying at the Logan Hilton," Liz said. "Have I seen you there?"

She shook her head. "I live here in Boston so I'm not staying at a hotel. I really did think…" She frowned, then held out her hand. "I'm Pamela Winters."

The name meant nothing to Liz, but she had a strong impression of knowing… For no reason, an image came into her mind of Jeannie's friend Mhairi, sitting on Jeannie's bed, shaking out her wild blond curls. She became aware that she was staring rudely at the woman. "My name is Liz Brooks," she said, then hesitated. "Have you ever visited Seattle?"

"I've wanted to. Nearest I got was Salt Lake City in Utah." Looking closely at Liz, she frowned, then shrugged. "Guess I was mistaken, or you've got a double somewhere."

"Maybe we met in a previous lifetime," Liz said, testing.

Pamela laughed, obviously taking Liz's suggestion as a joke.

Which was all it had been, Liz assured herself.

But afterward, back at her hotel, Liz found herself thinking of Mhairi again. She was sitting in front of the powder-room vanity, which was built into a niche in the wall, mirrored above on all three sides. Spraying her hair, she tried to tame it into submission before going out to dinner with a group of local travel agents who had taken pity on her solitary state. She glanced sideways and saw countless images of herself going off into infinity.

As she dragged a wide-toothed comb through her curls, pulling her hair to the back of her head, she stared at all those images of herself, wishing Matt were here so that he could answer the questions that were rattling around in her muddled brain. Should she call him? No. She had told him she wouldn't call or write while she was away. It would be a sort of test of their feelings for each other, a month in limbo, thinking things over.

Seeing Robert's face superimposed on Matt's, thinking for a while it was Robert making love to her rather than Matt, had shaken her even more than she'd let him know.

She shuddered. She had thought regressing into another world was weird, but having Robert haunt her in this one was weirder still.

Matt had been so understanding. Would his understanding have stretched to encompass the feeling she hadn't confessed to? she wondered. What would his reaction have been if she had told him she'd felt guilty at finding herself in his arms when she came back to herself? Guilty as if she'd betrayed Robert by making love to Matt.

In the cold light of dawn she'd begun to wonder if her attraction to Matt was real or just left over from her attraction to Robert. Deposited on Matt because he was *there*, a handy substitute.

Don't think about it, she told herself. *Think about Mhairi, it's less confusing.*

Or is it, she wondered, picturing the young woman's merry smile. She could see her clearly in her memory, hear the sound of her voice. Something about Pamela Winters had reminded her strongly of Mhairi. *Everything in life is significant,* Matt had said.

What would she ask him if she did call him? Hypothetical questions, of course. But if she *did* once live as Jeannie Findlay, then was it also possible for other people from Jeannie's lifetime to be living in this one? Specifically, was it possible for Mhairi to be *alive*?

The next thought followed logically on the heels of the last, zinging through her brain like a bolt of summer lightning. If it was possible for Mhairi to come back, could Robert have done so also?

Quite suddenly her heart was thumping in her chest like a yo-yo. With her gaze fixed on her own pale reflection, duplicated over and over in the side mirror, Liz allowed herself for the first time to wonder if Robert Charles McAndrew could be walking around somewhere in the world, living, breathing, smiling his roguish smile.

Setting down her comb, she put her elbows on the vanity counter and lowered her head into her hands. Was she gradually coming to accept the truth of reincarnation? Was she ready to do so?

She sat up straight and looked at herself in the center mirror. One reflection only. No, she was not ready to believe. She might never be ready.

Nevertheless, dining in the Bay Tower Room that evening she found herself looking intently at the faces of the men, rather than at the fabulous view of the waterfront and harbor, wondering if this one or that one seemed familiar to her.

And then a man with a Zapata mustache leered back at her and she realized she'd better quit. "Tell me about the

Faneuil Hall Marketplace,'' she said to the woman sitting next to her. "Someone told me I should visit it while I'm here."

She wouldn't think of any of it until she returned to Seattle next month, she decided. And she certainly wasn't going to attempt any regressions on her own. What she needed was a strong dose of twentieth-century reality. She had to reestablish her connection with today's world.

IT HAD BEEN decided during her absence that Ione would regress her and Matt would listen in. Matt had left a message on Liz's answering machine, giving her the time and date. He also told her he'd missed her, and asked her to call him as soon as she returned.

She didn't call, although she got in early enough on the day before her scheduled appointment. Still conscious of some ambiguity where Matt was concerned, she decided to wait to see him alone until after the next regression. If she saw him first in Ione's company, it might be easier to judge how she really felt about him.

"I have a weird question," she informed the two of them after the initial greetings were over.

She had no idea what reason Matt might have given Ione for this new arrangement, but Ione didn't seem concerned with finding out. Matt looked spectacular, Liz thought. He was wearing an Irish knit sweater with fairly tight-fitting blue jeans. Definitely a tactile man. And she was a tactile woman. God, she wanted to touch him. His hair was as unruly as ever. Her fingers itched to smooth it back from his forehead the way she had done when he made love to her. She wanted to kiss the corners of his fine elegant mouth. This was no leftover attraction, she decided, feeling enormously relieved. She hadn't been exposed to Robert

Charles McAndrew for a month. This was the real thing. She wanted Matt Lockwood for himself alone.

Hanging on to her equilibrium by a thread, she told Matt and Ione about her meeting with the woman who seemed familiar. "Apparently my brain made some kind of connection," she said. "Something about Pamela Winters made me think of Mhairi. I suppose it could have been some small similarity—a gesture, perhaps, a facial expression, the angle of her head. But I found myself thinking that if, and only if, I were the reincarnation of Jeannie Findlay, then maybe this woman could be Mhairi. And then it occurred to me that if that were so, it might be possible for Robert to be alive again somewhere. Or is that too weird even for you guys?"

There was a silence. It was as though all three of them had stopped breathing for a minute or two. It was Ione who finally answered her. Matt evidently intended to be a passive auditor during this session. So far he hadn't offered any comments, but he had looked at her searchingly when she arrived, as though to make sure all was well with her. Then he'd smiled his wonderful brimming smile, letting her know the magnetism was still alive between them.

"It's not weird at all," Ione said. "It's entirely possible." She looked earnestly at Liz, whose pulse had begun beating rapidly. "I will admit, my dear, that it's also possible the woman you met merely reminded you of someone you've forgotten, someone from your childhood or infancy perhaps. However, my specialty, if you want to call it that, is regressing couples who've reincarnated in the same period, couples who knew each other in a previous lifetime. Occasionally there's another person—a child or brother or friend, or, once in a while, a whole group—"

"I'm sorry," Liz interrupted. "I can't quite swallow all that. I mean, think of the coincidence."

"Coincidence? Or plan?" Ione smiled sweetly. She inclined her head to one side. "Tell me, my dear, how would you *feel* about meeting Robert in this life?"

Liz considered the question seriously. "I guess he wouldn't *be* Robert, would he?"

"Not so you'd notice," Ione said with another smile.

From the corner of her eye, as Ione spoke, Liz saw Matt shake his head sharply at the older woman. Was he afraid Liz would start searching the streets for Jeannie's lover? Or was it just that he didn't like people getting jocular about this kind of thing?

"I'd feel weird," Liz decided. She shook her head. "I guess I'd just as soon he stayed back there with Jeannie." She shuddered suddenly as a thought occurred to her. "God, he might turn out to be someone like Allen Harper. No, thank you."

"Who's Allen Harper?" Matt asked.

"Just a CPA I knew once. Terribly boring." No one *you* need worry about, her eyes assured him. "Let's just put the whole Mhairi episode down to my imagination, shall we?"

"What is imagination when it's not imagination?" Matt asked, smiling wryly at her.

She laughed. "You sound like a Zen Buddhist."

He raised an eyebrow. "And what does a little Scottish milliner know about Buddhism?" he asked.

She made a face at him. "Jeannie knew about halcyon days," she reminded him.

Ione was looking from Liz to Matt, smiling benignly. If Matt hadn't told her anything about their changed relationship, she was making some pretty shrewd guesses, Liz decided.

There was something hovering at the edge of her mind, something scary, connected to something someone had said, or the way someone had looked. Her mind ran back through the conversation. Before she could draw any conclusions, however, Ione was speaking to her.

"Shall we begin?" she asked.

Liz nodded and lay down on the couch.

"Remember, you have to want to do this," Matt said.

"Okay." She looked at Ione. "Do you mind not using that bit about not being able to open my eyes?" she asked. "It made me nervous last time."

"I'm glad you told me." Ione smiled at her gently. "We're going to try a slightly different tack this time, Liz. Matt says you were concerned about the secret Jeannie was keeping from Robert. Going back through the transcripts we came across a reference to Rory Douglas."

"Jeannie's former husband."

Ione nodded. "We thought that perhaps if we try to regress you to the time when Jeannie was married to this Rory Douglas, we might get to the heart of the matter. Are you willing to try?"

"Sure," Liz said.

But it didn't work. After Ione had successfully hypnotized Liz, she tried several different ways to get her to come up with something about Rory, but Liz adamantly refused.

Finally Ione said, "It was obviously a secret Jeannie didn't want to let go of. Maybe we can try a back-door approach. How about if you go to a time when Jeannie thought about Rory?"

Almost immediately, Liz was aware of a room forming around her. Jeannie's room. Robert was there, talking quite loudly about something. Jeannie's face was pink, and not from pleasure.

"I'm not going, and that's that," Jeannie was saying.

"But there's no earthly reason why you shouldn't," Robert protested.

"There's a verra good reason," Jeannie said. "I don't want to go."

"Please, Jeannie," Robert said softly. "It would give me such pleasure to take you to my house. I've imagined you there so often."

There was no resisting him when he smiled at her in that boyish, pleading way. Shaking her head, Jeannie went to get her hat.

"I'm afraid, Robbie," she murmured.

"Now Jeannie, why should you worry? You've visited other grand houses in your time."

"Aye, and went in by the servants' entrance," she said shortly.

"Then it's high time you went in through the front door, where you belong," he said.

Jeannie fastened her hat at its proper angle. He was a dear man, her Robbie, but he had no idea what he was asking of her.

Mhairi popped her head out of her door as they went by. She must have been listening for their footsteps. "Another picnic?" she asked with a sly smile.

Jeannie made a face at her. There were no secrets between her and Mhairi, but Robert had no need to know that. "How's the bairn?" she asked. Mhairi's babe had been born two weeks before, a fine healthy boy with his mother's bright curls.

Mhairi was immediately distracted, going off into rhapsodies of description of her perfect wee Thomas, and Jeannie and Robert were another five minutes before they could get away.

Robert's house was as large as Jeannie had feared, built of brick and situated some three miles west of the city in the midst of pleasant grounds. He insisted on walking her through all of it, the drawing room, two parlors, library, conservatory, morning room. There was a special room for dining with a gasolier hanging over an enormous table, another for billiards, a ballroom, numerous bedrooms, dressing rooms, a huge kitchen with a pantry big enough to contain Jeannie's entire flat. There was even a special room for smoking. And a bathroom with a gleaming white tub on a wooden base and a sink next to it, with a water closet nearby.

Almost everywhere ancestral portraits glowered disapproval at Jeannie for daring to enter their hallowed halls. She wondered which one of them was Black Robert. Best she didn't find out, she thought, she might just rip him out of his frame for what he'd done to her family. There was a portrait of a younger Queen Victoria with her handsome Prince Albert, painted at Balmoral, hanging in the dining room. The queen herself had presented it to his father, Robert told her proudly.

By the time the tour was done, Jeannie's leg was dragging, her hip aching the way it did when she overtired it, and she was thoroughly intimidated by the splendor of Robert's surroundings.

It was a cold day and there were fires in most of the rooms. "There's enough coal burning in this house to keep me in fires for a year," Jeannie muttered, taking refuge from intimidation by grumbling. She glanced up at Robert. "Do you no get lost sometimes?"

He grinned. "Not so far. But I do get lonely, Jeannie."

"Aye, I can see why anyone might. Though you've enough servants to keep you company."

"Jeannie," he said chidingly. "Do you not like my house? Would you not like to live in a house like this?"

"It's a fine house. Bigger even than my Lady Ross's mansion over in New Town. Cleaner, too."

"You didn't answer my question, Jeannie."

She looked at him helplessly. "I know that. I've no answer for you, Robbie. It's no a place I'd ever aspire to, so why would I be thinking I'd like to live in such a one or no?"

He had led her back to his bedroom, which he'd shown her earlier. It was easy to see what he had in mind. Jeannie felt her limbs weakening as they always did when she thought of lying with Robert. There was a fire burning brightly in the grate in this room, too, and a wealth of marble-topped tables. There were chairs with tufting in their backs, a chaise longue, books in glass-fronted cases, figurines and vases and a couple of stuffed birds. Besides all that there was a bed big enough for four to sleep in should they be so inclined. All of it in blue and garnet, with long windows letting in the weak wintry sunlight.

"I like this room best because of its view of the laburnum trees—a fine sight in the springtime," Robert said. Then he looked at Jeannie, who was still standing in the doorway. "You don't feel comfortable here do you, Jeannie?"

She shook her head, sorry to hurt his feelings. "It's the servants, mostly," she said.

His mouth tightened. She would not want him angry with her, she decided. "One of them said something to offend you?" he asked.

"Och, no, would anyone dare with you holding on to my arm the way you did?"

But they had *looked*. The only friendly face had been that of the housekeeper, a Mrs. Currie. Oh, Jamie Kintyre had smiled a welcome, but only because Robert was looking at him hard. Robert's secretary—Fletcher—had gazed at her suspiciously down his long thin nose.

One of the kitchen maids had giggled. By the time they reached the kitchens, Jeannie's hip had been paining her and she hadn't been able to avoid limping a little. Was that what the kitchen maid had found so amusing? Or was it her clothing that had struck the girl as out of place? The cook had knuckled her head for her and she had flung her apron over her face to stifle her giggles. Robert hadn't seen; he'd been too busy pointing out all the modern features he'd had installed. But Jeannie had.

"I just don't belong here," she said flatly.

Robert took her in his arms and kissed her with such tenderness her heart seemed to swell in response. "Of course you belong here," he said firmly after the kiss was done. "You belong to me."

About to argue, Jeannie subsided. Impossible to be angered when she was this close to Robert. But, oh, she did wonder that men thought a woman would be complimented to be told she was a possession. *I'm my own woman,* she thought stubbornly, but still she didn't resist when Robert led her to the bed and started to take off her coat.

"Perhaps it was my gloves," she muttered, still thinking of the kitchen maid.

She had knitted the gloves herself, to replace her old worn ones, needing the warmth these cold days.

"What's wrong with your gloves?" Robert asked, unpinning her hat and setting it aside on a chest.

"Well, for one thing, they're made from used wool. I bought this old cardigan from the ragman, you see, and unraveled it and wound the wool on a book in hanks. Then I washed it and let it dry and knitted it up. But it's a funny color, don't you think, halfway between gray and black?"

She spread her hands in front of her, looking at the offending gloves. "I don't know if there's even a name for this color."

Robert tugged the gloves from her fingers and laid them aside, then took her in his arms again. "You amaze me, Jeannie, the economies you practice. Is there anything you don't use twice over? I think you'd sooner go hungry than lower the amount of money you put away every week."

The truth hurt. Rory Douglas had said much the same to her several times, though not in such a kind, loving way. Robert meant no criticism by the remark, she knew, but she was still smarting from the servants' knowing glances, and made nervous by the bulk of Robert's house around her.

She blew up at him, yanking herself free of his arms. "Certainly I would go hungry, and frequently do. You will never understand, never, the yearning of a poor person to have enough money someday. Not a lot of money, Robert Charles McAndrew, just enough."

"I wasn't mocking you, Jeannie," he said, looking apologetic. "I think it's astonishing how you manage, your will to survive, to grow. I was admiring you, Jeannie."

Somewhat mollified, she allowed him to put his arms around her again. "You canna blame a Scot for behaving like a Scot, Robert," she chided him.

He grinned, looking down at her. "Do you know the story of the Scotsman who was run over by a carriage in Princes Street?" he asked. "He'd run out to pick up a sixpence. 'Death by natural causes,' the judge ruled."

Jeannie's laugh rang out, but her smile faded as Robert eased her toward the massive bed. "I'm not sure I want to get anywhere near yon bed," she grumbled.

"You don't think it will be nicer than the two of us crammed into yours like two sausages in one skin?"

She laughed again. How could she not? "But what if your servants hear us?" she asked.

"There's no one anywhere near this end of the house," he assured her.

She looked up at him, exasperated. "And you think they won't wonder when I don't come downstairs for an hour?" she demanded. "I've been in kitchens of grand houses, Robbie my lad, and you can believe me, there's plenty of conjecturing goes on about the habits of the likes of you."

"I'll try to be fast," he said with a lecherous grin that made her laugh in spite of herself. She couldn't stay angered at him, whatever the cause.

She had to admit, she thought some time later, there was a lot to be said for comfort. Feathers were much more relaxing than the chaff stuffed in her mattress.

She was lying next to Robert in the great bed, looking up at the swath of material draping its head. Robert was kissing her breasts. She had never liked Rory to touch her there, but when Robert did it, she thrilled to it. Why did she keep thinking of Rory today? Because she should tell Robert about him. This was not the time to do it, though.

There was nothing Robert did to her that displeased her, she decided. Now he was touching her in her secret place and he'd raised his head to look at her. He liked to look at her when he touched her there. She raised a hand to stroke his face and he turned his mouth to plant a kiss in her palm. "I love you, bonny Jean," he whispered.

She closed her hand over the kiss and gave him one on the mouth. "I love you, Robbie," she murmured.

How long, she wondered? How long till he tired of her? Not yet a while, she hoped. Not yet a long while.

"JEANNIE," a woman's voice said somewhere a long way away. "Jeannie, I want you to come forward a while. A week or two maybe. Come forward to some more significant time connected with Rory Douglas.''

Was this not significant? she wondered. Then she felt herself slipping deeper into the darkness that was like sleep, yet wasn't sleep.

"HURRY UP with those mugs, there's a good lass," Will Moffatt urged.

"I'm washing them fast as I can," Jeannie said, exasperated. "I've only two hands as you can plainly see."

"Saucy wench," the landlord muttered, but he backed away from the scullery. He'd felt the side of Jeannie's tongue before and he was something of a timid man.

Jeannie finished the mugs and went out to serve behind the counter, glad to be where she could avoid pinching fingers and hands that grasped certain parts of the body where no strangers' hands were allowed. Since coming to work at the Horse and Hounds, she had learned to move quickly past the customers. But one thing else she had learned as well: no man improved in nature by drinking. No matter how respectable he might be in his everyday life, give him a few pints of ale or a couple of drams of whiskey and he was Lothario himself.

It was Saturday—payday—and the overheated pub was packed to the rafters. Prostitutes were out in force, flaunting their silks and satins in the flaring gaslight, prowling like vultures after their prey.

Glancing past the brightly gilded spirit casks, plain wooden tables and motley collection of chairs, Jeannie was horrified to see Robert walk in. It was one thing for him to know where she worked in the evening—she was glad to have that worry off her conscience, truth be known. But for him to *see* her…not to mention how this rabble would jeer should he speak to her…

She walked past him rapidly, flinging over her shoulder to Will Moffatt, "I need a breath of air."

Robert took the hint and didn't speak to her until he'd followed her outside. Then he grabbed her wrist and pulled her toward him.

"Are you daft, Robbie?" she objected, then saw it wasn't passion that had motivated him but anger. His blue eyes were hot in a way she'd never seen before, his face pale, his mouth set in a straight line.

For a minute he stared down at her in silence as though choosing his words. His grip on her wrist was painful, but she suffered it, realizing that he was not only angry but in distress. "What is it, Robbie?" she whispered.

"Why didn't you tell me, Jeannie?" he demanded.

"Tell you what?" she asked, mystified. "You knew I worked here, you told me Jamie Kintyre followed me—"

"I'm not talking about that. I'm talking about Rory Douglas, Jeannie. Rory Douglas, the man you were married to once. Did you forget about Rory Douglas, Jeannie, or did you not think he was important enough to tell me about?"

It had happened then, the thing she'd feared from the start. Robert's secretary had made enquiries, she'd be willing to wager.

"I'm sorry, Robert," she whispered. "I was feared to tell you."

"What cause have I ever given you to fear me?" he demanded.

She shook her head. Useless to point out he was frightening her now.

"I want you to tell me about him," he said sternly.

"What point?" she asked wearily. "Since you know it already."

"I want to hear it from your own lips." He was beside himself, she saw. There was no reasoning with him.

There was a chill to the rain that spoke of snow to follow and there was not enough shelter under the overhanging eaves. Wearing only a thin blouse with her long black skirt, Jeannie was shivering, as much from fright as from the damp and the cold. But Robert, in his warm overcoat, did not seem to notice.

Jeannie let her wrist stay limp in his grasp. "I was married to Rory Douglas," she admitted. "The same Rory Douglas that robbed the Bank of Scotland in 1881."

"After befriending the cashier and two of the clerks."

"So they said."

"You want me to believe you didn't know about it beforehand?" he said grimly. "Was my bank to suffer the same fate?"

"Rory is dead," she said, thinking he must not know that fact. "He shot himself when his attempt failed."

"After killing two men."

"He was a boy, Robert. Twenty years old. He was desperate. We had no food, no promise of food. It was wrong, yes, but you must understand…"

"I understand that you lied to me, misled me, duped me. You helped him, didn't you? You were about to try the same trick on me."

In despair she looked up at him. He had finally released her wrist, but there was an expression of disgust on his face as he stared blindly down at her.

Turning from him, she started to run as best she could, not into the pub, but away from it, away from Robert. Her only thought was that she couldn't bear to see the man she loved look at her so.

At the corner, she glanced back before crossing the street. He was standing where she'd left him, standing very straight and tall under the lamplight outside the pub. He was staring into the darkness after her, but making no attempt to follow her.

She had reached the Lawnmarket, stumbling and slipping over the cobbles, her left leg dragging, before she realized she was drenched to the skin and shivering. It didn't seem to matter.

Her flat was dark and cold, so cold she could hardly light a match for the gas. Shivering convulsively she made several attempts to start a fire. The coal was poor quality and slow to burn, but eventually she kindled a small blaze and stretched her hands to it.

There was an old blanket in her kist, and her father's plaid lay stretched out on her bed. She should fetch one of them to wrap around her against the freezing cold. But somehow she couldn't find the energy to get up and cross the little room. Feeling exhausted she stayed crouched in front of the grate, finally sliding down into a heap on the uncovered floor. She was too grieved to cry, though it seemed all the tears in the world were bunched up in her throat.

It was over then, the lovely dream. She had known it would end. And now it had.

Several hours later she awoke and realized she had a fever. Her hair was still damp and she was shivering again, the fire having gone out, but her forehead felt as hot as a furnace and there was a severe pain in her side.

When she stood up her hip almost gave way, and she had to move slowly, like a bent old woman, from the kist to the chair to the bed. Her teeth chattered as she pulled the worn plaid over her. It had been foolish to run away as she had without her coat and shawl. She should make some tea—or some broth—to warm herself.

Och, no, she didna have the strength.... Already the

darkness was reaching for her, swallowing her up. Thankfully she let herself slide down into it.

"THAT WAS AMAZING," Ione said. Her eyes were wide behind her bifocals.

Liz came awake stretching and blinking as usual. Her head felt wooly, as though she were still running a fever. "It seemed a long way back this time," she said slowly.

"It was a long way back," Ione told her. "I had quite a time getting you to wake up."

"You mean there was a problem?" Liz sat up straight on the couch and swung her feet to the floor. "I could get stuck back there?"

"No way," Matt said. He was still sitting in the chair opposite her, looking at her now with his clinical expression in place. For Ione's benefit, she hoped. "Even if we left you to it, you'd wake up by yourself."

Liz sighed. "That's a comfort." She shook her head. "Gosh, poor Jeannie." She smiled wryly at Matt. "I told you all men were rats. Imagine Robert letting her run off in the rain like that."

"He thought she'd lied to him," Ione pointed out.

"Well, that's no excuse. Besides, she hadn't lied, except by omission. She had nothing to do with the robbery or its planning. She was completely innocent. Somehow she'd managed to survive the scandal, get her reputation reinstated, change her name back. Why should she ruin all that by telling Robert the truth? It was over, it had no relevance to the way she felt about Robert. In any case, she was afraid of losing him."

Matt's gaze was fixed on her face. "You remember all that?"

Liz laughed nervously. "I do seem to, don't I?"

"I will listen to the tape with great interest," Ione said.

"This is the most detailed regression I've ever run into—
even to the flaring gaslights, the gilded barrels. I'll make
you a copy, Matt."

Matt nodded, standing up. "I'll have Sally schedule an
appointment for Liz next week."

"Good," Ione said absently, intent on rewinding the
tape.

THE APARTMENT DOOR had barely closed behind Matt before Liz was in his arms. His kiss was warm, tender,
searching, reminding Liz forcibly of Robert's kisses.

She stiffened and he released her at once. "Problem?"
he asked.

She took a deep breath and fixed her gaze on the ridged
pattern of his Irish knit sweater. "Not too long ago I was
making love to Robert," she explained, then went on in a
rush before he could interrupt. "I know it was Jeannie, but
it *seemed* like me. And I've begun to wonder how much
of my attraction to you is left over from Jeannie's feelings
for Robert. There's guilt mixed in there, too. As though I
shouldn't be making love to you when I love…when Jeannie loves Robert."

"Poor mixed-up Liz."

He touched her hair and she lifted her head and met his
gaze. His eyes were gentle. "Maybe you could try to compartmentalize," he suggested. "Separate your feelings.
One block for Robert that belonged to Jeannie a long, long
time ago. Another block for me—all your own—now, today, here in the good old U.S.A."

"I'm not sure I can do that."

He put his arms around her and held her close. "What
do you feel now?"

His body felt so good against hers, solid and real and
warm. "As if I'd come home," she answered honestly.

"You are home," he told her. "And this is me, Matt Lockwood, ungrammatical but sincere, welcoming you." Ducking his head to hers, he kissed her very thoroughly, awakening every cell in her body to joyous life.

"Let's eat our pizza and see what happens next," he said when they came up for air.

Liz laughed. "God, you're so romantic," she teased. He had meant to make her laugh, she realized. It was too easy for things to get spooky in this reincarnation business. Laughter helped clear the air.

It had been Liz's idea to pick up a pizza on the way to her apartment. Matt had suggested taking her out, but she had pleaded exhaustion from jet lag. She *was* tired, but she had a feeling her main motivation had been to be alone with Matt. She wanted to gauge her response to him, find out once and for all if her feelings for him were genuine. Judging by that second kiss, she thought happily as she served the pizza in the kitchen, her feelings were one hundred percent flawless gold.

"How much do you remember about Rory Douglas?" Matt asked half an hour later. "Jeannie told Robert very little before she ran off."

Setting a piece of pizza crust down on her plate, Liz pondered his question for a moment. "I do believe I remember all of it," she said at last. "It seems to me that I read an account of the bank robbery in a newspaper. The police didn't tell me anything, they were more concerned with my part in Rory's plans than in telling me how my husband had died. I was so grieved and confused. I loved Rory Douglas. We married when we were sixteen—he was the first lad to look at me and not be put off by my limping. Our lives were not easy, but I loved him and they wouldn't tell me for the longest time how he had died. I thought I was going to prison for something I'd known nothing about, but they finally let me go for want of proof.''

Abruptly she sat up straight. ''Listen to me. I'm talking in first person, as if it was my memory, not Jeannie's.''

Matt looked at her steadily.

She took a deep breath. ''You believe it *is* my memory, of course.''

He nodded. ''I think you're beginning to accept it, too, Liz.''

She shook her head. ''No way. Don't go getting any ideas like that, Matt Lockwood. This is still an experimental exercise for me.'' She sighed. ''Poor Jeannie, though, she was very sick, wasn't she?''

''It would seem so.''

She was silent for a while, then she took a sip of the burgundy they'd opened to go with the pizza and started speaking again. As she told the story she felt as if she was reliving the horror and pity that had come over Jeannie as she read the account herself.

''Rory entered the bank at eleven o'clock in the morning, when the clerks were busy at their desks and the depositors few. Because of that, the police said he'd planned it well. Anyway, he spoke to the cashier through a glass partition and said, 'Open the door or I'll kill you.'''

Liz shook her head. ''Because he'd had drinks with Rory the night before, the cashier thought he was joking. He *laughed*. So then Rory jumped up on the counter and over the partition. From somewhere he'd obtained a gun. The cashier struggled with him and the gun went off, killing the man. Rory grabbed the money the cashier had been counting and ran out of the bank. A butcher who was just entering gave chase and other people joined in. They caught up with him at the end of a close. There was no way out and he must have been desperate. He shot the butcher, then turned the gun on himself.''

"And where was Jeannie all this time?" Matt asked.

"At home, sewing." Liz stared beyond him at the window, her gaze going beyond her own reflection in the glass, beyond the lights of Seattle, fixing instead on that other world that lived in the recesses of her own brain.

"She was a seamstress then," she went on. "Making sixpence a shirt. Rory worked on the railway. No, he'd lost his job. He was injured in the head in a train collision. In November, it was. The company settled with him for thirty pounds. For a while we made do but then the money was gone, most of it on whiskey. Rory hadn't been a drinker ever, but after the accident he was forever going out for a wee dram. He found a part-time job as a milkman, carrying twenty huge cans at a time up and down tenement steps. It was a bad winter and his hands were chapped and cracked with the frost and the cold. He'd cry sometimes, coming home. I'd have to hold his hands in mine to warm them."

She glanced at Matt, realizing she'd slipped into first person again. "It's so real, Matt. I can see him, a good-looking dark-haired boy, no more than twenty. He couldn't seem to think straight after the accident. He was always talking about getting rich, getting back what was due him."

She sighed. "It's so real," she said again.

Matt came over and pulled her up into his arms. It felt good to be held. Half of her was still back there in Edinburgh, grieving for Rory Douglas, half of her glad to be here in the twentieth century—warm, comfortable, safe.

"Did Jeannie explain it all to Robert?" he asked.

She shook her head against his shoulder. "I don't know. I only seem to know up to where Jeannie ran away from him and then crawled into her bed. That bed was *hard*, Matt—no softness in it at all. I don't know why the hell people call it the good old days. As far as I can tell they weren't, except maybe for people like Robert.''

He ran his hands soothingly over her back. ''It was Jeannie's life, Liz. Compartmentalize, remember.''

She moved a little in his arms. ''I've wanted to ask you something,'' she said, her voice muffled against his sweater.

''Ask away.''

''When I—when Jeannie makes love with Robert, like today, how does that make you feel?''

''Embarrassed as hell,'' he said, then laughed softly. ''I'll amend that. The last time, when we were alone, it was okay, just part of the regression. Today, with Ione there, was a whole other scenario. I think Ione suspects that you and I…well, anyway, Ione and I are old friends. She never misses a chance to tease me and she kept darting knowing glances at me, so I suggested she bring you forward. However,'' he added, setting Liz a little away from him and bringing his slanting eyebrows and brimming smile into full play, ''I've got to admit, it affects me in another way. I wanted you, Liz. Sitting right there in Ione's office, listening to you, watching you, I wanted you.''

His expression became serious. ''All the same, if you are still unsure of your feelings, or have any doubts about me one way or another, I'll wait until you are through with the regressions and can look at me more objectively.''

Liz gazed up at his lean, scholarly face, the level gray eyes, the wry sexy smile hovering around the corners of his mouth, the shaggy brown hair that seemed to invite her fingers. ''I don't see how I could ever look at you objectively, Matt.''

He laughed, then looked closely at her. "Do I take that as an invitation?" he asked.

Instead of answering, Liz put her arms around his neck and planted her mouth squarely on his, letting her lips part at once to his gently probing tongue.

A minute later, he took her hand and led her into her bedroom. Sitting with her on the bed, he helped her slip out of her sweater, removed her bra, then trailed a line of kisses over her breasts. "You are so lovely," he murmured as his lips found her already erect nipples.

Robert had kissed her breasts, Liz remembered, but she didn't feel as if Robert were here now. There was only Matt helping her to remove the rest of her clothing, stripping off his own, pulling her alongside him so that their bodies were pressed together.

It was difficult to tell where Matt Lockwood began and she stopped, Liz thought after a while. It was amazing to her how choreographed their lovemaking was, as though they had planned it out on paper beforehand, so that when she lifted a shoulder, his hand was waiting to slip under it. When her hands searched for warmth his hips were there to provide it. They turned, lifted, rolled and arched in precise contrapuntal movements that brought excitement and satisfaction to both of them.

Liz wasn't sure if time had stopped or expanded. It certainly didn't seem to matter, though she had lived her whole life with one eye on the clock, always punctual, always organized. In Matt's arms the very concept of time ceased to exist. She was aware only of his mouth, his hands, his tongue, his wonderfully firm body.

He was kneeling over her now, his hands moving slowly, exquisitely slowly, down from her shoulders. His thumbs brushed over her breasts, her belly, the patch of hair that was even brighter and curlier than the hair on her head. He lingered there, touching her lightly, his facial expression showing that he was totally engrossed, fascinated by texture and color.

When she wriggled her hips, wanting to encourage him to take her, he lifted his head and frowned playfully at her. "You're not allowed to move," he said sternly.

"Since when?" she demanded.

"Since right now. I've missed you for a whole month and I'm not interested in any fast sprint to the finish. I'm in the mood for a marathon."

"And I have no choice?"

"Of course you have. Just don't move."

She laughed, then lay obediently still, her gaze fixed on his face, imagining the moment when his expression would change and he would stretch himself over her and enter her, his mouth claiming hers, so that their bodies were touching, pore to pore, from head to toe.

No, first he wanted to play. She saw the mischievous curve of his mouth as he leaned his head down and touched her lightly with his tongue, then more demandingly. Then his fingers and mouth were working together to bring her arching upward, her whole concentration fixed on the place where his attentions were centered.

He entered her at the height of her explosion, taking her by surprise, sending her senses skyrocketing into yet another explosion and another, while he lay over her. Unmoving himself now, he smiled his wonderful smile at her, waiting until she lay gasping under him before starting to move again, deliberately, slowly, starting the whole unbelievably marvelous cycle over again.

She smiled up at him. "Sadist," she managed to say through her breathlessness.

He grinned. "Not at all. I'm just a patient person."

She loved his face, the way his eyebrows slanted when

he puckered his forehead, the strong shape of his nose, the star bursts radiating from the pupils of his gray eyes, the laugh lines at their corners, more lines bracketing his sensual mouth.

He was a rare man, Matt Lockwood, she thought contentedly—warm, sensitive, caring. She suspected she might be falling in love with him. It might even be possible, she thought, lying there smiling up at him, enjoying the smooth thrusting power of his lean but muscular body, the changing expressions on his face as passion took him over—it might even be possible that he could be falling in love with her.

How amazing it was, she thought, that so much cool flesh could produce so much heat. Lifting her hips to his, she found and matched his rhythm, feeling tremor after tremor go through her as they moved together....

Something was happening.

Alarm shot through her as a faint buzzing sound began in her ears. A familiar numbness was creeping over her limbs and body. She could still feel her body lying on the bed but the bed itself had become harder. To her horror, she could see Robert's brilliant smile flickering on the corners of Matt's mouth. At the same time Robert's bold blue eyes seemed to hover somewhere in the depths of Matt's gray irises. His body felt different under her hands, wider in the shoulders, narrower in the waist. With a supreme effort she stopped herself from calling out Robert's name.

It was growing dark now. She felt that she was tumbling through time and space, tumbling away from Matt, away from Robert, away from herself. Hands were pulling at her, lifting her, turning her, and she was hot, alarmingly hot, yet cold at the same time. Frightened, too, so frightened that she was going to die.

CHAPTER NINE

"HOW LONG has she been unconscious?" Robert's voice asked.

Jeannie wanted to tell him she wasn't unconscious, but she seemed to be down at the bottom of a deep, deep mine shaft and she didn't have the strength to make her voice carry all that way. She couldn't even see light at the top of the shaft, only a faint sprinkling of tiny dots of brightness, like faraway stars in an exceptionally dark sky.

"She comes and goes," Mhairi answered. "Most of the time she's delirious."

"It's all my fault," Robert said.

It was an astonishing thing. She had been dreaming that Robert was making love to her and now here he was. Magic. Why was she so surprised that he was here? She couldn't remember, she couldn't think—somebody kept bumping her up and down and her brain was all scrambled.

She was being carried. That was it. Robert had wrapped her in a warm blanket and now he was carrying her down the stairs. Her eyes seemed to be glued shut and she didn't have strength enough to speak, but she wanted to speak, wanted to tell him…

"It's all right, Jeannie," Robert said. "I'm not taking you to hospital. I'm taking you to my house."

She felt cold air on her face and then a few drops of rain and she was shivering again and coughing, then spinning down and down in the dark and the cold.

"I DIDN'T DIE," Jeannie said in a surprised voice.

Robert smiled down at her, his blue eyes shining. "So I see." He kissed her gently on the forehead. "Welcome back, Jeannie."

She looked around the huge, beautifully furnished room, herself in the middle of it in Robert's enormous bed, wearing a nightgown of the softest possible material, a white gown with little pink rosebuds all over it. She had vague memories of people she didn't know, women washing her, feeding her, putting welcome cold flannels on her forehead, taking off her nightgown when it was wet with sweat, replacing it with one that felt cool and dry. One woman had sat by her bedside often, knitting away with pale blue wool. Mrs. Currie, Robert's housekeeper. She had talked to Jeannie occasionally, her soft, country-woman's voice weaving in and out of Jeannie's feverish dreams along with the click of her knitting needles and the continual sound of Jeannie's coughing.

A man had been there, too—a tall angular man with a square gray beard and the smell of carbolic about him. A doctor. She remembered him putting a tube to her chest with his ear to the other end, shaking his head as he muttered about years of malnutrition, overcrowded conditions, lack of resistance to any infection that came along. Pneumonia. She distinctly remembered him mentioning pneumonia. He had looked very grave, listening to her chest.

Robert had been there, too, always, holding her hand, stroking her hair, talking to her. Calling her back when she wanted to rest, wanted to slip down into darkness. "How long have I been here?" she asked.

"Just over a week." Robert touched her cheek lightly. "You were extremely ill, Jeannie. The crisis came yesterday and your fever broke last night."

She wrinkled her forehead, trying to remember when she

had become unwell. And then she did remember. "You were angry with me," she said accusingly. "You thought I was going to rob you."

He touched her forehead, stroking wisps of damp hair away from it. "Dash it, Jeannie, I should never have suspected you. I am so sorry. I was completely distraught when Fletcher told me about Rory Douglas...."

"I knew it was yon Fletcher," Jeannie said in a voice filled with satisfaction. "But I didna have anything to do with the robbery," she added firmly. "I wouldna be party to such..." She had to stop as a fit of coughing overtook her. She had coughed all the time during her delirium, she remembered. Someone had given her a soothing syrup each time.

"Don't tax yourself," Robert said, helping her to sit up, putting pillows behind her shoulders. "Don't try to talk. I know all of it now. I talked to Mhairi and she told me the whole story, how Rory was hurt in the train collision, how poor you both were and hungry, and that you knew nothing of any of it until it was over and he was dead. She told me when she came for me, the day after you became ill. And you told me yourself, when your fever was so high." He smiled at her with something of his old teasing manner. "I should say you harangued me, Jeannie. You were very angry with me, shouting sometimes."

"Well and you deserved it, no doubt," she said complacently.

"I did. I should have known, Jeannie. I should have known you'd never do anything dishonest."

"Aye, you should have," she agreed. She drank the water Robert offered her, enjoying the warmth of his arm around her shoulders holding her, the feel of his hand over hers holding the cup. "I'm awfu' weak," she complained, leaning back.

"It will take a while for you to regain your strength, the doctor said. We have to give you plenty of good beef broth and the tonic he's had made up for you and you must rest.''

"Well, I canna rest long," Jeannie said. "I've work to do. Bills owing to the wholesaler, orders to fill."

"You'll rest as long as necessary," Robert said sternly. "Now that I've got you here, I'm not going to let you go."

She raised a hand weakly and touched his golden hair, loving the silken feel of it against her fingers. "Och, you're good to me, Robbie. But I canna stay here now I'm better." Her eyes closed. "It wouldna be right," she muttered. "I'll no be any man's kept mistress, Robbie. Not even yours."

She felt him take the cup from her fingers. "Sleep now. Don't worry about it."

The darkness was welcoming this time. Soothing and quiet. She sank down into it, letting it fold over her. Tomorrow, she thought. Tomorrow she would be well and she'd go back to work.

"IT'S ALL RIGHT, Liz," Matt said softly as she opened her eyes. "You regressed again."

She looked up at him, bewildered that it was so dark in the room she could see only the outline of his face. Her head ached, her ears felt stuffed with cotton, her eyes gummy. She was so sleepy. No matter how she tried she couldn't get her eyes to open all the way.

They had been making love. She had regressed to Robert in the middle of making love. "Oh, Matt," she murmured. "I'm so sorry. I didn't mean to go back. I *wanted* it to be you making love to me."

"I know. It's okay. Sleep now. Just sleep."

SHE AWOKE again to the smell of coffee brewing and the sound of someone rattling around in her kitchen. Alarmed for all of fifteen seconds, she remembered that Matt had stayed with her. She had come half awake several times in the night, had felt his arms holding her securely against his bare muscular chest and had drifted back to sleep immediately.

Shrugging into her blue terry robe, she padded into the kitchen. Matt was bent over the dishwasher, digging out a skillet from the back. He looked freshly showered and shampooed, his hair slightly damp, curling over his forehead and ears. He was fully dressed in his jeans and Irish sweater. Liz glanced out the window and winced at the brightness of sunshine on the white concrete wall around her veranda. "How much burgundy did I drink last night?" she asked.

Matt straightened, studying her face, looking so healthy and bright-eyed and vigorous she almost winced again. "No more than a glass."

"I feel definitely hung over."

He put his hands on her shoulders, looking solemnly down at her. "How much do you remember?"

"Everything. That was quite a night, wasn't it?" She felt awkward, embarrassed, unable to look directly at him. "I regressed spontaneously, huh? I thought I wasn't supposed to do that anymore."

"Subconsciously you must have wanted to."

"I guess so." She attempted a smile. "Do I smell coffee?"

"Why don't I bring you a cup in bed? You look as though you could use more rest."

She shook her head. "I always look like this in the morning. Three cups of black coffee, a slice of plain toast and a shower will fix me right up."

"I've made pancake batter," he said with a rueful grin. "Think you can face pancakes?"

She grimaced. "After the shower maybe."

The pancakes were delicious, light and fluffy, far better than her father's, though Jake had always proclaimed himself pancake king of the west. "I think I'm going to survive," she said as she laid down her fork. She still couldn't quite bring herself to meet Matt's eyes.

"I have an idea," he said cheerily, pouring more coffee. "How does a day on Mount Rainier sound? How about we get away from Robert and Jeannie altogether? Just you and me and the mountain."

"And a couple of hundred tourists?"

"Tourists we can ignore."

Feeling suddenly excited, she nodded in agreement. She loved Washington's majestic mountain, always felt her spirits lift when it was on view. She hadn't visited it in months. "I guess there'll be some snow," she murmured. "But we could hike some of the easier trails maybe."

"How about I run home for a jacket and hat?" He looked down at his shoes. "I'll pick up some stronger footwear, too."

"We could stop at your place on the way," Liz suggested.

Matt was clearing dishes into the sink and didn't answer for a moment. Then, in a voice evidently meant to sound casual he said, "Better if I go now, I think. Give you time to get ready."

He didn't want to take her to his house, she decided as she went into her bedroom to put on some makeup and braid her hair. Now why was that? Someone in his house he didn't want to see her? Or neighbors who might gossip? Why should it matter? He was divorced. Or so he had said. She was suddenly struck by how little she knew about his living arrangements. She didn't even know what area of Seattle he lived in.

On a sudden impulse she pulled a telephone directory out of a bureau drawer. There were quite a few Lockwoods listed, including a Meredith Lockwood. No Matthew, however. The yellow pages gave only his clinic number and address.

So his private phone was unlisted. Nothing wrong with that. So was her own. It was the only way to avoid being telemarketed around the clock. All the same she felt a little uneasy.

By the time Matt came back she'd made her bed, loaded the dishes, run a machine full of laundry and was dressed and ready to go.

"I guess you don't live too close," she said, hoping her attempt to be casual was more successful than his had been.

"Heavy traffic," he said ambiguously.

She wasn't going to worry about it, she decided. Today was an unexpected vacation; she wasn't going to worry about anything.

Warmly clad in down-filled ski jackets, knitted hats and hiking boots, they first hiked the Trail of the Shadows out of Longmire, stepping briskly through the forest on the wide path that circled the numerous mineral springs. They stopped to admire a bountiful crop of beautiful but deadly gold-and-orange amanita mushrooms and caught sight of a log cabin in a small clearing. Liz had forgotten the homestead cabin James Longmire's son had built. And she had never noticed the plaque that said it was built in 1888.

"Not so easy to get away, after all," she murmured, taking off her gloves so that she could feel the texture of the rough old logs. This house had been erected in the same year Jeannie Findlay had gone picnicking with Robert Charles McAndrew.

Matt put an arm around her shoulders and urged her onward. "Now who's seeing significance everywhere?" he asked her with a grin.

They drove up to Paradise and tramped the snow-covered Nisqually Vista Trail, which finished at an incredible view of Nisqually Glacier's snout. It was a lovely day, cold but bright, and the air smelled clean and clear. A couple of Clark's Nutcrackers, perched in a nearby fir, cocked their heads and scolded them for invading private space.

Later, after hot dogs and cocoa, they stood on the top floor of the visitors' center looking out at Rainier's massive, glacier-scoured summit and the saw-toothed peaks of the Tatoosh range that ringed the rest of the area. Liz felt clearheaded and light of heart. "This is wonderful," she murmured. "Last couple of times I came up I couldn't see anything but clouds." She sighed happily. "No wonder the local Indians called the mountain God. Look how close that sky is."

"It's almost as blue as your eyes." Matt put an arm around her. "I take it you're feeling better?"

"I feel great," she told him. "There's something about mountains that makes everything else seem small and unimportant."

She fell silent, still gazing up at the icy, sun-bright slopes of the summit. How many people had looked up at this mountain over the ages? How many had tramped through the snow, or hiked the mountain meadows in the summer? Often the snow didn't melt until mid-July. Then the meadows turned white again with avalanche lilies, blue with lupine, red with Indian paintbrush. Every year the same miracle of rebirth occurred.

Rebirth.

Not exactly rebirth, she amended. Each flower was a new one, not a complete replica of the old. What was that then, reincarnation?

Peripherally she was aware that Matt's gaze was fixed on her face, but the knowledge was secondary to the almost mystic hold the mountain had on her. She felt in tune with it, as she'd felt in tune with Edinburgh's Castle Rock. As she felt when she looked out from her balcony and saw the moon. Often as a child she'd spent school vacations on the Washington coast and had marveled at night at the constellations, so clearly visible away from the city lights. There was a stillness in her mind now, as there had surely been then, a recognition that the world was full of limitless possibilities.

"People really do believe we were here before," she murmured. "I don't mean here on this mountain, I mean here on earth."

She shook her head. "I want to be convinced, Matt, but something inside me is still switched on to reject. It's as though all my life I've perceived the world and my part in it in a certain way, and all at once you want me to perceive it differently. I have a feeling I'm waiting for absolute proof. But there probably isn't any."

His gray eyes held hers, so clear she thought she could see all the way to the back of them. "Give it time," he said.

Liz nodded, then said quietly. "There's no other possible explanation of all that's been happening to me, is there?"

He shook his head, then gave her his brimming smile and took her in his arms. They were alone for the moment, though they wouldn't be for long, judging by the distant clatter of booted feet on the ramp that led up to the top deck. There was a very solemn look on Matt's face. "I love you, Liz," he said softly.

Her heart turned over. Whatever she might have expected him to say at this moment, it wasn't that. She stared at him. "Just like that?" she exclaimed.

He looked puzzled.

"Most men would sooner cut out their tongues than say those words," she said, laughing. "I didn't have to hint or anything. You just came right out with it."

His expressive eyebrows slanted up. "I think I've mentioned before that your former choice of males leaves a lot to be desired." His smile turned rueful. "Is that all the response I get to my brave declaration?" he asked.

She smiled mischievously up at him. "My friend Erica said I should look for a man who makes my heart go pit-a-pat."

"And?"

"You make it bounce around like a rubber ball."

"Is that good?"

"I think so." She touched his cheek. "I love you, Matt. I think I fell in love with you the minute I saw you." She sighed.

"But?"

"But I still have this guilty feeling that I ought to be faithful to Robert Charles McAndrew. I can't seem to get away from it, no matter how ridiculous it seems."

He smiled, seemed about to say something, then changed his mind, kissing her again instead.

He'd never shown the slightest discomfort when hearing her talk of Robert, she realized. Not even when she'd described making love to him. Anyone else might have been jealous of her feelings for Robert. Allen Harper had been jealous when she mentioned the boy she'd had a crush on in third grade. Evidently Matt Lockwood was sure enough of himself not to worry about competition from a long-ago lover.

Somewhere in her memory something stirred, a feeling that if she really concentrated, she would realize...

"All we need know for now," Matt said, his gaze fixed lovingly on her face, "is that I love you, and it's entirely possible you might love me."

The elusive memory had drifted away. Perhaps it would come back later if she didn't push herself. "Doesn't sound like a fair exchange," she pointed out.

"It'll do for now. It'll all come out okay later."

She looked at him curiously. "You're sure of that?"

"I am."

About then a large group of children came up behind them and started running around the outside perimeter of the lounge, climbing up to look out of the windows. Matt and Liz started slowly down the circular ramp, hand in hand, stopping to check out the display areas, which Liz had loved as a child. Mount Rainier was first climbed in 1870, she read on a card. Jeannie would have been nine years old.

How impossible it was to free her thoughts completely of that other world. All day, it seemed, a small part of her mind had been occupied with wondering if Jeannie had stayed with Robert, if the two had enjoyed a happy ending after all.

Matt took her to dinner at the Copper Creek Inn at the foot of the mountain, where the food was excellent and the atmosphere rustic. It was a popular place and crowded. There was no chance to speak intimately. Which was just as well, Liz thought. Her mind was on overload, it needed a chance to coast.

"Tired?" Matt asked as they approached the outskirts of Seattle.

"Pleasantly so," Liz said. "It's nice not to do all the driving for a change."

"You're a good passenger. You didn't scream once coming down the mountain."

"Yes, I did. I screamed silently. Wore out the passenger brake halfway down, too, then I closed my eyes."

"Me, too," he said.

Liz laughed. "Thanks, Matt," she said. "It was a lovely day."

He nodded, then grinned suggestively. "It doesn't have to end, does it?"

She smiled at him. "I guess not." She hesitated, then plunged on, "My place or yours?"

He paused for only a split second, then he said, "Yours, I think. My cleaning lady comes on Mondays. By Saturday..."

Liz could not imagine Matt having a messy house. In his office, everything was in place. At her apartment he picked up and put away everything he used. And his car was spotless. You could tell a lot about a man by the way he treated his car.

"I don't mind," she found herself saying, pushing the issue just a little.

He glanced at her sideways. "I don't think you're ready for my house yet, Liz," he said firmly. "Let's take this one step at a time, okay?" Immediately he began talking about the alpine flowers that bloomed on the mountain in the summer months and if she'd ever seen them?

"Many times," Liz said, still wondering.

BY FRIDAY afternoon, when her next regression appointment was scheduled, Liz felt very anxious. All during the week, though she worked efficiently enough in the office or visited with her mother or father or talked on the telephone, arranging seminars and presentations, she kept feeling that she was nearing the end of Robert and Jeannie's story. She had nothing on which to base this fear, but it was quite strong. She was afraid that during the next session Jeannie would recover and decide her pride wouldn't allow her to stay any longer at Robert's home. They would argue and then agree to part. And Liz would have an anticlimax to deal with.

"Shall we attempt to pick it up where we left off?" Ione asked. "Jeannie had run off into the rain and seemed to be coming down with some kind of illness."

"Pneumonia," Matt and Liz said at the same time.

"Liz regressed spontaneously last weekend," Matt explained to his startled colleague. "I, well, I just happened to be there."

"Did you just happen to have a tape recorder with you?" Ione asked.

Matt shook his head, looking embarrassed, no doubt remembering that he'd been making love to Liz at the time. Tape recording the experience had probably been the farthest thing from his mind.

"I don't think we need to go through Jeannie's entire convalescence," Liz said.

Matt agreed. "Why don't we let you choose the time once you're under hypnosis?"

SHE CHOSE A DAY in January. Jeannie had stayed with Robert for almost three months. Her recovery had been slow, delayed by a troublesome cough that wouldn't go away. She was feeling fairly well, though, most of the time, and she had just come in from a walk in the gardens with Robert, snugly wrapped in the fine warm coat Robert had given her at Christmas. He had also given her several beautiful dresses and more underwear than one woman could wear in a year. She'd had nothing to give him but her love, but he'd seemed to think that was more than present enough.

Mrs. Currie was waiting in the room Jeannie had been given to dress in, next door to the bedroom she shared with Robert. There was a bed in the room and the servants were supposed to believe the fiction that Jeannie slept there alone.

Small and plump and always smiling, Mrs. Currie had been the first of the servants to come round to being Jeannie's friend. Some of the others had also accepted her now, including the kitchen maid who had once giggled at her. But Mrs. Currie had led the way, earning Jeannie's undying gratitude.

"I thought you might appreciate some help in dressing for dinner," Mrs. Currie said. "The master should really see about getting a maid for you."

"Och, I don't need a maid to help me take my clothes off," Jeannie said. "I'd be embarrassed." She laughed. "I used to think rich people could afford more privacy than poor people, but I've come to see they're rarely alone. Always someone poking in the chests of drawers making sure there's clean linen, someone walking in the bedroom unannounced to build a fire or take out waste water from the washbasin. There's no end to it."

She smiled at Mrs. Currie. "I'm no saying I don't welcome you in my room at any time, Mistress Currie—'tis just a matter of interest to me, the way the wealthy live. Also this having to change clothes so many times a day. 'Tis exhausting, keeping up with what's right to wear for morning, or afternoon tea, or dinner, or night, and which accessories go with what. 'Twas far simpler when I had but two dresses to my name, one for winter and one for summer."

Both women laughed. Jeannie had discovered early that Mrs. Currie's family came from the highlands just as hers did. Since then there had been no need to put on airs, even if Jeannie had been so inclined. Mrs. Currie knew all about her, and all about her situation here.

"As for a lady's maid," Jeannie went on, as she pulled out of the wardrobe the blue brocade dress she had decided to wear, "I'll no be needing one when I'm back in my flat in Old Town. There's hardly enough room for me."

"You're thinking of leaving soon then?" Mrs. Currie asked.

"I have to," Jeannie said simply. "This life is not for me. I'd sooner be earning my own living and saving for my wee shop. I feel useless here."

"The master will not be letting you go easily," the woman said.

Jeannie felt a familiar sadness come over her, just as it always did when she thought of being without Robert. "Och, I'll face that when the time comes," she said.

Mrs. Currie had been putting away Jeannie's new coat, after first brushing it and inspecting the fur trim that edged the front. Now she frowned. "Where are your gloves? They're no in your pockets where you usually stuff them."

"Och, I must have left them on yon table in the front hall," Jeannie exclaimed. "I'll go down for them. Could you be finding whatever underwear I'm supposed to wear with this gown?" she asked, laying the blue brocade over a chaise longue. It was a beautiful thing, cut low in the bodice, covered with garlands of flowers embossed in gold, the drapery over the shoulders tightly pleated and tied with knots of pale narrow ribbon. "I'll wear the satin slippers, I suppose, with the Louis XV heels."

Hurrying down the staircase, she realized she had little time to spare before dinner. It had been so fine and bright outside that she and Robert had lingered long in the garden after he returned from his day's labors at the bank. All the same, she had to stop on the landing—not only to rest her hip but to catch her breath. She had such trouble catching her breath nowadays. And her cough seemed so much a part of her she could hardly remember a time when she hadn't had it.

Slowing her descent, she walked down the second flight of stairs, then almost jumped at the sound of the front door knocker. Evidently all the servants were out of earshot, for no one came hurrying to answer it.

Jeannie looked down at herself. She was still wearing her old green serge frock. It had been good enough to go out walking in the gardens, she'd decided, not wanting to soil one of her pretty new gowns. But was it good enough to go answering doors?

"Och, what does the dress matter," she scolded herself. "Some poor body's waiting outside in the cold while I make all these deliberations."

Hurrying down the last few steps, she limped across the round entry hall and tugged open one of the double doors.

A tall gentleman stood on the doorstep, frowning down at her. Beautifully dressed he was, in black evening clothes with a pleated front to his white shirt and a white bow tie, with a half-caped overcoat over all. An older gentleman, with a fine head of white hair like a lion's mane, and an immense white mustache. A handsome gentleman, with a look of her Robbie about him.

Without thinking, Jeannie bobbed a curtsy. He seemed the kind of gentleman to whom a curtsy was due. "Good evening, sir," she said softly.

He smiled at her. "Good evening, young miss. And what is your name?"

"Jeannie, sir, Jeannie Findlay."

"You're new, aren't you?"

Jeannie hesitated. "In a manner of speaking, sir."

"Well, bonny Jeannie, please let your master know I've arrived." As he spoke he swung off his overcoat with a flourish and deposited it and his top hat, gloves and walking stick in Jeannie's arms.

"Who shall I say, sir?" she asked awkwardly.

"Robert Charles McAndrew," he answered with a twinkle in his blue eyes.

Robbie's father!

Jeannie might have stood like a lump, staring, for who knows how long, had not Travers, Robert's butler, arrived at that moment. Relieved to see him, Jeannie unceremoniously dumped her armload in his hands and hurried upstairs to Robert's study.

"It's your father," she informed him when she was through coughing after her exertions.

"Good Lord!" Robert exclaimed. "He usually lets me know when he's going to descend on me." He smiled ruefully at her. "What did he say to you?"

"He thought I was a servant. I didn't tell him any different. What could I say?"

Robert took her in his arms. "You could have said you were my own dear love."

Jeannie laughed. "I'm sure he'd have been overjoyed to hear that." She shook her head, stepping back. "Don't you worry about me, Robbie. My feelings are no hurt. I'll just stay out of the way now...I've a mind your father's expecting to stay for dinner."

"And the night probably. But there'll be no staying out of the way, Jeannie. I want you there by my side where you belong."

"Och, Robbie, you've gone daft. Your father would be shocked."

"Do him good." He looked at her sternly. "This is my house. I'll have anyone I wish at my dinner table. Away with you now and be sure to wear your prettiest dress."

"But Robbie…"

"Off you go. No argument."

She was very late coming down. Convinced it was the wrong thing to do, she had dallied while changing into the blue brocade and doing up her hair. But Robert had sent Travers up to find out what was keeping her and she'd no choice then but to go down.

Robert introduced her as, "My friend, Miss Jeannie Findlay," but she could see by his father's face that he'd been informed of their relationship. There was no twinkle showing now in the blue eyes that were so like Robert's, and his bow was so perfunctory as to be nonexistent.

The air in the dining room was frigid in spite of the flames leaping in the grate. It was obvious to Jeannie that Robert and his father had already had words before she came down. They were polite to each other, but Robert had told her many times that he and his father enjoyed a close companionship. There was no sign of it now.

Robert Senior was polite enough and he certainly tried to make conversation, with his son at least. Jeannie he simply ignored. There was a great deal of talk about "The Exchange," which meant nothing to Jeannie. Mr. Gladstone had addressed a large liberal meeting in Birmingham. The King of Korea had demanded the removal of the Chinese Resident, who had become persona non grata.

Persona non grata, Jeannie pondered. It sounded like someone unwelcome. Like her.

Robert Senior also had a lot to say about some well-known rich European family and a copper trust, and a visit some American gentleman had made to the Baron. Whatever all that was, her Robbie obviously disapproved of the entire transaction, which was somehow linked with the falling price of diamonds. "A syndicate with a few hundred million could pretty well control all the mineral lands of the earth," Robert Senior stated.

Uncomprehending, more nervous than she had ever felt in her life, Jeannie somehow managed not to make any mistakes in her manners as course followed course in apparently endless succession.

When she was finally able to leave the gentlemen to their brandy and cigars, it was with great relief. Robert insisted on escorting her out to the little drawing room where they usually had their tea served. "You did marvelously well, darling," he whispered. "It must have been terribly boring for you. I'm sorry. I wanted to make the conversation more general, but my father has definite opinions on what constitutes proper conversation for gentlemen."

"'Tis all right, Robbie," she murmured. "I should have stayed in my room, it would have been less awkward for you."

"And deprive me of such a beautiful sight?" he argued, looking at her with the bold beautiful smile that always made her heart tighten in her breast.

"Awa' with you," she said, smiling back at him.

It wasn't five minutes later that the argument started. At first Jeannie thought it was a continuation of the heated discussion they'd had about the copper and diamond trusts. But then she heard her own name, and Robert's father shouting, "You are insane, Robert! I'll hear no more about it."

His next remarks had something to do with Robert's lack of regard for appearances, something more about discretion and then a lot more in a lower tone that Jeannie couldn't catch no matter how much she strained her ears.

And then finally, unexpectedly, Robert's voice, clear and strong with a hint of defiance in it. "I love Jeannie, Father. She's given a meaning and purpose to my life that wasn't there before. She's the finest young woman I've ever known and I mean to marry her if she'll have me."

Shocked to the marrow of her bones, Jeannie almost dropped her teacup. She managed to set it down without accident, though it rattled in the saucer. Her first reaction was a thrill of excitement. To hear herself spoken of with such love, enough to be considered for marriage, would thrill any woman. But her second, more considered reaction was dread. Men like Robert Charles McAndrew did not marry women like Jeannie Findlay. It wasn't in the order of things.

Robbie's father hadn't made a sound since Robbie's announcement, she realized. Had he suffered an attack of apoplexy? She wouldn't be surprised.

Standing, one hand to her breast where her heart was pounding like the very voice of doom, she listened uneasily and heard only vague murmurs, until suddenly Robert Senior's voice rang out again. "You always would have your own way, Robert, even as a child. I blame your mother for spoiling you. But you're a man now, with a position in society to maintain. You must surely realize such a marriage would cast you completely beyond the pale. It would be the end of your career. You'll remember old Carstairs's son, who ran off with that foreign governess. Made a complete mess of his life. Such promise he had, but no, he would have his own way. A disgrace to his class."

Some murmured comment from Robbie indicated to Jeannie that he wasn't moved by this particular argument.

"But I forbid it," Robert Senior said sharply, obviously expecting this to be the last word.

Robbie's answer was just as sharp but unintelligible to Jeannie.

She must leave the room, she thought. Eavesdropping was not an acceptable thing to do. But the argument continued relentlessly.

"Marry her and I'll have no more to do with you," the older man said clearly. "Marry her and you will never be received in my home again."

"So be it," Robbie said.

Jeannie's breath stopped in her throat, so she had to cough. But she couldn't cough, mustn't cough. The two men had obviously not realized she could hear their argument. If they heard her coughing they would know.

Quickly, trying to tiptoe so she wouldn't be heard, she limped from the room. Gathering her flounced skirts in both hands she hurried across the hall, almost bumping into Travers, who was approaching the dining room with a decanter on a silver tray. Breathlessly she asked him to excuse her to the gentlemen on the grounds that she was unwell. Then she stumbled up the stairs, not caring if anyone saw her, and ran into her dressing room. Closing the door behind her, she leaned against it until she'd recovered from the fit of coughing so long suppressed.

Looking around wildly, she was suddenly struck by the incongruity of being surrounded by such luxury and taste. Of course she didn't belong here. She never had, never would. So what was she to do? She had to leave Robbie's house, for certain. How could she come between him and his family, between him and his career? But she could hardly run out into the night again, considering what a fix she'd got herself into the last time.

She must go in the morning then, but secretly. Robbie would argue with her, and she was no match for his arguments on his own ground. She needed to be in her own place, with her own walls around her, no matter how poor those walls might be. Luckily she had insisted on keeping up the rent on her flat.

When Robbie came looking for her an hour later she feigned sleep, lying in the small bed in the dressing room, pretending she couldn't rouse herself enough to talk to him. It was long after midnight before she finally did sleep, and her sleep was filled with dreams in which she was running and running and never getting anywhere.

When she awoke in the morning, Robert Senior had been taken to the train station by the coachman. Her Robbie had gone to the bank, leaving word with Mrs. Currie that he would return to take lunch with her at noon. He had something important to discuss.

After some thought, Jeannie had decided to take Mrs. Currie into her confidence. It would make her departure much easier. "I'll no take anything with me that wasn't my own when I came," she told the other woman. "But if you can arrange for Jamie Kintyre to take me home in the carriage, it would be a great help. It's an awfu' long walk, I'm no sure I'm up to it."

Mrs. Currie was disposed to argue, afraid the master would blame her for speeding Jeannie's departure. But Jeannie silenced her by telling her Robbie's plan to marry her. "No," the older woman agreed. "That wouldna do at all."

"He'd blame me all his life," Jeannie declared. "And even if he didn't, I would blame myself. Besides," she added, with her customary honesty, "I could no live a rich person's life. I'm happier working for a living, there's self-respect in that."

Well before noon she was climbing the stairs to her flat, carrying the one bag that held the clothing Mhairi had packed to go with her to Robert's house.

Mhairi was right behind her, of course, as was to be expected. "I didn't think to see you ever again," she exclaimed. "Your Robert sent his man to tell me you were recovered, but I've heard nothing since. Tell me everything that's happened. Don't leave out a thing!"

Mhairi wouldn't leave it alone, Jeannie knew, and something in her wanted to talk out the whole story of the past three months. So as she prepared paper and kindling and coal to warm the terribly cold room, she began with a description of Robert's household and the care he'd given her. She ended with the fight he'd had with his father the previous night.

"So here I am," she concluded wearily. "I'm recovered now, so it's time to go back to work."

Mhairi looked at her closely. "You don't look recovered."

"I've had a busy morning," Jeannie said with wry understatement, hauling herself to her feet.

"You're nobbut skin and bones."

"I was always skin and bones."

Mhairi sighed in resignation. "I'll put the kettle on for tea," she said.

Jeannie sat down on the edge of her bed. "I'd appreciate that, Mhairi. I'm awfu' tired, suddenly."

But before the kettle could come to a boil, she started coughing again, and she coughed and coughed for a long time. Mhairi supported her in her arms, looking worried, handing her a clean handkerchief of her own when Jeannie was done. Then she made the tea and carried a cup over, holding it to Jeannie's lips so she could drink.

"That's better." Jeannie sighed at the end of it. "There's nothing like a good cup of tea, is there?"

Glancing up when Mhairi didn't answer, she saw that her friend was staring in apparent horror at the handkerchief wadded up in Jeannie's hand. Following her gaze, Jeannie caught her breath as horror welled in her, too. The handkerchief was dyed a bright scarlet with blood. Blood that Jeannie had coughed up from her own lungs.

She had a sudden vision of the doctor's grave bearded face as he listened to her chest. Then she thought of how long it had taken her to feel better; how she'd never really felt as well as she should. And she *knew*, as Mhairi knew, as surely as if the name of her condition had been written on that same handkerchief. Both Jeannie and Mhairi had enough experience with the illnesses of relatives and friends and neighbors to know what blood coughed up from the lungs meant.

"Galloping consumption," she whispered.

She looked pleadingly at Mhairi, hoping for some word of disagreement. A laugh, perhaps, that would tease her for her exaggerated concern for her own health.

But the bleak expression on Mhairi's face only confirmed her fears.

"Get you gone," Jeannie said at once. "You canna risk your own health. Go now, awa' with you."

Mhairi walked slowly to the door, then turned. "If it was not for my wee Thomas, I'd take care of you, Jeannie."

"Do you think I don't know that?" Jeannie said softly.

Mhairi's eyes shone with unshed tears. "I'll come to the door every day," she insisted. "You must tell me anything you need, anyone I can fetch for you. Anyone." There was emphasis on the last word, and a straight look from Mhairi's amber-colored eyes to go with it.

"Robert's not to know," Jeannie said at once. "If he comes after me, he's not to know. I'll no have our love end with pity. I canna abide pity. I'd sooner fight with him over his father. Do you understand?"

"Aye," Mhairi said heavily. She had averted her head, perhaps not wanting Jeannie to see the pity in her own eyes.

HE CAME at half past one, running up the stairs two at a time. Jeannie had decided to bar her door to him and pretend she wasn't there. That would give him time to think things over. Surely on sober reflection he would realize marriage was out of the question. Robert was an ambitious man; he would not want to be a social outcast. And he was fond of his family—how could he risk being disowned? He would never need to know the nature of her illness.

She almost choked holding her breath while Robert hammered on the door. When he called her name, she wanted badly to answer, but she didn't. Later he'd come back, she knew. Later she might be over the shock and might have her arguments assembled so she could convince him.

At last he was silent. She heard his footsteps going heavily down the steps. She wanted to cry then, but Jeannie Findlay was too strong for tears.

SITTING THERE, she heard mad Harry come along the street below, playing his bagpipes. Usually his music was cheery if not overly tuneful, but today he was playing a dirge, a doleful thing full of wailing and sadness. The mad often had the second sight. Had Harry sensed death in the air?

Shaking her head abruptly, she stood up, smoothing out the skirt of her dress. It wouldna do to sit here indulging in self-pity. She would simply go on with the business of life, as she had always done, until there was no life left in her. That was the way to do it.

After putting away her things, she decided she'd best go

out to the shops and buy a few provisions. Perhaps she could find the doctor who had treated her at Robert's house and confirm her own diagnosis. Pulling on her shawl, pinning her hat at a jaunty angle, she unbolted her door and opened it.

Robert was standing on the landing outside, leaning on the stair rail. His face was as pale as the whitewashed walls, his blue eyes brilliant with pain.

"Mhairi told you," Jeannie whispered.

He nodded, then took her in his arms. "We'll fight it, Jeannie, if it is consumption. There's a doctor in America who's established a sanitorium. He uses an open-air treatment to cure the illness. We'll look for one in Scotland or England."

"I'll no go to England, nor to any sanitorium, or hospital," Jeannie said.

"Then I'll take you to Glendarra."

"To Black Robert's own house? I'd sooner die right here." Pulling away, she looked at his dear face as sternly as she could. "You must stay away from me, Robbie, and look to your own health. If I've infected you, I'll never forgive myself."

"I'll not leave you," he said firmly. "I've heard of a doctor right here in Edinburgh who has a dispensary for tuberculosis. We'll consult him. Perhaps I can find a house, a small house in the country where the air is pure and you can rest. Complete bed rest, that's what doctors are advocating now. We'll marry as soon as possible and live in the country until you've recovered. I can appoint an officer to replace me at the bank until we return."

Jeannie backed over to her bed and sat down, the strength gone from her legs. "You love me so much, Robbie? You'd not only defy your father, you'd defy death itself?"

He looked sad. "You heard my father then? I thought you must have done. I'm sorry. I tried to make him understand, but it wasn't possible."

He started toward her, but she held a hand up to halt him halfway across the small room. "I will no let you imperil yourself further. I've been nothing but trouble to you since we met. I'll no marry you, either. Your family's important to you. So is your career. I'll no let you give them up for me. It's over between us. 'Tis time to end it."

He sighed. "You're a stubborn woman, Jeannie Findlay."

She laughed, acknowledging the truth of that even as she fought the urge to cough. "You're a fine one to talk, Robert Charles McAndrew."

He nodded. "I know. I'm every bit as stubborn as you. Either I'll marry you or we'll live in sin." He smiled lovingly at her. "I'm going to find that house, Jeannie," he assured her. "In the meantime I'll have enquiries made about the dispensary I spoke of. We'll hire nurses for you, whatever is necessary."

Heading toward the door, he turned to look at her. She was to remember him for the rest of her life, the way he looked then, his eyes dark with concern, his golden hair somehow dimmed through his worry about her, but love shining as clear as day on his handsome face. "I do love you, Jeannie," he said.

Jeannie hesitated. Would it be better not to answer? All his talk of nurses and a wee house in the country and pure air was not going to help her survive, she knew. She could feel in her bones that she was going to die, had known she was bound to die as soon as she saw the scarlet blood staining Mhairi's handkerchief.

Would it be better to let him go without a word from her, give him time to think of the consequences? Och, no, she couldna let him go thinking she didn't feel anything for him. That would be the greatest lie she could tell him.

Summoning her brightest smile for him, she said with great feeling and complete truth, "I love *you*, Robbie."

And afterward she was glad she had let emotion triumph over common sense.

CHAPTER TEN

MATT WAS SITTING at Ione's desk, his head in his hands, fingers buried in his hair. He felt exhausted, used up, disappointed, not necessarily in that order.

Straightening, he saw that Ione was watching him, affection warming her eyes. "You going to be okay?" she asked.

"I was hoping Liz would go farther," he admitted wearily.

Ione nodded.

"Who is it talks about 'the rest of the story'? Paul Harvey?" He worried his hair with one hand. "We didn't get it, that's for sure."

"Maybe there isn't any more," Ione said gently. "Maybe Jeannie died before Robert came back."

"But in my own regressions I would surely have come up with Robert finding that out, wouldn't I? I learned almost everything else. Liz's regressions were more vivid, more detailed, but they agreed with everything I experienced." He laughed shortly. "I was anxious all week, sure I'd finally get to know what happened after Jeannie found out she had tuberculosis."

"Liz was disappointed, too. Perhaps we should have gone on."

Matt shook his head. "No, you did the right thing, ending the session. She was very tired." He laughed again, more genuinely this time. "At least she finally admitted she'd misjudged poor Robert—he wasn't a villainous seducer after all.''

"You love her, don't you?" Ione said unexpectedly.

He sat forward. "She's great, Ione. Intelligent and compassionate and straight. Everything she is is right there on her face. She doesn't play games, she's never devious, what she thinks, she says. On top of that she's got a terrific sense of fun." He grinned. "Yes, I love her. Not just because she was Jeannie, either, though that has to have some influence, of course."

"You're going to see her later?"

"I told her I'd come by." He hesitated. "I was thinking I might take her to my house but I'm not sure she's ready. She's confused as hell about her feelings for me getting mixed up with her feelings for Robert. So what happens if I come along and wave a magic wand and say, hey presto, no need to worry, we're one and the same? Some truths you don't tell people—they have to accept them by themselves. I'm afraid Liz would blow up in my face and tell me to get lost."

"She's a bright young woman—she must surely suspect the truth."

Matt shook his head. "Not so far. She's still hung up, worrying that she's confusing her feelings for Robert with her feelings for me. Question is, will taking her to my house speed up the process or make her reject everything?"

"And if you don't take her to your house?"

"She's beginning to wonder why I don't. I sure don't want her to start distrusting me."

"Sometimes you have to take a risk, my friend."

He sighed. Standing, he reached for the tweed jacket he'd draped over the back of his chair earlier. "Wish me luck," he said.

Ione's smile was full of compassion. "You know I do."

Driving to Liz's apartment a half hour later, Matt made the decision that had to be made. "How about I fix dinner at my house?" he said when she opened her door.

Her gamin smile flashed out at him. "I was beginning to wonder..."

"I know." Closing the door behind him, he took her in his arms and kissed her. "You feeling okay now?" he asked.

She sighed. "I suppose so." She laughed in an artificial way that wasn't at all like her. "I'm feeling sort of peculiar, to tell the truth. Logically I knew Jeannie had to die sometime. Everybody dies. But I didn't expect her to die *now*. And I sure didn't expect to be left hanging. I had the feeling today I'd find all the answers. Instead I ended up with more questions. When Robert left, the things that seemed to be in Jeannie's mind—how afterward she remembered him looking that way, afterward she was glad she'd told him again that she loved him—it seemed so final. Yet it doesn't seem finished."

She smiled tiredly at him. "Doesn't make a whole lot of sense, does it?" Without waiting for a response, she pulled herself free. "Let me get a coat. Can I bring something to help with dinner?"

"Nope. I'm well supplied."

"Maybe you'd like a glass of wine before we go?"

He was worried by her brittle smile, her sudden hostessy manner. The skin around her lovely eyes looked strained, he thought. Maybe this wasn't such a hot idea.

She didn't say a word as he drove up in front of his house, but he saw her face whiten, then close. In silence she got out of the car and stood on the sidewalk looking up at the redbrick facade and the wraparound veranda and the gingerbread detailing. He thought of all the months of work he'd put in on this house, the stripping and refinishing of woodwork, the restoration of wainscoting and wood flooring, the intricate work on the ceilings and window frames and doorjambs.

"What a wonderful old Victorian," Liz said brightly. "I should have known you wouldn't settle for a boxy apartment, Matt."

In the round entry hall she asked, in the interested voice of a new acquaintance, "Did your wife live here with you?"

"I bought the house after the divorce," Matt said. "Meredith wasn't interested in old architecture. She wanted everything in primary colors—contemporary and uncluttered. Minimalist is her favorite word. I, on the other hand, have this very definite emotional response to—"

"Don't I get to see the rest of it?" Liz interrupted.

"Of course." He gestured for her to precede him, and she tripped lightly in and out of the living room, the library, the dining room. She examined the kitchen, which Matt had totally gutted and redesigned along more convenient lines, while preserving its historical integrity. Brightly she glanced at a high medallioned ceiling here, a chandelier there, a smile fixed on her face like that of a little girl who has been told to be polite. Dutifully she admired the beautiful curving staircase and the stained-glass window on the landing, the upstairs bedrooms and bathroom, the long lovely hall.

Then she led the way downstairs again, still without making any comment. Matt was puzzled by her lack of questions. He'd expected her to be shocked, of course. She had visualized Robert's house even more vividly than he and had described it to him and Ione. She had to know this house was as similar as it was possible to get. On a much smaller scale, yes, but so similar it had stopped him dead in the street when he'd first seen it twelve years ago.

"When I first saw the house I was in my early twenties, still going to medical school," he told her, keeping his voice cheerful, trying to ease the shock for her. "I loved it at once, but it wasn't for sale. I couldn't have afforded it if it had been. I made a practice of walking or driving by here at least once a week. It came on the market soon after Meredith and I were married, but as I told you, it isn't a type that holds any interest for her, so I had to let it go to someone else. The new owner didn't do any restoration, so I kept hoping he might decide to sell. It seemed criminal to let such a wonderful old place sit here unloved, falling to pieces. And then about a month after the divorce was final, there it was on the market again. I didn't hesitate, didn't even haggle."

Liz had nodded a couple of times as he spoke, but she wasn't meeting his eyes and she seemed to feel terribly uncomfortable. He could almost feel her vibrating with the need to be gone from here.

"Liz," he said softly. "Don't you have any questions for me?"

Her eyes met his, so blue, so candidly surprised. "My goodness, Matt, why should I have any questions? I can see what a terrific job you've done on this house. You've really worked hard. It's...lovely. Should we go in the kitchen now?"

The kitchen. The one room that was different.

"You're hungry?"

"Famished."

He had to admire her courage, he thought as the two of them worked to prepare dinner. It was quite obvious that she wanted to bolt through the ornate double doors of the front entrance, but she wasn't about to give in to her emotions. She was going to stick it out, stay in the house that had given her such a shock.

They had decided on pasta, and Liz had volunteered to make a pesto sauce. As Matt tossed a green salad and prepared garlic bread, he watched her clipping away at the clump of fresh basil he'd washed for her, chopping garlic, measuring pine nuts and oil and Parmesan cheese into the blender. Every movement was crisply efficient. She didn't once look up to catch his eye.

Throughout the meal she talked—about an article she'd read about Rio de Janeiro; the arctic weather that had recently hit Seattle, bringing with it a few light flurries of snow; an exhibition of sculpture she'd gone to during the week. And all the time her gaze was concentrated on the food in front of her, on the wall behind Matt's shoulder, on the fingernails of her own left hand.

And then, finally, her voice trailed away and she set down her fork and buried her face in her hands.

He stood up, walked around the table and put his hands on her shoulders. "It was a mistake to bring you here, wasn't it?" he asked softly.

She shook her head without raising it. "I can't think why I'm behaving like such an idiot." Her voice was muffled in her hands.

"You're not an idiot at all. It was a shock. I should have prepared you. I thought you were ready."

She sat up straight. "I've no idea what you're talking about, Matt. Ready for what?" Her eyes glanced brightly at him over her shoulder, but didn't really focus on his face. "No, don't answer that," she said. "You're so serious this evening. Let's talk about something else."

She was still taking refuge in denial. "Liz," he said tentatively.

She stood. "We'd better do something about all those

dishes. I hope I didn't put too much garlic in the pesto. What did you think?''

He put his arms around her and pulled her close and held her tightly. Then he kissed her, tenderly at first, then, as her lips responded, more searchingly. Her arms went up around his neck and he felt himself relax for the first time since he'd made the decision to bring her here. It was going to be okay. She might be denying everything else, but she wasn't denying her feelings for him.

''You know what I'd like to do,'' she said, when they came up for air. ''I'd like to make love without talking. It seems to me I've been talking all day. I took my dog and pony act to a tourism trade show in Bellevue this morning and made about two hundred and fifty direct contacts. Then there was the regression and that long discussion with you and Ione afterward. And I've certainly been a motor mouth since we got here. So how about I zip my lips and we just go upstairs and get into your lovely big bed and shut out the rest of the world?''

She was still denying, of course, but there was a possibility that making love might help her adjust to the shock she'd received. Matt was willing to do anything that would help her adjust, and he was ready and eager to make love to Liz under any circumstances.

He smiled in agreement, letting all his love for her show on his face.

''How about pretending we've just met?'' she asked. ''We don't even know each other's names, but we're crazy about each other.''

If she pretended she didn't know his name she wouldn't have to worry about calling him by the wrong one. Denial again. But probably harmless. ''Sounds good to me,'' he said. Her grateful smile looked more genuine than it had all evening.

THE BEDROOM was large, but not intimidatingly so, and the bed was a fairly modest queen-size. It was the *type* of tables and chairs and fabrics that echoed Robert's bedroom, Liz decided, rather than the actual proportions of the room or furnishings. The swag of blue cloth that had hung over Robert's bed—so like the swag that hung over hers—was missing here. Perhaps it had seemed too feminine for a twentieth-century man living a bachelor's life.

The evidence was all there, answering the question she hadn't yet been able to formulate even to herself. But she didn't even want to *consider* the question, or the evidence. It was all too much for her. She hadn't yet absorbed the shock of simply seeing the house—that cataclysmic moment when her two separate worlds had brushed against each other.

Slipping out of her sweater and gray slacks, she watched Matt unbutton his shirt. His eyes were dark with concern as he looked at her. As well they should be. She had the feeling if she didn't hang on very tightly she would fly apart into a million pieces.

"Liz?" he said questioningly as she hesitated, looking at him.

She put her finger to her lips, reminding him he wasn't supposed to speak. Somehow she managed a smile and he grinned ruefully in response.

He had taken off his trousers and shoes and socks and was removing his shirt. She loved the sturdy look of his thighs, the long bones in his slender legs, his flat stomach and well-developed chest and shoulders. Her own firm flesh was due to strenuous jazzercise sessions three evenings a week, plus jogging around Green Lake on alternate days when she was home, along any likely looking path when she was traveling. She never had asked Matt how he kept himself in such great shape.

She couldn't ask him now. She had decreed silence. What an understanding man he was. He knew her emotions were running on overload. By agreeing to her suggestion he had taken a major part of the pressure off her.

Strangers.

Looking at him, she found herself getting excited. This stranger was beautifully made.

He was naked now. Waiting for her. Obviously ready for her. Quickly she slid out of her panties and bra and walked into his waiting arms.

"Liz," he murmured again as her mouth met his. She pursed her lips, reminding him, and he laughed softly.

Everything was just fine. She was able after all to put out of her mind the way his house looked, the terrifying equation the sight of it had produced in her brain. She didn't have to worry about any ghosts walking into her head to haunt her as she made love to him. They were strangers to each other. Just two shapely, healthy bodies winding around each other, touching in intimate places, coming together out of a need that was as old as time.

He leaned above her, his gray eyes glinting with light and love. With hand signals he made her roll onto her stomach, then he began massaging her, his hands moving slowly from her shoulders to her waist, his thumbs seeking out and easing tightness wherever they found it. He worked on her legs, bending them, kneading her thighs, her calves, delicately tugging each toe.

Her body was tingling by the time he turned her over again. Still smiling lovingly at her, he soothed her arms, her abdomen, and finally her breasts.

He had succeeded in relaxing her completely and she was grateful. Kissing him gently, she pushed him lightly onto his back and signaled that she was taking over.

He grinned and closed his eyes, letting his body relax

instantly, totally. She kissed each of his flat nipples delicately, and felt the tremor that went through him. Then she
concentrated on kissing his lips for a while, putting a lot
of time and attention into her delightful task, coaxing a
response from him that threatened to bring him off his
back and over her again. But she kept her hand on his
chest, letting him know he was to stay where he was. She
was in charge now.

Slowly she trailed kisses down over his smooth chest to
his flat stomach, enjoying the wonderfully clean, mildly
salty taste of him. Inch by inch she explored him with her
mouth and her tongue and her fingers, letting her hair trail
over his body as she moved, knowing by his unnatural
stillness and the rasp of his breathing that she was exciting
him unbearably.

When she finally raised her head, she caught her breath
at the desire on his face. She had been wanted before, but
she had never been wanted like this. Straddling him, she
brought her mouth down to his, then let him roll her over
onto her back. She was happy to take a more submissive
role once more.

Matt's usual patience was missing now. His mouth was
hot, demanding a response that she was eager to give.
When he took her face in his hands and dragged his lips
along her hairline, she felt the edge of his teeth against her
flesh. Tilting her head up, he kissed her again and again,
taking, urging, ravishing. His hands were holding her head
still so that she could not have escaped his foraging mouth
if she'd wanted to, which she didn't. Her own mouth was
aching as if she couldn't get enough of him.

I love you, she wanted to cry out, but she forced herself
to obey her own injunction, to carry out the fantasy of two
strangers loving each other in silence.

Her pulse was pounding in her ears. She felt wild, wanton, her body straining upward, wanting him. Her hands pulled at his body, persuading him over her, into her.

She let out her breath in a long sigh that mingled with an answering sigh from Matt. He was inside her, part of her, they were joined. The impatience was over, the violence of their loving was unnecessary. They were together. They could take their time.

Their patience lasted all of one minute, then Matt was kneeling over her, gazing down at her. He looked like the stranger he was supposed to be, his gray eyes hooded, somber, passionate, his mouth stern. He was lifting her with him, setting the rhythm again, the familiar rhythm her body longed for whenever she was away from him. And she was moving to the rhythm, lifting and rubbing against his wonderfully smooth body, then dropping again, moaning deep in her throat over the weight of him, the heat of him, the *feel* of him inside her. Shudders ripped through his body, answered immediately by a swelling surge of irresistible power that crashed through her and lifted her in one last intense, unendurable spasm.

They slept.

And woke again to renewed passion, which they exhausted almost at once. And slept again, joined, slipping down together into cool quiet peace.

The rain woke her, drumming on the roof, splashing through the drainpipes, running down the windows. Matt was looking at her, might have been gazing at her for hours for all she knew.

"Hi, stranger," she whispered.

"Hi, yourself."

She raised herself on one elbow and traced the line of his sensual mouth with one finger. "You are some kind of great lover," she told him.

His hands cupped her buttocks, feeling warm and comforting and familiar against her flesh. "Not so shabby yourself," he replied.

"I want you to do something for me," she said.

He looked a question at her. His eyes were the color of the dawn outside the windows, gray and shining. "It's important to me," she added.

He waited.

"I want you to regress me. Not Ione. You. I want to find Jeannie again. I want to know what happened." She put her fingers to his lips as something negative flickered across his face. "Please don't give me the standard lecture on ethics. I know all that stuff. I'm asking you as my friend, my lover, my love, to do this for me."

"Okay," he said on a long sigh.

"ARE YOU READY, Liz?" he asked an hour later. They were seated in Matt's living room, Liz leaning back in a deep, tufted armchair with her feet on a hassock, Matt straddling a wooden chair, his arms folded on top of its back. The drapes were drawn across the windows. They were both fully dressed in sweaters and jeans.

"Find a spot to fix your gaze on, okay?" Matt said. "How about that carved medallion on the picture rail there? Let yourself relax now, feel the relaxation flowing through you, floating through you. Let your eyes close any time you're ready. Listen to the sound of my voice. Concentrate on the sound of my voice."

It was comfortingly warm in the room. Matt had lit a fire in the fireplace and she could hear it crackling. The best sound in the world, the sound of a log fire. She could feel the air folding in around her, vibrating through her. Her whole body was tingling gently.

"Where are you, Liz?"

"It's dark," she said. "I can't see anything."

"Nighttime dark, or some other kind?"

"Emptiness dark. Nothing around me but emptiness."

"What is your name?"

"Liz Brooks."

"I want you to feel yourself floating backward, Liz. Feel time slipping away past you as you float backward. Count the years—ten, twenty, thirty, forty, fifty, one hundred years. Can you see the passage, the familiar passage?"

"It's dark," she said again.

There was movement beside her. Fingers touched her forehead, pressing lightly. "Let yourself relax," the voice said. "Let it happen. Ask your inner mind to take you to a place where you can see Jeannie. Visualize Jeannie in your inner mind."

Afterward she thought it was like movies she had seen of movies being made—a director calling out, "Lights, camera, action." One minute it was dark all around, the next the "otherness" was upon her and she was sitting on Jeannie's chair in Jeannie's room working on a little capote made of point d'esprit lace with a band of rich passementerie and an aigrette tied with a knot of rose-colored ribbon.

She had begun work on the bonnet the day after Robert had last come, for something to occupy her hands. Now that she could not work for customers, now that there was no hope of opening her wee shop in New Town, she had decided she might as well use up some of the materials she had on hand for herself.

She jumped, startled, at a knock on the door. Robert? Hope spiraled upward from her heart, then faded as she recognized Mhairi's signal.

"Did yon doctor come?" Mhairi asked, standing just outside the doorway, which was as far as Jeannie would let her venture.

"Aye," Jeannie said with a tired grin. "He left not half an hour since as you well know. What kept you so long?"

"I was bathing Will." Mhairi blushed as she realized she'd admitted watching all traffic to Jeannie's door. Then she set her small round chin stubbornly as if to say, "Why should I not when you need to be watched?" "Well then, what did he say?" she demanded.

Jeannie set the lace bonnet down on the table and folded her hands on top of it. "What do you think? We're no daft, you and me. It's consumption—tuberculosis the doctor called it."

"And?"

"He gave me some medicine that he doesn't expect to help me much and says I have to go to hospital."

"Are you going?"

Jeannie shook her head. "I'm waiting for Robbie."

"Jeannie," Mhairi began, but Jeannie cut her off with a look.

"I asked him, the doctor, if there was much chance of me recovering whatever I did, and he said no, there wasn't. 'Tis not just in my lungs, you see, 'tis scattered. He thinks I was probably infected as a child, which made me more susceptible to reinfection. The danger, he said, was increased by malnutrition, fatigue and overexertion as well as mental strain. Not to mention a bout of pneumonia. He had a suspicion before, he said, but not enough to make a pronouncement." She managed a wry smile. "The disease, he added, as if I didna ken, is most prevalent in areas of overcrowding and poverty."

Mhairi was silent for a minute, obviously struggling not to cry. Then she said very softly, "You canna wait for Robert. It's been a week. He's no coming, Jeannie."

It was Jeannie's turn to set her chin. "He said he'd come. He'll come."

Mhairi sighed. "And you'll go with him, expose him to the risk?"

Jeannie shook her head. "What do you take me for? I'll go to the house in the country when he finds it, I'd be foolish not to. But I'll no let him stay with me." She sighed deeply and picked up the lace bonnet again, examining the stitches as if it was very important each one was almost invisible.

"You must no look so tragic, Mhairi," she said briskly. "I've no had such a bad life. Better than some. And the past few months with Robbie—I've had more happiness than some people experience in a lifetime. Some pain, too, perhaps, but love's worth it, for all that."

"You still believe he'll come?"

Jeannie nodded. She had to believe. What else did she have to cling to?

It was three days later that a different knock sounded on her door, a tentative sound. Jeannie, who had arisen that morning short of breath after a prolonged bout of coughing, called out weakly, and the door opened to reveal Mrs. Currie. A respectable widow, Mrs. Currie always dressed in black. But to Jeannie, suddenly, there seemed more meaning in the older woman's clothing. Her eyes were swollen, too, she could see from across the room.

"Have you been ill, Mistress Currie?" she asked, getting slowly to her feet. "I'd offer you some tea, but I think it best you come no farther—I'm no in good health myself."

"Aye, so the master told me, before…"

"He's away then still? I thought he must be. Did he have a message for me? I'm surprised you found me."

"Jamie Kintyre brought me," Mrs. Currie said. "I insisted he had to, that you should know."

Jeannie realized that her hands were clasped tightly to-

gether at her breast. Her face was burning hot as though
her fever had returned. And her legs were trembling under
the skirt of her old green dress. She wanted to say something, anything to stop the woman from saying words that
were even now parting her lips. But her mind was empty,
as if it might never fill with words again.

"He's dead, Jeannie," Mrs. Currie said.

Well now, had something gone wrong with her hearing
suddenly? And her sight, too. Mrs. Currie's face seemed
to be retreating from her, and the air in the room was
pulsing with an erratic yet rhythmic sound. Surely it was
loud enough to drown out the words she had said—words
she could not have said.

"That's nonsense," Jeannie said faintly. "Robbie was
as well as could be when he came here. Upset, yes, but
full of plans. His face was healthy looking and his voice
was strong." She was abruptly angry. "How could you
say such a thing? You were my friend, I thought. This is
a cruel kind of trick you're playing on me, Mistress Currie."

"He was out looking for a house," Mrs. Currie went
on inexorably. "The estate agent said he'd found two that
he liked, and he wanted to go back alone to see both of
them and make a choice. He was so eager, the agent said.
Even though there was a storm coming, he insisted he had
to go."

Her words kept coming and coming, with an echo to
them such as Jeannie had heard in empty buildings sometimes. Empty buildings, empty rooms. She had heard that
echoes sometimes could be heard in mountainous areas. In
her mind she pictured mountains. She had always thought
it would be a fine thing to climb a mountain, to stand on
top and look down on the world, perhaps even reach up
and touch the sky.

Mrs. Currie was still talking. Why did she keep on talking? Better God should strike her dead than that she should give utterance to such words. "They think his horse might have been frightened by lightning or thunder, or else he stumbled in a hole. They didna find the horse, but they found Mr. McAndrew, lying at the side of the road, where he'd been thrown. He'd been dead some time, the estate agent said."

Jeannie remembered a time when she was a small girl and had stayed a winter with her grandparents in their small cottage. She had gone out to visit a friend's house and lost her way home in a snowstorm. It had been so cold. She had stumbled along for what seemed like hours, going round in circles probably, her feet and legs and body gradually becoming numb with cold so there was no feeling in her. Then like a miracle she had found herself on her grandparents' doorstep. It had taken a long time for her to get warm. Where was the miracle of warmth now when she needed it?

"No," she said.

"I thought I should tell you," Mrs. Currie said. "It was four days ago they found him."

Four days ago she had started sewing on her bonnet, wanting to be pretty when he came for her.

"The funeral was yesterday. I take it you didna see the newspaper."

"I've no been out to buy a newspaper," Jeannie said, relieved to have something so ordinary to say. If she hadna bought a newspaper, then the notice could not have been in it. Robbie couldna be dead.

Dead. Such a short word. Four letters. Like love. There ought to be a longer word for such a monstrously final thing.

Sitting down on her chair, Jeannie stared and stared at

the older woman's face, thinking that any minute now Mrs. Currie must surely disappear and then she could wake up and find out she had been dreaming. She'd fallen asleep, that was it; such a disturbed night she'd had. And this was a terrible nightmare.

"No," she said once again.

"I'm sorry, Jeannie," Mrs. Currie said. She said something else, too, but Jeannie couldn't hear what it was. She was back in that long-ago snowstorm, stumbling around in circles, trying to find a place that was warm. The wind was howling all around her and she couldn't hear, couldn't see, couldn't feel.

"Liz," Matt said. "It's okay, Liz. Everything's okay."

She shook her head, opening her eyes. Tears were streaming down her face. Matt was standing over her, looking down at her. His face was very pale.

"How can you say it's okay?" she demanded, her voice breaking.

"It was a long time ago," Matt said. "It happened a long time ago."

What difference does that make, she wanted to shout, but she couldn't keep shouting at Matt even if she did feel very angry with him. Why was she angry with Matt? she wondered. It wasn't Matt's fault that Robert had died. It wasn't anybody's fault.

But Robert was dead, all the same. Robbie was dead.

Jeannie's Robbie. Not her Robbie.

Compartmentalize, Matt had told her once before. Her two worlds might have brushed up against each other, but they were still separate. She had to keep them separate.

Sitting up straight, she fixed her gaze on the window and the bare oak tree outside and took a deep breath, fighting for control. As though her movement had startled them, a dozen little brown birds suddenly billowed out of the tree and wheeled in front of the window, then settled back down in the tree again. How had they known to move all together like that? What instinct was born in them to act in unison?

"I was expecting Jeannie to die, not Robert," she said indignantly, swiping at her tears with the back of her hand. "If I'd known Robert was going to die, I'd never have asked you to hypnotize me again."

"You wanted to know," he said gently.

She shook her head, then stood abruptly. She had to get away from this house. Her body was telling her to run, run from here and the knowledge of Robert's death. "It's time I was going home," she said evenly.

"No," he protested at once. "We have to talk about this, adjust to it."

She looked at him pleadingly. "I have to be alone, Matt. Please understand. I can't possibly talk about it now."

He put his arms around her. She let him hold her, but her body was stiff. "I have to be alone," she insisted again. "I'm okay, I can handle it. I've got it all compartmentalized now, the way you said to. I just have to be alone for a while."

He stepped back, releasing her, looking down at her with great concern. At last he nodded. "Okay, I'll drive you home."

She'd forgotten that she didn't have her car with her. "I'll take a taxi," she said.

"Liz," he protested. He looked under the weather himself, she realized. His face was still pale, the area around his gray eyes strained.

"Please," she said. "I have to get it all straight in my head, okay?"

He studied her face for a long moment, then sighed.

"Okay," he said. "You'll call me when you feel ready to see me?"

"It might take a while."

"I'll be waiting."

CHAPTER ELEVEN

LIZ HAD NEVER BEEN intimately acquainted with grief. Her mother's parents had died when she was in her teens, but they had lived in England and she had seen them only rarely. Her paternal grandparents were still alive, living in Florida. No intimate friend of hers had ever died. She had lost pets, yes, but not until they were fairly old and could be mourned with an accompanying appreciation of their long and happy lives.

She had not known that grief could wrench her body with actual physical pain. She had not truly known anguish. There would be no more regressions, she realized as she rode home in the taxi Matt had reluctantly called for her. She could not bear to go through Jeannie's death, too. So she was doubly bereaved. It was over, all over. How empty life would seem without either of the people who had come to mean so much to her in so short a time. It seemed as though all the color had leached out of her days, leaving only an empty grayness.

The emptiness surrounded her the rest of the day, though she functioned as much as usual, cleaning her apartment as she always did on Saturdays when she was home, going to the market for fresh vegetables and fruit, the supermarket for other needs. All day she seemed to be surrounded by a wall of mist that separated her from the people she came in contact with. She felt alien, separate, alone. Without planning to she bought a bouquet of pure white chrysanthemums and arranged them in her prettiest vase on the dining table.

Robbie was dead.

The thought came to her again and again, and tears started in her eyes each time. She could see him clearly in her mind, so sturdily built, so elegantly dressed, his linen so immaculate, his hair shining gold in the sunlight, his eyes so boldly blue. In her memory he was always smiling, looking at her with love.

He died a hundred years ago, she kept reminding herself. But for her, he had died that morning.

She remembered reading that when someone suffered the loss of a limb, that person felt the phantom shape of it afterward, as if it were still attached. Would Robert and Jeannie stay with her like that, she wondered, or had they been cut away from her forever?

After a sleepless night she knew she needed to be with someone. Not Matt—she still wasn't ready to confront the questions that surrounded Matt's presence in her life. In a mood of calm detachment that seemed preferable to her former emotional exhaustion, she decided to visit her mother, maybe invite her out for breakfast. Catherine would be up and dressed by seven-thirty; she always rose early, even on Sunday.

At nine o'clock Liz walked out of the elevator in her mother's ultramodern building and knocked on her apartment door. It was a couple of minutes before she heard movement inside, and then Catherine opened the door. As soon as she saw Liz, she appeared unaccountably taken aback.

"I wasn't expecting you, darling," she said slowly, blocking the doorway so Liz couldn't enter.

Liz stared at her. Her mother was wearing the monogrammed Pierre Cardin terry robe Liz had bought her the previous Christmas. Never in living memory had she seen her mother still in her robe at this time of the morning. Not only that, but Catherine's glossy brown hair was tousled. And her long, elegant feet were bare.

"I thought I'd take you out to breakfast," Liz explained. "I guess I should have called first. It never occurred to me that…"

"Heavens, there's no need for you ever to ring me up before coming over, darling." All the same, she made no move to usher Liz in. "It's just such a…surprise," Catherine went on.

She glanced furtively back over her shoulder, and light suddenly dawned in Liz's mind. "You have a visitor?" she whispered.

"Is that so amazing?" Catherine asked, arching her smooth eyebrows.

"Well, no, of course not," Liz stammered. But it was, and she was suddenly overcome with embarrassment. Backing away, she mumbled, "Listen, I'll see you later, okay?"

"Don't be silly, Elizabeth. Now that you're here, of course you must come in." She looked at Liz directly, as if seeing her clearly for the first time. "Are you unwell, dear? You look rather peaked. Perhaps I should take your temperature."

Liz smiled involuntarily. That had always been Catherine's first response when she complained of illness as a child. If the thermometer showed a normal temperature, Liz went to school. No pretense had ever seemed possible until Liz discovered she could hike the mercury up a couple of degrees if she shook the thermometer sharply upside down. Once she had overdone it and registered a fever of one hundred and five, which had been belied by her cool forehead. Catherine had kept a wary eye on her during the procedure after that.

The memory made the tight band across Liz's heart ease a little, and she was able to smile again more naturally. "I didn't sleep too well is all. I'm fine, really. And I will see you later. I'm not about to intrude."

"Nonsense," Catherine said briskly. "You're going to find out sooner or later, it might as well be now." Taking Liz's arm, she urged her into the small hall, then gestured toward the kitchen. "Come in and have coffee. We've finished breakfast, but I can make you some bacon in the microwave if you like."

Jake was sitting at Catherine's glass-and-chrome dining table, which filled one end of the kitchen. He was reading the Sunday paper when Liz awkwardly allowed herself to be propelled into the room. His hair was tousled, too, but then it always was. However he didn't usually have a salt-and-pepper shadow around his chin and upper lip, and he didn't usually visit his ex-wife in the robe that matched hers, also a present from Liz.

Liz stopped dead. "Good God!" she exclaimed.

Jake grinned at her like a small boy caught stealing cookies from a jar. "Morning, Elizabeth," he said in what was obviously supposed to be a casual voice.

They were both calling her Elizabeth this morning.

Liz felt totally disoriented, her mind swept clean of anything intelligent to say.

Catherine giggled nervously. But Catherine never giggled.

Liz swallowed hard. Twice. Still no words came out.

Catherine set a cup of coffee on the table across from Jake and gestured toward a chair. "I expect you're a little surprised," she said.

Liz finally found her voice. "Surprised is not the word. Thunderstruck, maybe? Flabbergasted? Astonished?"

Catherine giggled again. Jake smiled at her, his blue eyes bright with affection.

Liz sat down. She had to. Her knees had buckled under her. "What, may I ask, brought about this entente cordiale?" she demanded.

"You're not shocked, are you?" Catherine asked. "After all, your father and I were married for a long time. Just because there was a divorce doesn't mean we can't establish friendly—well, I suppose it's more than friendly—relations.... There's no real reason why we can't—" She broke off and looked appealingly at Jake. "Why am I floundering around so? We're all grown up. It must be obvious to Liz that..."

"Just shut up, Catherine," Jake said tenderly.

Liz shook her head. "No, I'm not shocked," she said. "I'm delighted. I'm just having a hard time assimilating..."

"Me, too," Jake said. "It was your mother's idea. 'We need to have a long talk,' she told me last night. 'You might as well come prepared to spend the night,' she said."

"That doesn't mean I planned...what happened," Catherine protested. She was blushing furiously. Another phenomenon. "I just didn't want you rushing off home too soon. I wanted us to have a chance to really talk things out, see where we're going."

"And where *are* you going?" Liz asked.

Jake and Catherine exchanged a glance that was positively conspiratorial, then Catherine said briskly, "I think you'd better let me fix you some breakfast while we tell you first where we've been." She busied herself in the refrigerator, adding over her shoulder, "You start, Jake.

Tell her about Dr. Demetrius. That part was your idea, after all.''

"*My* Dr. Demetrius," Liz exclaimed. "You went to see her?"

"We didn't know she was *your* doctor," Jake said, looking puzzled. "You told me Dr. Lockwood. Matthew Lockwood.''

"I've seen both of them," Liz said.

Jake shrugged. "Well, the duchess and I only knew about Dr. Lockwood. I called him up and asked him to recommend someone we could see. He told me Dr. Demetrius specialized in couples with marital problems.''

"He didn't say a word," Liz murmured. "Neither did Ione—Dr. Demetrius.''

"We asked them not to," Catherine said. She was fiddling with the buttons on the microwave oven, obviously still flustered.

"I doubt they'd have spoken to Liz about us anyway," Jake pointed out. "It wouldn't be ethical.''

"Matt's very hot on ethics," Liz said.

Catherine looked over her shoulder. "Matt?"

"Later," Liz said. "We're dealing with your story here.''

Jake was gazing down at the newspaper in front of him, not looking at Liz. "Your mother and I talked on the telephone about you, honey. We were both worried about you, about the strange experiences you were going through. I came over here a couple of times and we discussed our concern, and somehow got into discussing our own lives.'' He looked at Liz suddenly, his blue eyes candid. "I've never stopped missing the duchess," he said. "Found out she was lonely, too.''

Catherine touched his shoulder lightly as she passed him to put bread in the toaster. It had been many years since

Liz had seen an affectionate gesture between her parents. The small incident moved her, almost bringing tears to her eyes.

"We decided to call your Dr. Lockwood. Your mother said you didn't want her going to see him, and we respected that. We didn't know you'd consulted Dr. Demetrius, too."

"There was a problem," Liz said slowly. "I'll explain it to you later." She frowned. "Did you meet Matt? Dr. Lockwood?"

"Briefly," Jake said. "The first time we went to the Institute, he was coming out of Dr. Demetrius's office and she introduced us."

"What did…" She had to stop and take a sip of coffee to clear her throat. "What did you think of him?"

"Nice young fellow," Jake said promptly. "Your mother liked his eyes."

"He has a trustworthy face," Catherine said. "Honest. Honorable. Intelligent." She giggled again. Giggling was evidently becoming a new habit. "Not to mention that he's absolutely gorgeous."

That comment earned her a mock-frown from under Jake's bristly eyebrows. She made a face at him, looking suddenly about sixteen years old. Then she concentrated on buttering Liz's toast and serving it to her along with the bacon. "I suppose I could have poached an egg," she said vaguely. "I'm sorry, darling, I didn't think…"

"This is fine," Liz said. "For God's sake, just tell me the rest of it. I'm going crazy with curiosity."

Jake laughed. "Not much more to tell, honey. We started seeing Dr. Demetrius when you were in Boston. We've probably seen her four times since."

"She regressed you?"

He nodded. "Separately and not too successfully.

Though I did manage to come up with glimpses of a life in colonial America, which fitted in with your mother's odd experience years ago." He paused. "You told Elizabeth about that?" he asked Catherine.

Catherine nodded and came to sit down beside him. "Dr. Demetrius tried to get me to go back to that time, but I couldn't seem to summon it up. I got a few vague impressions and fleeting sensations that I had lived before in other places, but nothing very definite to go on. We're going to keep trying, though."

"The one thing that did come up for both of us," Jake said, "was the fact that we do still love each other." He was looking at Catherine as he spoke, and her hazel eyes were shining as joyously as his face.

Tremendously moved, Liz stood and went to put her arms around both of them, kissing them each in turn. "I'm so glad," she said softly. "I've always wanted you two to get together again, but I'd about given up hope. You were always sniping at each other."

"Yes, well, it's a habit we got into," Jake said, looking sheepish. "It's one of the things we talked about last night, before—" He broke off.

Liz laughed and went back to her seat, finding that she could now eat the bacon and toast her mother had prepared. Earlier she had been sure she had no appetite at all. Her parents' happiness was almost palpable, and somehow it was helping to alleviate her grief.

"What we've decided is that we're old enough now to be kind to each other," Jake continued.

"And to accept each other the way we are, rather than trying to change the other to suit some preconceived image of the perfect partner," Catherine added.

"Wow!" Liz exclaimed. "That must have been some conversation."

"It ranged a lot," Jake admitted. He laughed. "Even if it did get cut off by more pressing concerns."

Catherine blushed again.

"Does all this mean you're going to remarry?" Liz asked.

"We're going to wait a while," Catherine said. "We thought it might be more fun to court each other first."

"Some kind of courting," Jake murmured, and they all laughed. Then he stood. "Champagne," he said. "This occasion definitely calls for champagne."

"At nine-thirty in the morning?" Catherine protested.

"Don't you remember when I'd come home from a long mission and we'd go out for Sunday brunch at the base?" he asked. "We always had champagne to celebrate my homecomings. You used to mix yours with your orange juice—it made it healthier, you said."

Catherine's face had softened as he talked. "I'd forgotten those days," she murmured. "That was a long time ago."

"Good days," Jake said.

Catherine nodded. Then she glanced sheepishly at Liz. "I expect you think your parents have lost their minds?"

"If you have it's a pretty good condition to be in," Liz told her.

A minute later Catherine went off to track down champagne flutes and Jake went to fetch a bottle from the liquor cabinet in the living room. "I suppose we'll have to put ice in it," Liz heard him grumbling to Catherine. "What do you say, honey—when we're together again, we'd better have champagne on ice at all times."

"Splendid idea," Catherine replied.

When we're together again. The words had a wonderful ring to them, Liz thought. Of all the surprising developments…

Somehow she must try to join wholeheartedly in her parents' celebration, she told herself. She must not mar this special occasion with her own grief.

Even as she thought this she felt tears welling in her eyes again. To distract herself, she picked up the newspaper her father had been reading and idly turned the pages. She was scanning, not reading, keeping her mind off Robert.

Her father always read the sports section first, then the comics, then the editorials and world news. The real estate section had not been unfolded. There was no real reason for Liz to hesitate when she reached that section. Perhaps the name Lockwood had leaped out at her. Familiar names did that.

The story was not about Matt, however. It was about his wife. His ex-wife. Apparently Meredith Lockwood was a program coordinator for Washington State's housing commission. The newspaper's real estate editor had interviewed her concerning some peculiar conditions attached to financing a home with state bond money. The entire discussion was beyond Liz's understanding—money matters were not one of her strong points. Instead her eye was drawn almost immediately to the photograph that accompanied the article.

The woman in the photograph had a very intelligent, pretty face and long straight hair that was parted in the middle and held up at the sides with combs or barrettes. There was something very familiar about her. Had she seen a picture of Meredith on her tour of Matt's house, Liz wondered? No, she hadn't seen any personal photographs at all.

It came to her then, what the likeness was. Her breath caught in her throat.

"I married Meredith for all the wrong reasons," Matt

had said. "Mostly because she reminded me of someone I'd known a long time ago."

"Your first love?" Liz had queried, and he had nodded.

She looked like Jeannie. Meredith Lockwood looked like Jeannie Findlay. She had reminded Matt of Jeannie, and that was when he had begun to believe he was in love with her. Later, he'd found out he was mistaken.

Jeannie. And Matt.

Liz's two worlds had collided after all. She had known they would if she ever allowed herself to consider them side by side. She had known for some time. Perhaps even from before she had looked up into Matt's eyes and seen Robert's face instead.

Meredith could not have reminded Matt of Jeannie unless he had known Jeannie. And there was only one way for Matt to have known Jeannie Findlay.

"What's wrong, honey?" Jake asked.

Liz took a keep breath and folded the newspaper, with Meredith's picture on the inside. "Nothing's wrong," she said. She had meant to speak lightly, but her voice caught in her throat and the words came out sounding strangled.

Jake set a glass of champagne in front of her, and carried another to his own place. Catherine sat down beside him, her eyes fixed on Liz's face. "I thought you didn't look well when you came in," she said. "Then you seemed all right and I forgot. What is it, darling? Have you caught that horrible flu that's going around? One of my friends had it and it was three weeks before she could even lift her head off the pillow, she said."

Liz seized on the excuse. "Maybe a cold," she said. "I'm a little sniffly."

Jake held up a hand like a policeman stopping traffic. "You never were a good liar, Liz my girl," he said flatly. "And you always did get red around the eyelids when you cried. I know nowadays you young people get into some peculiar shades of plum and pink in your eye makeup, and I know you and the duchess never did give me credit for seeing much beyond the end of my nose. But it looked to me when you came in as if you'd been crying your eyes out and it looks to me now as if you've had some kind of shock. I want to know what's going on. Does it have anything to do with this handsome Dr. Lockwood?''

''Indirectly perhaps,'' Liz said. Pushing the newspaper aside, she sipped the champagne, then held her glass up, forcing herself to smile. ''I thought we were going to drink a toast?''

Jake clinked his glass against hers, then Catherine's, then set it down untasted. Catherine did the same. Both of them fixed their eyes on her face.

''It's a long story,'' she said as lightly as she could manage.

''We're not going anywhere,'' Catherine said with a glance at Jake. The two of them were holding hands under the glass table, Liz saw. Holding tightly. Obviously they were worried about her. She would have to try to lay their fears to rest.

It was difficult to get started, but once she began, the story of Jeannie and Robert poured out of her. Both Jake and Catherine had always been good listeners where she was concerned and it was obvious that the story fascinated them. They didn't interrupt except to occasionally exclaim softly and to exchange a glance of astonishment now and then. Liz tried not to leave anything out. She even confessed her relationship with Matt and her earlier concern that her attraction to him had been left over from her involvement with Robert.

''And so he died,'' Jake murmured when she was done.

"Poor tragic little Jeannie. How would she manage without him?"

Liz shook her head. "I'll probably never know. I suppose she'd have to go into a hospital, even though she was afraid of such places. She was expecting to die, that's for sure. Apparently there weren't any drugs to treat the disease in those days."

Catherine got up and left the kitchen, returning in a couple of minutes with an encyclopedia. "They discovered the causative organism, the tubercle bacillus, in 1882," she said after reading in silence for a while. "There wasn't any protection against it until a French biologist developed a vaccine in 1924. Here we are—the first specific chemotherapeutic agent became available in 1944, when an American bacteriologist named Selman Waksman discovered streptomycin. In 1948 something called PAS was discovered. Together these two drugs revolutionized tuberculosis treatment." She set the book down and looked sadly at Liz. "Much too late for Jeannie."

Sitting down again she gazed at Liz in silence for a minute. "You believe now, don't you? You believe you were Jeannie Findlay?"

"Yes." It was the first time Liz had admitted this even to herself. But she knew she had been coming to it for some time. "When I came out of the regression yesterday morning, I felt as if I'd just lost someone very, very dear," she said slowly. "I don't know how to handle it. It's never happened to me before."

"It gets less painful," Catherine said softly. "I know that sounds easy to say, but it happens to be true. You never forget, but it gets easier to bear. After a while you can even smile about your memories of that person without feeling any pain at all."

Jake nodded. "It takes time," he says. "You have to give yourself time."

"Perhaps you should take a holiday," Catherine suggested. "You haven't had one for a long time. I can certainly manage if you want a few days. A couple of weeks?"

Liz shook her head. "I'd probably be better off working," she said. "If I can just convince myself that Robert died a hundred years ago, I think I'll be okay."

They were all silent for a few minutes, then Jake reached out and put his big hand over Liz's, which were clasped in front of her on the table.

"I could go to Scotland," Liz said abruptly, startling herself. "No," she countered almost immediately. "What help would that be?" She mulled over the idea a moment more. There was something about it that appealed to her strongly. "I have a feeling it would comfort me to go back to Scotland, to Edinburgh," she said slowly, looking from Jake to Catherine. "Does that seem foolish to you?"

"To go to the place where you were once so happy?" Catherine murmured. "No, not foolish at all. As long as you realize it's you—Liz—making this pilgrimage in the twentieth century."

"A pilgrimage," Liz echoed softly. "A journey made as a mark of respect. I like the sound of that." She nodded. "I'd like to see the castle again. Jeannie really loved that old castle." She managed a smile. "Remember when I used to draw it all the time, Mom? Isn't it astonishing to think it was because Jeannie always wanted to draw it and couldn't?"

"Not so astonishing, really," Jake said. "Inexplicable things happen all the time. We tend to dismiss them because we pride ourselves on our intelligence. If we can't explain them they can't have happened—that's the way our twentieth century minds work.''

Catherine was looking at him approvingly. Her father had come a long way in the last ten years, Liz decided. She remembered her mother exclaiming once, just before the divorce, ''That man's never had an abstract thought in his life.''

''You think I should go then?'' she asked.

Catherine and Jake exchanged a long glance. It had been years since they had consulted each other before giving an opinion, Liz realized. The fact that they were doing so, even though silently, boded well for their future.

''Yes,'' they said, speaking together with one voice.

''What will you tell Dr. Lockwood?'' Jake asked.

''I don't know if I will,'' Liz said.

''You can't just go off without letting him know,'' Catherine protested.

Liz shook her head. ''I can't talk to him right now. Maybe I'll write him a note, tell him I have to take a trip. I'll let him think it's a business trip. I have to get something straightened out in my own mind before I talk to him again.''

''Something you haven't told us?'' Jake asked.

Liz nodded. ''Something I haven't even allowed myself to believe until now. Something he kept from me. I'm not even sure I can forgive him for doing so.'' She glanced at the newspaper and felt a tremor go through her.

Her mother and father were both looking puzzled, for which she could hardly blame them. But they didn't question her further. When she left they hugged each other fiercely. ''We want you to be happy, Liz-girl,'' her father murmured against her hair.

''We can't be totally happy until you're happy, too,'' her mother added.

"Now, Catherine, don't go putting responsibility for our happiness on our daughter's shoulders," Jake chided her.

Catherine glanced at Liz in apology, then looked at Jake solemnly. "You're right," she said.

Both Liz and Jake gaped at her, then Jake grinned from ear to ear. "That I should live to see this day," he said gleefully. "Did you hear that, Liz-girl? Your mother said I was right."

A moment later Catherine was in his arms, laughing as hard as he was, and Liz decided it was time for her to leave.

CHAPTER TWELVE

LIZ ARRIVED in Edinburgh five days later. Five days in which she had not responded to Matt's messages on her answering machine. Five days in which her grief over Robert's death had alternated between denial, anger and deep, deep sorrow. She was grateful that Matt hadn't come to her apartment or to the office to confront her. On her answering machine, his voice was kind. He was just calling to let her know he was thinking about her, he said. He wanted her to know he was there for her whenever she was ready to come to him. She wasn't sure she would ever be ready.

Edinburgh was colder than Seattle. Liz had to fight her way along Princes Street the day after her arrival. The wind, blasting along the thoroughfare almost lifted her off her feet, singing against her clenched teeth, buffeting her down-filled jacket and cutting straight through her jeans to her shinbones, making them ache. She tried to pull her knitted hat further down over her ears, but her hands were awkward in mittens and the hat kept springing up again. Her nose was going to drop off from frostbite, she decided. But she didn't really mind the cold—it gave her something to fight against and it was impossible to think when your bones were frozen to the marrow.

The gardens were a little more sheltered. When she reached the bench she was able to sit fairly comfortably for several minutes, getting back the breath the wind had sucked out of her.

The castle loomed sternly above her on its ageless rock. Somehow she had thought that when she saw it she'd feel better, but if anything she felt emptier than ever. Concentrating on the gray stone walls, she tried to empty her mind, hoping to summon Jeannie back by sheer willpower. She didn't want to regress again, she just wanted to feel close to Jeannie one more time, before letting her go. But there was no mist softening the landscape, and the noise of twentieth-century traffic, carried in her direction by the wind, made concentration impossible.

She would have to find some other way to get in touch with Jeannie, she decided, and she spent a couple of hours wandering the narrow streets, going in and out of shops, trying to decide which building in the old town had housed Jeannie's flat. But though some areas seemed more familiar than others, she couldn't decide if that was because she'd lived there, or because she'd walked them on her previous visit.

At last, disconsolate, she wandered back to the small hotel where she was staying. It had seemed best to avoid any of the Prince hotels. She was here on a private quest, and she didn't want business intruding.

In the morning she ate a solitary breakfast in a nearby restaurant that served the best oatmeal she'd ever tasted. "Steel-cut oats," the proprietor told her. "None of that steamed and rolled nonsense for me."

Looking out the window at the cobbled street, Liz suddenly remembered Mrs. Currie asking Jeannie if she'd read about Robert's funeral in the newspaper. Leaving the restaurant, she made her way to the offices of a newspaper that the restaurant's proprietor had told her had existed forever—well, for at least a hundred years.

The newspaper not only had records, it had them on microfilm, with a machine to read them by. Using the excuse that she was thinking of writing a travel article and wanted to back it up with some history, Liz was given access to the files.

She began in September, 1888, and found a mention of Robert Charles McAndrew almost at once. How weird to see his name in print like that. And what a shame newspapers that old had not used photographs, even though the Victorians had been such camera buffs. Not only was it hard on the eye to search through columns and columns of print, it would also have been so exciting, so comforting, to see a picture of Robert.

The newspaper quote had been taken from a speech Robert had given before a large number of "notable individuals." He had spoken of a significant weakness in the Scottish economy—the enormous gap between the very rich and the very poor. One quarter of the national income, he'd said, was divided among five thousand very wealthy men—professionals, businessmen, large landowners. These men enjoyed a personal income two hundred times larger than that of the lowest sort, while the other seventy-five percent of the whole population earned less than thirty pounds a year.

Someone had pointed out that laborers must work for a mere pittance to enable their employers to sell their goods at a low rate, or there would be no work for them to do at all and they would starve. "Do you suppose they do not starve now?" Robert had demanded in reply.

Scrolling through the microfilm, Liz found one other mention of Robert—in a list of people who had attended some charitable function. He had said on that occasion that a banker couldn't shut himself up in his office. He had to care about his city and the problems of its people.

And then Liz came to his obituary. Robert Charles McAndrew Is Dead, was the blunt headline above a sizable article. The facts of his fall from a horse were given in detail. An eminent gentleman, the newspaper called him. A man of keenest intellect. In all his daily endeavors, his management and policies had been sound, fair to all.

He had been buried in the beautiful churchyard at Glendarra, the family's Scottish home, which had belonged to the McAndrews since the twelfth century. An uncle, a Lord Armstead, had been chief mourner. The funeral had been kept as private as possible, but a large group of friends and neighbors had attended.

Liz rewound the film and put it back in its box, returning it to the young woman who had helped her set up the machine. Then she went out into the wintry streets and walked again until she was exhausted.

Surprisingly she slept well that night and awoke feeling refreshed and optimistic. Perhaps seeing Robert's death recorded in that ancient newspaper had made a difference. The language had obviously belonged to a previous century, just as Robert had. Somehow the experience had helped her distance herself from Robert, though she was still aware of that phantom feeling of something missing— yet still there.

She spent the next two days exploring the country around Edinburgh not admitting to herself that she might be looking for the place where Robert picnicked with Jeannie, though that was what she was doing. She didn't find it, however, and contented herself with visiting Linlithgow, the palace Ian Cameron had told her about. There she was shown the little room in which Mary Queen of Scots had been born, the dungeons, torture chamber and secret stairway, and a sixteenth-century fountain in the courtyard. She explored the castle ruins at Tantallon and the crumbling seafront fortresses that lined the bays and headlands of East Lothian.

And always she came back to Edinburgh and to Castle Rock. The rock, she had learned somewhere, was one of the first places in Scotland to be inhabited, first by the predecessors of the Picts, then by the Picts themselves. Celtic chieftains made it their fortress. Then the Angles replaced the Celts, being replaced themselves by the Scots. She began to feel the rhythm of centuries marching on, people coming and going, living and dying.

It was such a formidable rock, such a formidable castle. Sitting on her bench on a windless though still cold morning several days after her arrival, she gazed up at the rock, thinking that she was probably ready to go home. The castle wasn't going to help her. Only time, as her father had told her, would do that.

Quite suddenly she became aware of a presence nearby. Someone or something had come to sit on the bench with her. The presence was too large to be a squirrel, and the squirrels had more sense than to be abroad on such a chilly day anyway. Why was she so reluctant to look? She knew who it was. She had known all along that he would follow her here.

Taking a deep breath, Liz turned her head.

Matt was sitting at the other end of the bench, looking impossibly handsome, wearing jeans and the ski jacket and gloves he'd worn when they hiked on Mount Rainier. He was bareheaded, his brown hair as untidy as usual—obviously in need of a barber's attention. He smiled at her, the cold gray light of the sky reflected warmly in his eyes.

Her heart turned over. She felt the urge to move at once into his arms, but held herself back, reminding herself that she was angry with him, terribly angry. "How on earth did you know where to find me?" she asked.

"Your mother called me the day you left," he answered. "She told me she didn't want to interfere, but that she was worried because you'd seemed disturbed."

"Like hell she didn't want to interfere," Liz said with a wry grin.

"As for knowing you would be here, on this bench," Matt went on, his face solemn, "I found you here before, remember? On September 6th, 1888."

Robert was suddenly alive again in her mind, looking down at her, smiling at her, his blue eyes so bold. *A witty woman as well as a pretty one. You don't mind me looking at you, do you?* Jeannie had thought he was the most beautiful man in the world. Involuntarily Liz smiled at the memory.

Evidently encouraged by her smile, Matt smiled in return. "Robert asked you if you knew what the date was, remember, so he could determine if you had a concussion or not." His eyebrows slanted upward. "You do know now, don't you?"

She sighed. "That you were Robert? Yes, of course. I can't think why I avoided knowing it for so long. I shut my mind to it, I guess. I wasn't sure I believed it until I saw your house. I didn't want to admit it to myself—I didn't see how I could admit it and still go on loving you. But then I came across a picture of your ex-wife in the newspaper and saw how much she resembled Jeannie physically. I had to admit it then."

Her voice was stiff. She took a deep breath. She seemed to be very short on oxygen all of a sudden, remembering why she was angry with him. "You deceived me, Matt," she said accusingly. "You knew all along, at least from the first regression in your office. That's why you acted so strangely for a while. You knew! But you didn't tell me. You let me go blundering on, worrying that it might upset you to have me talking about loving Robert, worrying that I couldn't love you and Robert at the same time.''

She stood and started away from the bench, away from Matt. ''You shouldn't have come here,'' she said.

He was behind her, his hands on her shoulders, holding her back when she wanted to run away. Oh, the touch of his hands, the nearness of him. She suddenly remembered how it felt to be near him, both of them naked, bodies pressed pore to pore along their length, hands exploring, mouths twisting together frantically.

''I love you, Liz,'' he said softly.

''You deceived me,'' she said dully.

''I had to.''

He turned her around, still holding on to her, compelling her with the sheer force of his personality to look at his face. His eyes were intense, his mouth stern. ''Don't you remember the first time you came to my office?'' he asked.

''Of course I do.''

''Do you also remember how sure you were that there was some other explanation for what was happening to you? You weren't about to believe in reincarnation. So how would you have reacted if I had said, tah dah, I'm Robert, fret no more my love, I'm here again, ready and willing to go on with our love affair?''

She didn't respond for a minute. Almost against her will, her anger was dissipating. What he said made sense, she had to admit. ''I'd probably have socked you with my purse,'' she said with a sigh, then she rallied. ''Later,'' she added. ''You could have told me later. When I couldn't distinguish between you and Robert making love to me, you could have told me then. You could at least have told me before I saw your house!''

''I debated telling you,'' he said earnestly. ''But it seemed to me it would be better if you arrived at the truth by yourself, without too much prompting from me. You hadn't yet accepted reincarnation, so how could I hope you would accept me? And then when Ione asked how you'd feel if you ran into Robert in this life, you said you'd sooner he stayed back there with Jeannie." His smile was tentative. "Add to all that the fact I'm a dedicated coward," he went on. "I was desperately afraid of losing you altogether, of having you reject everything—including me." His eyes searched her face hopefully.

At last she nodded. "I guess I can understand that."

With a sigh of relief, he kissed her lightly, then drew her back to the bench so they could sit down. Perhaps his knees felt as weak as hers did, she thought.

"I read Robert's obituary in the newspaper a few days ago," she told him. "I went in the—do they call it a newspaper morgue in this country? Whatever. I went there a few days ago and read the old newspapers on microfilm. And there it was."

"Creepy," he said, his eyes still studying her face.

"Very." She took a breath. "I think it helped, though. I feel I can accept his death now." She looked at him sternly. "I think the thing I find hardest to forgive is the fact you didn't warn me about Robert dying."

"I didn't know, Liz. It was as much of a shock to me as it was to you. I was expecting Jeannie to die. My own regressions took me as far as Jeannie's discovery that she had tuberculosis and no farther. It didn't occur to me that the reason I stopped there was that Robert had died."

She remembered now that he had looked pale and shocked when she came out of that particular regression. Why hadn't she remembered that before?

She glanced up at the castle, feeling suddenly awkward in his presence. He had come all this way to make sure she was okay. He had deceived her only to protect her, to give her time to accept the impossible. He had never stopped loving her. But she had come very close to denying her love for him.

"I used to draw the castle, compulsively, when I was a child," she said. "I didn't tell you that before because it seemed too weird. I didn't even know what castle it was until my mom told me." She glanced at his face. "Did you ever draw the castle?"

He shook his head. "I drew only Jeannie. That's all I had in the beginning—my memory of Jeannie. I had no idea who she was. I liked Scottish things, though, just as you did. Scottish music, especially. Even the sound of the bagpipes, which is usually an acquired taste. Then, when I first saw the house—the house I'm living in now—I regressed spontaneously. I saw Jeannie clearly, but my regression wasn't as detailed as yours. The later regressions followed along like yours, though, when Ione hypnotized me, but they ended when Jeannie became ill."

She wrinkled her forehead, looking at him. "I wanted to ask you something. You said maybe I'd lived in Persia, remember? Were you joking?"

"You lived in Persia, yes," he said firmly. "You knew your place then, too," he added with a smile. "You wouldn't have dreamed of running off on your own to foreign places."

"You were there then?" she asked. "In Persia?"

"And in Denmark," he said.

Something suddenly struck her as funny and she couldn't resist sharing it with him. "I wasn't in the Cistercian monastery, was I?" she asked.

His wonderful brimming smile showed up for the first time. "I hardly think so. I didn't see you in the regressions anyway." He laughed. "Unless I had you hidden away."

There was a silence, but it was not an uncomfortable

one. Somehow the humorous exchange had helped clear the air between them. She was no longer angry, could not think now why she should have been angry. She should have remembered that she could trust him, that he wouldn't have deceived her without reason.

A long-ago memory stirred in her mind for no immediately apparent reason. "Do you like magic shows, Matt?" she asked him.

He looked puzzled. "Very much," he said.

"I used to love them when I was a kid." She looked up at the castle again as she sorted through the memory that had come to her, suddenly recognizing the symbolism of it. "I saw one once that featured a close-up table—you know, where the audience can crowd around and watch the magician close up? The magician had two large metal rings that were joined together. He gave them to me to examine and I was really thorough, I checked them out very closely. Boy, there wasn't going to be any fraud with me right there watching. And I was satisfied. There was no way those rings were going to come apart. But they did, very easily in the magician's hands. And then he joined them back together."

She looked at him again. "It was a trick, of course— sleight of hand, prestidigitation. But it worked."

He was listening patiently, his gray eyes curious.

She smiled at him. "My separate worlds," she explained. "I was determined to keep them separate, but in spite of my efforts they came back together anyway. Robert and Jeannie. You and me. One world separated only by time."

He let out a long breath she hadn't realized he was holding. "You accept it all," he said softly.

"I do." She touched his cheek with her gloved hand, then took off the glove so she could feel the warmth of him against her fingers. "I love you, Matthew Lockwood," she said. "And the great thing about all this is that I know now that love really can last forever."

His arms went around her and he held her as close as he could, considering the bulk of their winter clothing. There were no ghosts present now. That whole shared history would always be there in the background, though, Liz thought—enriching their life together, coloring it, but not interfering with it.

"I love you, darling Liz," Matt said. "I was so afraid when you ran away from me. I didn't want to have to wait until some other life to get you back again. I need you too much in this one."

He kissed her, a warm, searching kiss that set her pulse thumping and her blood shooting through her veins and arteries, warming her, making her feel more fully alive than she had ever felt. "You are going to marry me, aren't you?" he asked.

She grinned, teasing him by hesitating. "I understand you know my parents are consulting Ione," she said.

"I couldn't tell you. It was up to them to let you know. I take it they did?"

She nodded. "Evidently their reconciliation is working very well. So I asked them if they were going to remarry and they told me they wanted to court each other for a while first."

His brimming smile had come back in full blinding force. "You want me to court you?"

She shook her head and gave him her lips again. After a long, satisfying time, she said, "I don't need to be courted. I'm won. A hundred years ought to be enough time for me to make up my mind, don't you think?"

She inclined her head. "Maybe I should remind you,

though, that my job often takes me away from home. Is that going to be a problem?''

He laughed. ''Here we go. Cards on the table. Cautious Liz making sure everything's clearly understood.'' His grin took any possible sting out of the words. ''One of the things I love most about you is your insistence on speaking straight out.'' His smile became wry. ''I handle a seminar or two in other cities myself from time to time. Is that a problem for you?''

She shook her head. ''Think of the homecomings.''

''Oh, yes, indeed,'' he said softly.

Liz took a deep breath. It was time to stop waffling around. Past time. ''Yes, I'll marry you, Matt Lockwood,'' she said firmly. ''The sooner the better. But you have to promise me first you'll never ride a horse.''

''I've always been wary around horses, as a matter of fact,'' he said with a laugh. Then he kissed her again. And again. And it seemed to Liz she could suddenly imagine how these gardens would look in spring, with a warm sun shining and new buds forming on the trees and birds singing. She would like to see that, she thought.

''You didn't look terribly surprised to see me here,'' Matt said after a while. ''I could tell you were angry with me, but you didn't seem surprised.''

She grinned. ''How could I be surprised? You told me you'd come.''

He looked puzzled.

'''And fare thee well, my only luve, and fare thee well a while,''' she quoted to him.

His response came back immediately, along with a radiant smile that had a lot of Robbie in it. '''And I will come again, my luve,''' he said softly. '''Tho' 't were ten thousand mile.'''

His arms tightened around her and his mouth closed

over hers once more. As he kissed her, her blood began singing through her body again, her pulse echoing in her ear as though she held a seashell to it.

But over and above her bodily sensations, it seemed to Liz that she could hear Jeannie's voice saying to her, as she had once said to her friend Mhairi, "Och, aye, love's worth it for all that."

Every day is

A Mother's Day

in this heartwarming anthology
celebrating motherhood and romance!

Featuring the classic story "Nobody's Child" by Emilie Richards
He had come to a child's rescue, and now Officer Farrell Riley was
suddenly sharing parenthood with beautiful Gemma Hancock.
But would their ready-made family last forever?

Plus two brand-new romances:

"Baby on the Way" by Marie Ferrarella
Single and pregnant, Madeline Reed found the perfect husband in the
handsome cop who helped bring her infant son into the world. But did his
dutiful role in the surprise delivery make J.T. Walker a daddy?

"A Daddy for Her Daughters" by Elizabeth Bevarly
When confronted with spirited Naomi Carmichael and her brood of girls,
bachelor Sloan Sullivan realized he had a lot to learn about women!
Especially if he hoped to win this sexy single mom's heart....

Available this April from Silhouette Books!

Where love comes alive™

Visit Silhouette at www.eHarlequin.com

PSAMD

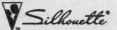

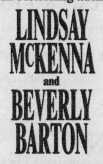